28 DAY BOOK

CRIMINAL GOLD

Visit us at www.boldstrokesbooks.com

CRIMINAL GOLD

by

Ann Aptaker

2014

CRIMINAL GOLD
© 2014 BY ANN APTAKER. ALL RIGHTS RESERVED.

ISBN 13: 978-1-62639-216-8

THIS TRADE PAPERBACK ORIGINAL IS PUBLISHED BY
BOLD STROKES BOOKS, INC.
P.O. BOX 249
VALLEY FALLS, NY 12185

FIRST EDITION: NOVEMBER 2014

CREDITS
EDITOR: RUTH STERNGLANTZ
PRODUCTION DESIGN: STACIA SEAMAN
COVER DESIGN BY SHERI (GRAPHICARTIST2020@HOTMAIL.COM)

Acknowledgments

I'd never have made it without this incredible, talented, loving crew in my life, who were there when it really counted: Allan Neuwirth, Risa Neuwirth, Jody Gray, Debby Solomon, Peter Winter, Barbara Rosenblat, Mikaela Lamarche, Dorian and Jeffrey Bergen, and my fabulous sister Yren Berry, who's a lot smarter than I am.

Special thanks to Susan Herner, who stood by me in the difficult beginning, to Shelley Singer, who taught me how to do it in the first place, to Janice Hall, for her patience with me on a cold night in Greenwich Village, and to my brilliant editor, Ruth Sternglantz, who challenges me, because I need it.

Dedicated to a memory.

CHAPTER ONE

New York City
March 1949
Just before midnight

I am Cantor Gold. I'm one of those females who confuse you, maybe even intrigue you, even if only a little, which is still more than you might care to admit. According to upright citizens—you know the type, busybodies like your next-door neighbor or the schlemiel who signs your paycheck—I'm a dangerous person, a threat to the very fabric of society. Well, maybe I am; my way of life and way of love certainly tug at society's threads. But if you ask me, those threads could use some serious tugging. The fabric of society is too damned tight for my taste, threatens to cut off my air. Especially lately, what with all your hot-for-love GIs rolling stateside during the last four years, all pepped up since they clobbered the Nazis and the rest of the Fascist gang. The fellas expect their cozy little nest to be exactly the way they left it, with their wives waiting in the kitchen or their girlfriends daydreaming on the front-porch swing. The Johnnies are marching home and they want their women back, back from me, if they only knew, from a dame tagged *butch*.

Look, there were lots of lonely ladies during the war who needed a soft shoulder and a little companionship to help them through all those empty, scary nights, so let's just say that whenever I could I did my bit for the war effort.

And don't get all drop dead about the butch tag, its whiff of the brutish or clumsy, because I'm neither. Brutes don't have the soul to court a woman's passions as I like to court them. And clumsiness, in my outlaw love life and rogue profession—I smuggle art and other priceless treasure into the Port of New York—clumsiness could get me killed or locked up.

I've been locked up, just once, spent a night in the city slammer about six months ago, and it didn't have a goddamned thing to do with the smuggling racket or the rough stuff that comes along with it. Nope, it was for dancing at the Green Door Club with a sweet little redhead whose blue eyes were as clear and pretty as the Central Park lake in springtime. Christ, what a night, courtesy of one of City Hall's periodic anti-vice flimflams. The cops raided us, hauled everyone off to the lockup, where they bloodied us but good. I've been beaten up before, by cops, by gangsters—it happens in my line of work—I knew I could handle it. But a lot of the girls were just innocents led to a slaughter.

Yeah, you heard me, I said slaughter, because when the cops raped those girls, it was as bad as beating them to death. A potbellied sergeant in a sweaty white shirt and a wedding ring too tight for his pudgy finger started the party. When he unzipped his fly and his pecker popped out, it was so swollen and red it looked like it had been skinned alive. This sonuvabitch sergeant pulled the red-haired kid from the crowd while another sweaty cop held me back with a billy club pressed across my chest. The sergeant slammed the kid against a wall, pulled up her skirt, and pulled off her panties with such force the silk cut her thigh. Then he pressed her head to the wall. Her eyes got big and round, searching frantically for me, but I couldn't push past the cop with the billy club. I felt helpless and sick to my stomach when the sergeant ran his fat fingers around the kid's nipples while he hollered at the rest of us, "Take a look, perverts! This is how it's natural, how it's *legal!*" Then he rammed his pecker into her, over and over, her back scraped bloody against the wall. One of the other cops turned a radio on, turned the music up loud to drown out her screaming, but it didn't help. I still hear her screams in my sleep through Perry Como singing his hit parade tune, "A, You're Adorable."

But I bet the red-haired kid's dreams are a lot worse than mine, and not just about the rape. When the cops were done with her, she tried to wash herself at the only sink in the holding tank, but someone had puked in the sink and the police matrons never bothered to clean it up. The matron at the desk nearest us outside the tank was a skinny dame whose well-pressed uniform marked her as the type who valued cleanliness, so I asked her if someone could come clean the sink. She didn't even bother to laugh.

That crummy night killed off any stray thoughts I might've had about maybe going legit, working a regular job, fitting myself into the fabric of society. Why bother? The straight-backs who run the world with their laws and their hired truncheons mark people with my romantic predilections as criminals just for living, so I figure I don't owe the rest of their rules and regulations any allegiance. Frees me up all the way around.

Like tonight, out here on the East River on this beautiful March night, a bottle of good Chivas scotch to keep me company while I sit in my boat, tucked up against a stone support tower under the Manhattan side of the Brooklyn Bridge. My boat's a dandy fifteen-foot utility job with a hefty engine for speed, low to the water and with good lines for maneuverability. She'll outdance a cop cruiser anytime, but I don't figure we'll have to rhumba to that numba tonight. Red Drogan and I have the night's business timed as tight as a racetrack clock.

Meantime, with my black sweater and watch cap blending me into the shadows and the Chivas going down smooth, I can relax a little and take in the terrific view of the ships and tugboats sailing the harbor beneath the Manhattan skyline. The sea air provides the pleasure of a bracing sting along the scars on my face: a small one shaped like a knife above my lip, a jagged slash on my left cheek, and a sharp curve, like a sickle, above my right eye. Each one is a souvenir of my outlaw ways and my brazen freedom.

The pleasures of the river are also my protection. The rhythm of the harbor, the wind telling tales in my ear: these things keep me sharp, alert me to danger. Cops think they can outwit me by hiding inside the harbor's booming noise. What those boys don't get, most of 'em anyway, is that a smuggler stays alive by listening for what's on the other side of the foghorns and the buoy bells, hearing past the bellow of the big ships and the growling engines of tugboats. I'd hear a prowling cop boat through all of this tumult and still pick up the rolling lilt of midnight traffic crossing the bridge a hundred feet over my head, a steady whoosh soothing as a sweetheart's whisper.

The whiskey is doing a good job of warming me against a chill that's rolling in on a light fog. I like fog. It dresses up the harbor, puts a silvery halo around the big March moon, and wraps the famous skyline of Lower Manhattan in a luminous stole. Just look at all those tall, slender skyscrapers, classy and arrogant as society dames watching the dazzling theatrics on the docks below. And what a show! The waterfront shimmers bright as footlights on Broadway, lighting an all-night razzle-dazzle dance of steel cranes and brawny men who wrestle the nation's goods in and out of port.

I am a speck in this enormous harbor and all its goings on, an unnoticeable outlaw speck who clears a hefty income by slipping some of the world's most fantastic loot into the hands of private collectors and swooning curators of famous museums. Next time you're on upper Fifth Avenue along Central Park, wandering through the rooms of—well, let's keep the name of the joint quiet; if you and your family pause to look at a famous Italian painting or maybe an ancient Greek urn that catches your eye, chances are you can thank me for the pleasure.

So you see? Life is full of pleasures, enough to go around for people like you and people like me. And the night's still young, barely midnight. A rather delicious pleasure is waiting for me after my business on the river is done, a royal bauble passed, and a sack with the royal sum of twenty-five thousand dollars tossed in my lap. That kind of money will warm me very nicely and heat up my after-hours night on the town with the lovely Rosie Bliss, a cabbie with the skills of a first-rate getaway driver, a taste for my outlaw life, and an interesting fondness for the scar above my lip. Rosie also worries about me, says I'm getting reckless, says that maybe I have an unconscious death wish. I tell her that people with a death wish don't shop for a new car, and I've been looking at the line of '49 Buicks.

So, no, no death wish for me. If I'm out for a wilder ride these days, it's because I'm free of recent distractions, free from things that sapped my energy and ate me up alive, unreliable things like dreams of hearts and flowers and growing old with the ladylove of my life…

Sophie…Sophie de la Luna y Sol…her long black hair swaying along her shoulders, the way she'd tilt her head when she fussed with an earring, a timeless gesture, as if she'd learned about earrings in a previous life as a contessa.

Those distractions disappeared when she did, when the city swallowed her and the night hid the crime. I went a little mad after that, aching to the bone with missing her, hating myself because I couldn't protect her, and going crazy because I didn't even know who or what I couldn't protect her from. I spun in every direction to look for her, scraped every corner of the city for any trace, even badgered every doorman on her block for any scrap of information. I called in every favor from every pair of eyes and ears along the docks and on the streets. I questioned her mother and father and kid brother so many times, they finally got a restraining order against me. The madness almost deep-sixed me until I saw that my only way out was to rip life's sweeter emotions from my soul. Love wouldn't matter to me anymore. I wouldn't lose anyone I loved ever again.

Dammit, Drogan's late. He should've been here by now. He's cutting it too close. We'd timed tonight's handoff down to the seconds between the scheduled runs of the harbor cops. One of their patrol boats should be sliding under the Williamsburg Bridge up at Delancey Street any minute. Won't be long 'til it's under the Manhattan Bridge, that lacy piece of work less than two minutes north of me at Bowery and Canal Street.

Another pull of the Chivas helps kill the tension, then I tuck the bottle under my arm and slide my hands into the pockets of my chinos. My right hand takes comfort in the cold steel of my Smith & Wesson .38 while my left hand wraps around a leather pouch containing a silver-and-emerald doodad that's a hundred and seventy-five years old.

I'll tell you a secret: a hundred and seventy-five years may as well be the day before yesterday in the better class of the art and treasure trade. But with an emerald the size of a walnut and a lady's name engraved in the silver in French and Russian, then we're talking about a brooch that graced the bosom of a particularly zesty Russian empress. I took possession of the thing about a half hour ago from the bursar of an incoming liner, a guy who's been a reliable courier for my goods. The tricky part came after, when I sailed it past a couple of US Customs lookouts and between the boats of the New York Harbor Police. Talk about your pleasures.

There, up ahead—and it's about time—Red Drogan's tugboat. With Gregory Ortine on it. I can almost hear the sleazy social climber salivate. Ortine's the fussy type, been pestering me for weeks about these arrangements. I had to explain to him a thousand times that we'd make the handoff under the bridge soon after I got the brooch, that I'd set things up this way so the brooch would never touch land, never be traced to American shores from the time I picked it up until Ortine takes it wherever he's planning to take it. I told him to tie up his yacht outside the twelve-mile limit of territorial waters, then motor his launch to a set of coordinates south of Ellis Island to meet Drogan. I don't want the registration number on Ortine's launch showing up in New York Harbor tonight, so I told him to come into port aboard Drogan's tug. And I warned Ortine not to tell me or Drogan where he moored his yacht or where he's planning to go afterward. That's the kind of information that could jam me up later in case of trouble. I told Ortine that if he lets that information slip, even blurts it by accident, the deal's off. I'd toss the pouch into the river—minus the brooch, of course, but Ortine wouldn't know that.

Drogan's tug, on the other hand, is a working boat and a familiar sight in these waters, so there'll be no reason for any patrolling cops to pay attention when he glides the tug under the bridge. The shadow of the bridge will cover us when Ortine tosses me the sack with the twenty-five G's and I toss him the pouch with the brooch. Everyone will then just sail away. Drogan will ferry Ortine back to the Ellis Island rendezvous spot and collect his own payoff from the guy. If Ortine stiffs Drogan out of his cut, Drogan will roll him for the brooch and throw him overboard. I hope that doesn't happen. Ortine's flush with clip-joint money and has social aspirations that need a show of good taste, like having an art collection. He's exactly the kind of long-term customer I like to develop.

For my part, Ortine's twenty-five grand will nestle snugly beside his ten-thousand dollar down payment sleeping peacefully in the safe in my office.

I muzzle the urge to make a dash for Drogan's tug. I've been in the smuggling racket long enough to know when to hang back, make the money come to me.

But all bets are off when a siren howls! The shriek rips the air, bangs back and forth against the bridge's stone tower, and tears into my eardrums. Goddamn harbor police: a patrol boat is barreling toward the bridge.

I don't know if her crew's spotted me. Don't know if they're even after me. The cops could have their eyes on any one of the vessels on the river tonight. I can make a run for the pier nearest me, Pier 21 at Dover Street, slip my boat through the pylons under the pier, and then disappear into the action on the docks where rough guys with grappling hooks who load big ships and take their orders from the Mob aren't known to go out of their way to clear a path for the cops. I'm dressed just like a lot of roughnecks on the waterfront. If I keep my head down, chances are the cops won't spot me.

But I'd be going home twenty-five grand light. No pleasure in that. No way around it. If I want my dough, I'll have to outrun that shrieking police boat. I can lose the cops after I get my cash. Believe me, I know how.

I take a quick slug of whiskey to kick my gut, then push off from the tower. The prow clears the bridge and I'm ready to start my engine, make a run for Drogan's tug.

Something slams down on my boat, loud as a hard smack on the ass. The city and the sky wrench sideways—what the *hell* am I doing in the air?

The black river is rushing at me, then I slam into it with a wallop that almost tears the skin off my face before I'm sucked down where it's goddamn freezing and goddamn dark. My legs pedal like crazy. I get my arms into the act, finally break free of the river, cough it out of me so I can grab some air. A blazing bright searchlight nearly blinds me, but I can see through the glare what's left of my capsized boat.

A woman is sprawled over the hull. Her red dress shines.

CHAPTER TWO

They've laid her out on the deck of the police boat. The famous cheekbones are all banged up. The silky body is broken at angles, her red sequined dress twisted in every direction, the sight of her as heartbreaking as a kid's Raggedy Ann doll in a trash can. You'd hardly recognize her as one of the most beautiful faces to ever grace a gossip column. One of the cops on the boat, an older guy, shows a little class when he lays a blanket over her, tucks it around her torn shoulders.

But she won't need the blanket to warm her. Her skin can't feel the chill in the air or the needles of river spray flying around us. She won't feel her bones bang around from the bounce of the boat. She can't feel the boat. She can't feel anything.

In life the lady had plenty of things to feel good about, expensive things like diamond jewelry and classy cars, most of it paid for by big shot Sig Loreale. But even a big shot gets stuck in the mud sometimes, and Loreale got stuck a couple of years back, caught taking the skim from some cheapjack garbage scow operation. The dough was small change for Loreale, who makes more serious money in all sorts of rackets, the biggest being his contract murder outfit, but it was enough to send him to Sing Sing for eighteen months. He's getting out tonight, as a matter of fact, and for the last few weeks the newspaper scribblers, radio spielers, even those Brylcreemed yakkers on that new box, the television, have all been jabbering about Loreale finishing his stretch at midnight tonight. It's a few minutes past that now.

The poor guy won't have his sweetie to come home to.

Loreale's dead ladylove goes by the name of Opal Shaw; though I wonder about the Shaw moniker, with its Highland Lass ring to it. Not with those cheekbones and hair as black and wavy as a shadow rippling on the river. By the look of her, I'd say the Shaw was probably wrenched out of something else—Schwartz, maybe, or Scalisi, the sort of names I knew in the Coney Island neighborhood of my rowdy childhood. By the look of her...

She was something to look at, all right. Before Loreale went to prison, there were plenty of pictures in the papers of Opal and Loreale arm in arm at the city's hot spots. They'd have late suppers at Sardi's with the after-theater crowd, sip martinis in a blue-and-white zebra-skin booth at El Morocco with the swellest of the swells. Opal would be wrapped in expensive furs. Plenty of mink, sure, but the more exotic kinds, too: leopard, ermine, even tiger. From what I could see in the pictures and in newsreels at the movies, Opal Shaw looked as supple and elegant in fur skins as the creatures who'd worn them on their bones before her.

She sure drove the gossip columnists crazy. A society scribbler wondered how a night-crawling party girl like Opal Shaw landed the notoriously reclusive businessman Sig Loreale, who was rumored to have ties to the underworld, or so the papers said. Another slobbering gossip-meister went gaga over Opal's long hair, compared her to the sleek danger of a prowling panther. If that reporter saw her now, dead on the deck of a cop boat, her famous black mane wet and tangled around her busted-up face, he'd have to lose the panther angle and compare her to something else, maybe a squid.

The bulky mass of Sergeant Bram Feek inserts himself into my reminiscences of Miss Shaw as gently as a boulder rolling over a flower bed. Feek has to shout to be heard over the engine, a shout that explodes from his mouth like an ogre's belch. "What's your story tonight, Gold?" Feek's the skipper of the patrol boat. He'd beat me up if no one was looking.

I'm soaked and cold to the bone, so it's tough for me to shout or even make civil conversation through my chattering teeth. "I was...out for a sweet little cruise on a fine night, Sergeant." I bet Feek is warm and cozy inside his big blue police slicker.

River spray and moonlight are kind to the sergeant's thick mug, make him look less like an unmuzzled pit bull, more like a dented Christmas-tree ornament. He kills my good impression of him when he grins, spits, aiming for my face, but the wind carries Feek's spit backward into the river spray. He knew it would. I can see it in his entirely too satisfied grin. "So," he says, "it's a fine night, is it?" He's grinning at me like he's enjoying a fantasy of killing me. "One night you'll play it a little too cute, Gold, and when you do"—his grin is really nasty now, a stretching slit of hate across his yellow teeth—"look for me at the head of the long line of cops muscling each other outta the way to be the lucky fella who gets you locked up."

Locked up. Hearing those words come at me from a cop's mouth makes me edgy, makes me remember my lousy night behind bars, and makes me wonder, too, how long I can outrun the danger of my life. If the sad day comes when the Law snares me, I hope it's not until my twilight years when sharing a cozy prison cell with a pretty little murderess might not be so bad.

Meantime, I'll take my pleasures where I find 'em and right now I'm about to grab a small one at Feek's expense. "I wouldn't jump the line too soon, Sergeant. The department should be less concerned with locking me *in* and more concerned with who's getting *out*. It's a sure bet that Sig Loreale will be interested in what happened to his ladylove." My numb lips and chattering teeth must make my own smile as grotesque as Feek's, an idea that gives me great pleasure as I flash the smile at him. His clumsy counterpunch, a showy sneer meant to vanquish me, or at least annoy me, makes me giddy instead. I have to turn around and look at the action on the waterfront or I'd laugh right in his rotten face.

We're coming up fast to the docks. The pier at Dover Street is already mobbed with so many reporters and press photographers pushing their way out of the wharf shed that the morgue's meat wagon is having a helluva time getting through. The photographers are popping their flashbulbs fast as a firing squad. What a bunch of ghouls. I swear, those characters must sleep with their clothes on and police-band radios crackling beside their beds. Look at 'em, elbowing the morgue boys and each other to get a good spot, get the first grim picture of the big shot's dead dolly. The twirling light on the meat wagon shows up their true colors, smears all of 'em blood red.

Feek's looking at the hubbub on the pier, too. His bulldog nose flares like he's caught the scent of something cops fear more than the danger of the job: aggravation. There's nothing that tangles up a cop more than the aggravation of buttinsky reporters, except maybe buttinsky politicians, and Opal Shaw's big splash is a sure hook for both. Feek rubs his mouth like he's craving a stiff drink but would settle for a tall bicarbonate of soda. "Goddamn sonsabitch reporters. They had to go squawk about Loreale gettin' outta prison tonight. And now his woman is nothin' but a dead fish on the deck of my boat. *Christ!* Next thing, I'll have the goddamn police commissioner round my neck and the mayor round my ankles." Feek eyes me, studies the scars on my face as if they're drawing him a picture.

He says, polite as a professor, "You're a member of the criminal class, Gold, so what do you think happened to the hoodlum's dame? Maybe she might've wanted to cash it in? Maybe she wasn't as happy about Loreale comin' home as she was supposed to be? Or maybe she might've had a little help goin' over the bridge?"

"How the hell should I know? Nobody paid me to catch her."

Feek sneers at me again. I guess he didn't like my answer.

The patrol boat slows as we get close to the pier.

The last thing I need in my line of work is my face plastered all over the city's morning dailies. I hang back until Feek's crew carries Opal up the ladder, then I wait until the camera crowd and pen pushers and radio gossips swarm around the main action of Opal being laid out on a gurney and wheeled across the pier. Nobody's paying any attention to me when I start to climb up, but I pull my soaked woolen watch cap lower, keep my head down anyway.

A rough yank on my sweater pulls me backward, fast. I slam against Feek. His knuckles dig into my spine as he twists the back of my sweater, stretching it across my chest, tightening the wet wool around my neck. He slides his stubbly chin over my left shoulder, gets cheek to cheek with me. His day's growth of stubble scrapes my face like sandpaper. His breath, a sour gas stinking of cheap cigars and old cheese, turns my stomach almost as much as having his body pressed against my back.

"Not so fast, Gold! Don't think you're gettin' away from me just like that."

If Feek wasn't choking me, I'd vomit from the stench

coming out of his mouth. His stubble grinds my cheek as he tilts his head down. The brute's ogling my chest. He spits a small laugh, the filthy sort that made your mother wash your mouth out with soap. "Well, you coulda fooled me," he says. "I doubted you had a pair!"

I'd like to wash Feek's mouth out with his own blood.

I grab as much air as I can, but Feek's fingers are tightening the neck of my sweater. He's not trying to kill me, just prove he has the power to shut me up.

I won't let him shut me up, not as long as I'm alive and kicking. Between choked gasps and gurgles, I manage to grind out, "Get your...eyes...off my pair, Feek, and I...won't ram the...heel of my shoe...into yours." My right foot is up between Feek's knees.

Feek snaps me loose but grabs my arm again fast, spins me back around, shows me his pit-bull's teeth, shows me who's boss. He even barks, "Get up there on the pier! A detective radioed the boat. Two of 'em wanna talk to you. They got a few questions." He pushes me toward the ladder, pushes my head hard enough so my face slams against the wooden slats. What is it with cops slamming people's heads?

I'm spitting splinters out of my mouth as I climb up.

If the two gold shields standing over me wonder why I seem unsociable, I could tell 'em I've got twenty-five thousand reasons at the bottom of New York Harbor and one more reason right under my derriere: the iron stanchion they shoved me down on is ice cold through my soaked chinos.

These two boys are just like all the other night shift detectives who've tried to lord it over me through the years: out-of-style overcoats, scuffed shoes, faces as ashy gray as their shapeless fedoras, and feral, bloodshot eyes that never seem to blink until sunup. One guy's snarly, the other's quiet, scribbling notes with a stub of a pencil on a pad of paper. The snarly one does all the talking.

"Did you know the victim?"

"I've seen her picture in the papers," I say.

"What about Sig Loreale? Know anything about him?"

"What everyone knows. Papers say he's getting out tonight."

"What were you doing in the harbor at this hour?"

"Nice night, nice moon. Say, did ya see it shine through the fog?"

"What about that tug heading your way?"

"Which tug? This is New York Harbor, for chrissake."

The cops give me a blanket from the morgue truck to wrap myself in while we jabber. I give them nothing but conversation. When the conversation is over, the snarly cop takes the blanket back and the quiet cop hands me a dime for the subway, since everything I'd had in my pockets—my billfold, the brooch, and my gun—is now at the bottom of the East River.

They let Opal keep her blanket, though, when the morgue boys slide her into the meat wagon.

❖

Cash and crime never stop flowing in the City of New York. They just make less noise at certain times of night in certain parts of town. Around here, for instance, in these dark streets and alleyways behind the docks, where waterfront gangs do business for the Mob bosses, you can't hear the crackle of dirty money changing hands in the damp rooms above the tradesmen's shuttered shops. You won't hear the muffled groans of some poor schnook who's behind on his loan payments, getting beaten to a pulp in a moldy corner of one of the old brick warehouses. You can't hear the whispered deals being made in the back rooms of City Hall or in the basement of the criminal courts building a few blocks away. The only noises out here on Ferry Street tonight are the moans of the foghorns drifting in from the harbor and the squish on the pavement of my waterlogged deck shoes. My only companion is my own shadow sliding around me on the sidewalk whenever I pass under a street lamp. The only money I can lay my hands on is the police department's dime in my pocket.

The last time I had only a dime in my pocket I was a randy kid under the Coney Island boardwalk, and even though a dime got you a whole lot more then, it didn't get as much as I wanted. Same story now. Best it can get me tonight is a phone call or a ride on the subway.

I've been keeping an eye out for a phone booth. I spot one at the corner, start to pick up my pace, but I'm stopped short by a guy's phlegmy voice suddenly behind me. "Stand still, don't turn around, you don't gotta see me. All you gotta do is listen. Be at Mr. Loreale's place later." The guy makes his point with a gun to my spine. The cold barrel stings through my wet sweater. But it's not just the icy steel that makes me shiver. It's feeling the vibration of the vast web Loreale's spun through the city. He's been out of the slammer only minutes, and he already knows what's happened tonight and my part in it. He knew where to send this guy to shadow me.

I say, "What's *later*."

"Late enough so he can get back in town, soon enough so he don't hafta wait long. Know where his place is?"

"Doesn't everybody?"

"Don't gimme any smart lip. Just be at Loreale's place."

"You have a car? Give me a ride to my apartment so I can change into dry—" But the gun is gone from my spine, the guy is gone from the street. Just as well; I wouldn't want that fishy article knowing where I live.

I head for the phone booth I'd spotted in front of a rope supply place on the corner. Funny, how a sight as common as an empty telephone booth can beckon like a haven in the darkness, its shiny blue-and-white enamel Bell Tel sign holding out a promise that when I close the door my freezing flesh will get a little relief from the night chill.

I step inside. The door keeps the chill out, all right, but the overhead bulb is busted. How many other little indignities are gunning for me tonight? I have to tilt my head just right to allow enough light to dwindle in from a street lamp so I can see the dial. I pull the cops' dime from my soggy pocket, feel around for the coin slot, and drop the dime. It clatters down, ringing its bells and jangling my nerves, until it lands in Ma Bell's lap and she gives me a dial tone so I can dial Judson Zane, a talented young jack-of-all-trades who works for me. No one types faster than Judson. No one is better at digging deep into the city to find people who can perform certain necessary services but don't ask questions. The only person Judson hasn't been able to find is Sophie, though he works his sources first thing every morning and last thing every night. He hasn't turned up anything yet, and until he does, we just don't talk about it.

Judson's phone rings, keeps ringing. The way my luck's running, it would fit right in if he's not home. Or maybe my call is interrupting one of his interesting nights. The town's debs and coeds are crazy about Judson, his skinny build, wire-rimmed glasses, and all. I don't know what he tells them he does for a living, but I don't worry about it, either. Judson's code of secrecy is more impenetrable than the vault at Fort Knox.

He finally answers on the sixth ring.

"It's me, Judson," I say. "You alone?"

"Yeah. Did everythi—"

"I'll fill you in later. I need you to drive downtown, come pick me up. I'm at the corner of Ferry and Cliff. And look, I've already had cops in my face and a gun in my back and I'm out twenty-five grand, so do me a favor and make it snappy. And bring your office keys."

"What the hell—? What are you talking about, out twenty-five grand? Didn't Ortine come through with the cash? Cantor, I spent *weeks* setting up a cold trail of customs stamps just so Ortine could squeeze that big emerald in his tight fist."

"You'll read all about it in the morning papers, Judson. Hell, you might even hear about it on the radio while you're driving down here. Listen, get a hold of Rosie. I'm supposed to see her later, but if she's still hacking, you'll have to stop by the office and put in a radio call to her cab. Tell her to meet us at the office right away. And bring your rain slicker."

"But it's not raining."

"Just bring it. Believe me, you'll thank me later."

"See you in fifteen minutes."

Fifteen minutes to go nuts with myself just standing around in the dead of night in Lower Manhattan, watching old newspapers fly around on the cobblestones, my eye catching headlines: the scribblers are still bellyaching about Joe Louis retiring from the fight ring a couple of weeks ago; old Joe Stalin died last week, which is sad for his wife and kids but maybe nice for millions of Russkies who won't be rounded up to rot in Siberia; President Truman is busy sunning himself in Key West, Florida, though I'm sure he took the time to send a thoughtful note to Stalin's widow; and Sig Loreale is getting out of prison.

I wish I had my bottle of Chivas to warm my innards and maybe drown the sickening memory of Opal Shaw broken and bleeding on the hull of my sinking boat. And I could use a cigarette from the pack of smokes that the East River swallowed up along with everything else. The fifteen minutes creep along, a torture of shivers from lousy memories and my increasingly cold flesh, until the glow of the curbside street lamp slides along the chrome on the fender of Judson's blue Chevy. He bought it this past December, when the showrooms were making rock-bottom deals to move the last of the '48 models. Saved himself a bundle.

His rain slicker is on the front seat. I put it on, get into the car. An old Cole Porter tune, "All Through the Night," is playing on the radio when we drive away.

I say, "Were you followed?"

"Nope. Zigzagged through Times Square, used a trick Rosie taught me to get through the Bow Tie. If there was anybody on my tail, they're still stuck in the cabbie traffic in front of the Hotel Astor. And, oh yeah, thanks for not getting my car seat all wet. What'd you do? Get caught in the wake of Drogan's tug?"

"Didn't the radio spielers fill you in?"

Judson turns the radio down low, says, "I roamed the dial for any bulletins. Ortine's name never came up. Neither did yours. Just quickie cut-ins about Sig Loreale's lady taking a dive—oh no, for cryin' out loud, Cantor. Please tell me you're not tangled up in that."

"That's what I'm tangled up in. The lady crashed right down on my boat. Nearly killed me."

"And the emerald?"

"At the bottom of the river. Along with my boat. Let me have one of your smokes."

Judson unzips his lumber jacket, the brown leather whispering in its lifelike way, and reaches into his shirt pocket for his pack of Luckies. He hands me the pack as I press the cigarette lighter on the dashboard of the Chevy. With one of Judson's Luckies between my lips, I say, "You reached Rosie?"

"Yeah. She's hauling a fare from the Copa to Seventy-Third and Park, but she'll meet us at the office after. Cantor, what the hell are you getting into?"

The dashboard lighter pops out with a click. I grab it and bring it to the end of the cigarette, my nerves overdue for a deep, calming drag. The lighter's hot coil glows bright red, the same color as the swirling light on the coroner's meat wagon. I see Opal Shaw all over again.

CHAPTER THREE

Every muscle and bone in my body needs a stiff drink and a hot shower by the time Judson pulls into the alleys behind a row of small warehouses and factory buildings along Twelfth Avenue. A tumbler of Chivas is my usual medicine of choice for what ails me, but tonight I doubt any amount of booze will kill the bitter taste of losing my small boat and that big emerald. That's a lot of money at the bottom the East River. And even if I guzzle the juice 'til I'm blotto, I doubt I'll ever get rid of the memory of Opal Shaw all twisted and busted up. Nobody deserves to die like that, broken and tossed away like useless goods.

But a scotch and a shower will at least warm the ache out of my muscles and smooth the goose bumps off my flesh. Relief from those irritations is very near now, inside the one-story brick job I own at the end of one of the alleys.

It's a perfect setup for my racket: a nondescript building at the corner of Twelfth Avenue with the Hudson River's passenger ship piers across the street and the protective shadow of the West Side Highway overhead. By night, unless a liner's coming in, the streets around here are as empty as an old lady's handbag. The cheap luncheonettes where dockworkers grab a sandwich and a cuppa coffee are closed.

The worn-out souls who eke out a living doing piecework in the neighborhood's small-time factories have gone home to their shabby apartments.

By day, though, it's a different story. The neighborhood's a horn-honking tangle of delivery trucks, handcarts, and taxi cabs that can tie up any cop car that's trying to get to me before I can stash whatever needs stashing—that is, if the cops even knew I own the place. My lawyer buried the title so deep, in so many layers of paperwork, you'd need a pickax to get to the bottom and you'd still never find my name.

And chances are you won't see many cops around here anyway. Like all the piers in the Port of New York, those docks across the street are Mob turf, sewn up tight through the pistol local of the longshoremen's union, where union votes are tallied with bullets, squealers wind up dead, and cops are paid to stay clear. So if he knows what's good for him, the only reason for a cop to show up around here is to have a friendly drink with one of the boys and pick up an envelope stuffed with cash, some of it mine.

As for any other Joes and Janes who might be innocently wandering around outside, their attention is nicely diverted by some of the more glamorous activity that goes on across the street along the twelve-block stretch of piers called Luxury Liner Row. The most famous ocean liners in the world dock over there, so why pay attention to my scruffy hideaway when you can ogle the sleek lines of the *Queen Mary* or the *Ile de France* and their first-class passengers? Who knows? You might even see the Duke and Duchess of Windsor coming down the gangplank, or better yet, a movie star, maybe that cute Betty Grable showing off those million-dollar legs.

But if anyone ever does notice my squat little building, they'd never guess that the blacked-out front door opens on nothing but a wall, that the real access is through the maze of alleyways in the back, or that my building's ramshackle exterior camouflages a big-money business with a false wall in the basement that conceals a room-size vault. Inside that vault are treasures that curators and collectors would kill for. *Do* kill for. Collectors like Gregory Ortine, who right now is probably thinking about killing *me*.

That idea nips at my heels as I get out of the car.

Judson unlocks the sliding steel door at the back of the building and walks inside, making sure the steel shutters are bolted before he turns a light on at his desk. But I don't wait for the light. I want that shower and I need that drink and I don't need light to find my way to my private office. This place and its secrets are as much home to me as my apartment.

I'm out of my wet clothes by the time I turn my desk lamp on. The lamplight settling around the room makes me feel cozier already, right at home among the grade A furnishings I've brought in, all of it earned by the sweat of my brow and my finger in the Law's eye. The lamplight brings out the patina of my walnut desk, deepens the color of the oxblood sofa, and throws soft shadows across a pale green club chair whose leather is so smooth and supple that sitting in it is like being embraced by a mistress who's worth every dime she costs you.

I even sleep here sometimes, on the couch, if I need to babysit a treasure before delivery or if I have to lie low until certain situations cool off. Tonight may be one of those situations, depending on who's in a more murderous mood: mobster Sig Loreale or clip-joint racketeer Gregory Ortine. But I'll be okay if I have to stick here tonight. There's food in the icebox, plenty of coffee, and I always make sure there are two virgin bottles of Chivas backing up the bottle that's already working.

A glass of scotch comes with me into the shower. The hot water soothes my scars and massages my knotted muscles, but it's the whiskey that oozes life and heat into my gut, opens me up for the luxury of that first warm, moist breath after I turn the shower off. The steamy air rolls through me, cleans out the poison of Sergeant Feek's dirty mind and stinking breath. But the death of Opal Shaw still haunts me, and with the memory of Miss Shaw's death comes the problem of Sig Loreale and what he wants of me.

I'll know soon enough, and I'd better be sharp when I meet with Mister Big Shot. He can spot weakness a mile away.

I take out a dark green silk suit and a light blue cashmere pullover from the closet across from the washroom. With each piece of clothing I put on—the trousers, the cashmere, a pair of powder-blue silk socks, brown oxfords, and an alligator-band wristwatch—I'm restored to my favorite mood: brazen. Even my hair is brazen, an intractable brown mop that no barber can tame. Some women like it, some don't. The ones who don't are usually too tame of spirit for me anyhow.

The last bits of my outfit are in the safe behind my desk. I grab a set of spare keys from the top shelf: car keys, office keys, the keys to my apartment. But my fingers wrap tight around a specific key, the key to Sophie's apartment on East Sixty-Third Street where I'd spent the night from time to time after she went missing. I figured I'd protect the place, keep an eye on her furniture, her clothing, all the little personal things Sophie used to pick up and put down.

There's a framed photo in the safe, too. I took it from Sophie's apartment. It's a picture of me and Sophie, an enlargement of one of those Times Square twenty-five-cent photo booth snaps taken when we went out for breakfast after the first night we made love. We're grinning at each other like love-struck teenagers with a secret, a secret as exciting as it was dangerous, a secret that could get us locked up or beat up, but that morning we didn't care. We'd found paradise in each other and together we'd face whatever danger the world's hatred would throw at us. I kept the photo on my desk for a while but finally had to stow it in the safe. Seeing it every day was driving me over the edge again.

I don't go to Sophie's place much these days. Like I said, I'm free of that madness now. I keep the rent up to date, though, in case Sophie finds her way home.

I stash my key ring in my trouser pocket, take a spare billfold, a backup driver's license, and a hundred cash in small bills from a strongbox that also contains Ortine's down payment of ten G's. Nice wad. He'll want it back. I don't want to give it to him.

A shoulder holster and the spare .38 I keep at the office finish up my dressing routine. I load the gun's chambers, snap the barrel back, and slip the gun into the rig. No doubt I'll have to hand it over to one of Loreale's thugs before I'm ushered into the boss's presence, but odds are good I'll get it back afterward, and with Ortine and *his* thugs on the prowl I'm not about to hit the street naked.

After I grab extra rounds and put them into my trouser pocket, I close the safe, slip my suit jacket on, and top it off with a blue silk pocket handkerchief. The deep green of my suit shimmers in the lamplight. I like silk suits. I like the way silk feels and I like the way silk shines.

Okay, I'm ready to face the big bad boogeyman named Sig Loreale.

There's a quick tap on my office door, followed by a breathy "Cantor?" It's Rosie.

"C'mon in." The door opens, Rosie steps inside. Judson follows her. Rosie must've driven here straight from her last cab fare. She's still wearing her driver's duds and cap.

The glow from the desk lamp sits even better on Rosie than it does on my silk threads or my fine furniture. Light always sits well on Rosie, settles naturally on her peaches-and-cream complexion, turns her blond hair the color of mist. But don't let the dainty-damsel details fool you. Rosie Bliss handles an automobile better than any wheelman in town. She can slice through clogged New York City traffic with the daring of a race-car driver and the precision of a brain surgeon.

She also has a way of sitting down that never fails to attract my attention, an effortless, subtle sashay that flows naturally from her most luscious parts. I watch with pleasure as she unzips her jacket and sits down in the club chair with a gently rolling motion that carves curves in the air around her. Her blue work shirt doesn't do justice to her breasts, full and luscious as a Classical Venus. But that's all right. I know what's there. I've gotten lost in them often enough.

Rosie pulls out a pack of smokes from her jacket pocket and lights one up. Through an exhale of smoke that curls around her face as seductively as a belly dancer's veil, she says, "I was hoping to go home and get all dressed up before we go out. Plans changed?"

"Sorry, Rosie. Yeah, plans changed. An appointment suddenly came up, but I don't want my car spotted there. And I have things I want Judson to do here, so I need a ride in the cab."

"Where we goin'?"

"Sig Loreale's place."

Judson sits down on the couch with a thump I didn't think possible from a kid with such a skinny build. He's looking straight at me, eyes wide behind his glasses, an expression on his face like he's figuring the arrangements and cost of my funeral.

Rosie says, "Yeah, it's been in the papers all week about Loreale gettin' out tonight. What's it got to do with you?"

"You hear what happened to his lady, to Opal Shaw?"

"Nope. Didn't have the news on in the cab."

"Opal took a dive off the Brooklyn Bridge, landed on my boat." I give Rosie and Judson the whole story, from pushing off under the bridge to make a dash for Red Drogan's tug, all the way through to the guy with the gun at my back while he delivered Loreale's post-prison social invitation. "And listen, Rosie, I'll keep you out of this as much as I can, but I don't want my Buick on the street at Loreale's place. It's better if I leave it in my spot in Louie's garage in case the cops have an eye out for it, now that they've fished me out of the river. They don't need to know I've got business with Loreale."

"Sure, I'll carry you," she says. She takes a deep drag of her smoke, looks at me in a way I like. There's nothing tame of spirit about my beautiful soldier. She handles trouble with a wink and a kiss. It's even how she handles me. Rosie knows that sharing sex and crime with me doesn't mean sharing my heart, at least not all of it, and that my bed entertains other women. If she wants more of me, she hasn't said so. Rosie's too smart to corner me.

Speaking soft and low, giving every word an erotic promise she knows I go for, she says, "Working with you is a lot more fun than hauling cab fares. And the side benefits aren't bad, either." Rosie's smile comes at me sideways but with perfect aim, hitting me in the juiciest of places. I give her a smile back, let it pass the message that after I take care of Loreale's business, we'll make time for those side benefits before sunrise.

Judson says, "And what about Gregory Ortine? That vicious son of a bitch is almost as dangerous as Loreale."

"*Almost* as dangerous. I'm putting him in your lap for a while, Judson. I want you to stay here and get hold of Red Drogan, find out what went on with Ortine after the louse up on the river. Then tap your other sources and get a current line on Ortine, find out where he is and what he's up to. I'll check in with you later."

I take a pack of Chesterfields, a book of matches, and a penknife from my desk drawer, then grab a brown tweed overcoat and green checkered cap from the closet. On my way through the office I run my finger along Rosie's shoulder. "Let's go."

CHAPTER FOUR

Some people are born dangerous. I figured it out when I was just a ten-year-old kid in scruffy dungarees in Coney Island during the wild days of Prohibition and I'd see Solly Schwartz walking around. He was a short roly-poly guy with a monkey's grin, but he could cut you in half with one swipe of his steel-gray eyes. Everybody in Coney Island—the soda and ice cream peddlers on the beach, candy butchers along the boardwalk, glad-handing thrill-ride operators, and singsong barkers who'd lure the suckers into the fun houses and arcades—they all knuckled under to Fat Solly, forced to pay kickbacks and protection money to Coney Island's brutal boss of the underworld.

But in the hard world of dangerous men, Solly and his gang of bruisers were no match for the sly genius of the young Sig Loreale when Loreale and his assassins started muscling in. Sig had three things Fat Solly didn't: a strategy, the brains to carry it out, and a disciplined bunch of murderers to enforce it by killing not only those who got in Sig's way, but also his rivals' girlfriends, wives, their kids, even their household pets, as a warning to any potential interlopers. The outfit's methods ran the gamut from a simple shooting to breaking a mark's arms and legs and hurling him into oncoming traffic, or binding a guy in rope from his neck to his feet, then tying bricks to his ankles and tossing him into the Atlantic Ocean for the fish to nibble his eyes out. And those were only the ones we heard about, stories whispered in the clam bars, the bathhouses, my school yard. We knew there were plenty more we didn't hear about.

Sig's businesslike ruthlessness was sleek and modern, never seen before by the clannish old-school Coney Island bosses. Solly and his crowd couldn't muster a quick-footed defense against it, couldn't stop Sig from grabbing the amusement ride and sideshow skim offs, the illicit whiskey operations, the gambling joints and sex trade, all the moneymaking fun of Coney Island.

One hot and sticky August afternoon during a lull in Sig and Solly's gang war, I was having a swell time at a Kewpie-doll concession, shooting BBs at a moving line of painted tin ducks, when a strong-arm thug grabbed me by the rope belt around my dungarees. The guy just about lifted me off the ground. The Kewpie-doll huckster looked the other way when the thug grabbed me. I flailed and yelped like a terrified pup, but the huckster didn't lift a finger. He knew the price of interfering.

The thug hauled me to a shabby room above Hobart's Gypsy Danceland, a dime-a-dance joint near the Wonder Wheel ride. I'd have choked on the stifling air in the room, bristly with sand and dust, except I was too scared to breathe. It didn't help that the Wonder Wheel's hurdy-gurdy music was muffled by the closed window, made the music sound far away, and put my cozy world of childhood fun terrifyingly out of reach.

A pale, skinny guy walked in and killed that childhood world altogether when he pulled the window shade down. He turned a light on, a naked overhead bulb whose glare made the room even uglier, colored the dusty air yellowish-green. He knocked on a door to another room. I don't know if he knocked loud or lightly, but it sounded like a firing squad to me. I closed my eyes real tight, crinkled my face, a kid's defense against being scared.

But when I heard the door open, my eyes opened, too. I guess a kid's curiosity is stronger than a kid's fear. Coming through the door was a guy who was a lot older than me but a lot younger than my old man. His face was as flushed and fleshy as boiled meat but he was as well tailored as the Percival van This-and-Thats whose pictures advertised expensive cars in magazines. His thick brown hair was neatly combed and he wore a natty gray suit despite the suffocating heat. His stride was powerful, deliberate, with that no-nonsense air of authority that makes people obey. His only concession to the heat was the loosened knot of his floral-pattern tie and the open collar of his white shirt, the high-collared kind popular in those days. His gray eyes drooped like a cocker spaniel's, but there was no doggy friendliness in that face. In the glare of the naked lightbulb the guy's eyes were empty as a vacant lot.

I tried not to cringe when he walked right up to me, put one of his eerily cool fingers under my sweaty chin, and lifted my face. Looking up at him was like staring into the inhuman face of the night-walking boogeyman who frightens little kids into pulling the bedcovers over their heads. He was Sig Loreale, master killer. I was in his gang-war headquarters.

He spoke to me slowly, and the way he put space between his words gave them a threatening power. His voice was rough but whispery, like gravel grinding sand. "You are quite the little operator. Oh yeah…sure…I know all about your finders-keepers racket."

My stomach turned over. I'd been found out by a grown-up. The deadliest of all grown-ups!

And then things got even worse. He said, "That is some nerve you got, scrounging on the beach while the people pack up to go home. Those are poor people. Immigrants, most of 'em, hardworking immigrants. Same as your momma and poppa. Same as mine."

He knew who my parents were. He knew what I was doing on the beach. He really *was* the boogeyman. He knew *everything*. He could come to our apartment. He could kill us all.

I wanted to run away from that room, run home and warn my mom and pop, but Loreale kept his eyes on me, those droopy gray eyes whose hard stare was a warning not to move, just to listen. "How do you think your momma would feel if she knew what her American-born bundle of joy was up to, eh? What would your poppa think if he knew that you pick things up that fall from people's pockets and bags? What would he say if he knew that you don't give the items back, as he would want you to do, but that you stash everything in a strongbox you got buried under the boardwalk? Well, I will tell you what he would think. He would be ashamed of you, that's what."

And then Loreale tilted his head back, his eyes crinkled, his lips widened into a smile. His mouth opened but no sound came out. He was laughing, a silent, gruesome laugh that almost scared the water outta me. It took every ounce of my pint-sized willpower not to pee in my pants, an effort that had nothing to do with my pride but with the raw terror that Mr. Loreale wouldn't like it if I peed in my pants, and I'd wind up being the next victim whose eyes were nibbled by fish.

He shook his head as he finished laughing, then said, "But...I got to hand it to you. You got a good head on your shoulders. I hear that you weed out your trinkets, take only the best to the secondhand peddlers down the Lower East Side. I've seen you lug your satchel of stuff up the stairs to the

Stillwell Avenue train station. A regular little Santa Claus you looked like." The way he smiled at me was almost fatherly, if my father was a murderer. My old pop couldn't kill anybody, not for all the money in America.

Loreale lifted my chin again. His fingers were still cool. He didn't sound fatherly anymore. "Look, I don't give a damn about your little beach racket. Go ahead, make a living. You're entitled. Just get out from under the boardwalk. Find another spot to hide your trinkets." He didn't threaten me, didn't say *or else* to scare me into obedience. He didn't have to. His reputation and my imagination were scary enough.

Even all those years ago, Loreale was spinning his web. He knew everything going on in Coney Island and who was doing it. But I wasn't thinking about that then, about how he knew about my family and my finders-keepers operation. I was just grateful that Loreale nodded at the jamoke who'd brought me up to that hot room above the dance hall, the nod meaning the guy could take me right back out again. I was still alive. I could start sixth grade in September.

Sig and his mob won the turf war, won it so clean the Law couldn't connect him to any of the bloody, burned, and dismembered corpses that littered the back rooms of the clam bars and fun houses and, yeah, under the boardwalk. The war was Sig's masterstroke. It gave him the means to fine-tune his murder operation, lay the foundation for a killing-for-hire business he eventually built into a shadow corporation more powerful in this town than City Hall. These days, his murder and rough-'em-up services are contracted by bosses and big shots, by bosses of crime and by big shots you didn't know are in crime. Think about that the next time you're enjoying a cuppa coffee while you read the gossip column or business news in your favorite morning paper.

Rosie's rolling along West Fortieth Street toward Fifth

Avenue. I'm in the backseat, just another anonymous late-night fare in the darkened backseat of a cab, not worth a cop's notice. We're on our way to an office tower, a doozy built in the '20s, the Jazz Age, when the town stayed drunk on bootleg whiskey and dressed for the party in high-style architecture. When the Depression crashed the party and sent everyone home without even enough for carfare, Loreale was able to buy the building for pennies on the dollar and set himself up in the penthouse.

The place is a sleek black brick pile dolled up with Gothic-style gilt work on top. During the day, when sunlight hits all those gold pinnacles and arches, the penthouse shimmers like a luminous royal crown. By night, lit only by the lights of the city and the glow of the moon, the building's dark mass disappears, leaving just the rooftop glowing in the sky, a brilliant golden crown for the king of killers who lives inside.

Rosie's craning her head for a look out the windshield, trying to see the top of Sig's tower. She says, "You think Loreale's gotten in yet? I can't make out from down here if the lights are on in his place."

"It's only about an hour's drive down from Ossining," I say. "Sig must've had one of his boys pick him up." I check my watch; it's one in the morning. "If Sig and his driver aren't back yet, they should be here any minute."

"What about the doorman? How you gonna get by him at this time of night, looking the way you do? I mean, that's a swell outfit you're wearing, Cantor, but you'll confuse the poor Joe, just like you confuse all the poor Joes. And you know as well as I do, better, even, that Joes don't like to be confused. Makes 'em nasty, turns 'em dangerous."

"There's no doorman after business hours, Rosie, maybe just a night watchman—"

"Same difference."

"—who's probably one of Loreale's boys. Could be I've met him before. Anyway, Loreale must've passed the word that I'm expected. I doubt there'll be a problem."

She makes a sharp pull to the curb in front of Sig's building. The maneuver knocks me sideways on the backseat. It's Rosie's way of letting me know she's not crazy about my take on the situation.

"This won't take long," I say when she brings the cab to a stop and I'm able to sit up again. "I'm sure Loreale wants to grill me about what happened to Opal Shaw on the river, and since I have no idea what was going on with Opal before she crash landed on my boat, there isn't much for him to grill me about. Believe me, I have no intention of lingering after I give him my story. I figure to be back in twenty minutes, maybe a half hour." I start out of the cab.

Rosie's arm moves fast over the top of the front seat, her hand grabs the sleeve of my overcoat. "And if you're not?"

There's something about a woman's face at night, when the furtive light of street lamps uncovers thoughts she wants to keep secret, that makes me want to kiss her. Light from a curbside street lamp is uncovering Rosie's secrets. They're irresistible. I take her face between my hands, kiss her.

I want to satisfy the desires of her mouth, especially when her tongue lightly traces the scar above my lip, but I don't dare linger. I'm not sure which is more dangerous: being tardy when summoned by Sig Loreale or letting Rosie take too much of me. I take my lips from hers, whisper, "Since when have I ever kept a lady waiting?"

Rosie loosens her grip on the sleeve of my coat. I get out of the cab.

I wonder if the daily tenants who walk through that soaring glass-and-bronze entrance into Sig's big black tower— ordinary business folk in three-piece suits and gray fedoras, their white-gloved secretaries and red-lipsticked steno girls whose high-heeled shoes click along the marble hallways—I wonder if they ever feel a stomach-churning dread of the quiet, well-groomed businessman who owns the building and who makes his home in the penthouse. Or maybe the simple prudence of writing their rent checks on time, getting through the workweek, and otherwise minding their own business numbs them to the idea that a killer owns the air they breathe five days a week.

On the other hand, people seem to like rubbing elbows with gangsters. So maybe Sig's tenants get a kick out of their proximity to the underworld's biggest big shot. Maybe tomorrow morning, if they pass Sig in the lobby on his way out to breakfast at Bickford's cafeteria, when he'll likely be dressed in the conservative businessman's attire he favors, the women will smile nervous little smiles at him, the men will tip their hats to welcome him home. And that night, when they sit down to dinner with their families, they'll tell them all about the Mr. Big Shot in the lobby and feel the thrill all over again.

Sure, it's easy for them. The nine-to-fivers only work in Sig's building; they don't live on his side of the Law. I do. I know the power of his reach too well to fool myself about the deadly reality of Sig Loreale. Right now, my stomach's churning with plenty of sickening dread, just like it did on that hot afternoon in Coney Island when Sig's thug dragged my terrified, squirming ten-year-old self into the boogeyman's presence. My stomach turns over every time I'm face-to-face with Loreale.

I press the brass button for the night bell. The button is cold from the chill in the air. Stings my fingertip.

Then I wait, obedient, a vassal outside the glass door.

A light finally goes on in the vestibule. A regular sort of old fella in a blue janitor's uniform shows up, but he doesn't unlock the door. I've never met this gray-haired geezer before. It's pretty clear by his sneery annoyance that he's pegged me as someone who's not a tenant dropping by the office for a little late-night paperwork. He waves me away. I knock on the glass. All I get is the sight of him walking back into the lobby. I ring the night bell again, then pound on the glass, hard, make enough noise to reclaim his attention, and when he turns around I mouth the name "Loreale." He stares at me for a second or two, he looks scared, the kind of scared that comes with aggravation you can't escape. The guy turns back around to the lobby, shouts for someone, but I don't catch the name. The sound is muffled by the thick glass door.

But I hear Rosie shouting, "Cantor, what's goin' on there?" Before she finishes her question, I see another guy step into the light in the vestibule, a guy with pomaded red hair and a jaunty twinkle in his light blue eyes. He has the congenial manner and style of a successful used-car salesman tricked out in a dapper charcoal double-breasted suit, starched white shirt, and finished off with an up-to-date yellow tie with a black stripe down the center.

Now I'm getting somewhere: I know the guy.

I give a quick wave over my shoulder to Rosie, a signal that everything's okay. Then I hear the cab's ignition turn over, the engine idle smooth and steady. I bet Rosie's keeping the doors unlocked, too, in case I have to jump in fast. My beautiful soldier isn't at all convinced that everything's hunky-dory. She's wise to the ways of business done at night.

I don't waste my time anymore with women who aren't wise to the night. They can't take care of themselves, get swallowed up and disappear, leave me empty-handed and alone on the sidewalk.

The guy in the vestibule is Leon "Pep" Green. I've seen him around town running errands for Sig, even while Loreale was upstate. Sig gave him the moniker Pep because of the joy and energy—the pep—he brings to his job, which isn't salesman. He kills people. A silenced bullet to the head is Pep's trademark method, though word's gone around that he's developed the taste and skill for the even stealthier quiet of a well-aimed ice pick.

The cheery smile Pep gives me lets me know he recognizes me, too.

He signals to the old fella to unlock the door. The guy pulls a ring of keys out of his pocket, unlocks the door, then scurries away, shrinking into his janitor's uniform like a jittery crab pulling deep into his shell, wanting no part of the goings on between the merry murderer Green and a peculiar article like me.

I open the glass door, step inside.

"Hello, Cantor," Green says. "Always nice to see you. Business been good?"

"Your boss is expecting me."

"What's the matter? Can't you even give a civil greeting? I'm just trying to make a little friendly conversation."

"I wasn't aware we're friends."

"You're not friends with Loreale, either, but somehow you got a personal invitation. C'mon, follow me. He wants me to send you up on his private elevator. I gotta frisk you first, though."

Pep's a pleasant guy, as murderers go, but I don't want his paws on me. I open my overcoat and suit jacket, take my gun out, and hand it to him. "Here, I'll save you the trouble."

"I still have to pat you down, Cantor."

He's smiling his best close-the-deal smile while his hands come at me. I push him away.

"C'mon, Cantor, you know I gotta do this."

"And you know I won't let you. You want to know what

I got underneath? This is the best you're gonna get." I pull at the crease of my trousers, hike the cuffs up above my ankles. "See? No gun, no hidden shiv strapped under my socks."

Pep's suddenly not too peppy at all. Like most guys, especially guys who are just henchmen for a more powerful guy, he doesn't like being pushed aside by a dame, whether it's by a dame in tight skirts or a dame like me. Particularly by a dame like me. Pep's cheery smile is gone. His mouth tightens into a thin, straight line. The light blue of his eyes shines a dark silver. A savage face is bleeding through the friendly one, both of them convincing, both of them real.

And then the friendly salesman seeps through again, smiling, his light blue eyes twinkling again.

He gives me the creeps.

He cocks his head for me to follow him across the lobby.

The click of our shoes against the black tile floor echoes into the dark maw of the vaulted ceiling, three stories high. The main lighting is off for the night. There's only a dim luster from the frosted-glass sconces along the lobby's black marble and mirrored walls. But even the glow from all those lamps can't make it up to the ceiling, can't penetrate the darkness looming over my head.

Pep inserts a key into a bronze plate on the wall beside Loreale's private elevator. The doors slide open. I step inside, turn around, see Pep reach for the intercom phone next to the elevator, probably alerting any muscle upstairs that I'm on my way. He flashes me his best salesman's grin as the doors close.

I forget about the murderer downstairs, concentrate on the murderer upstairs, spend the time it takes to ascend to the top of the tower reminding myself that after each of my encounters with Sig Loreale I've walked away alive. Good odds. But as a gambler friend of mine is fond of telling me, the odds eventually turn. Always.

CHAPTER FIVE

I've never been invited up to Loreale's place before tonight and never really wanted to be, either. I'm not keen on heavy socializing with death. Sure, I've met with Loreale since that hot August afternoon in Coney Island, especially since he started buying my goods in the autumn of '45, around the time he met Opal, but it's always been in impersonal places, at one of his front businesses for instance, like his garment factories, or one of his warehouses or trucking firms, where I'd hand Sig a work of art and one of his flunkies would hand me a valise stuffed with cash. The cash was the only pleasurable part of the deal. Being face-to-face with Sig Loreale might not be as scary as when I was a little kid, but not by much.

The elevator finally opens on a green marble hallway that could be equally at home in a bank or a mausoleum. There's a door at each end of the hall. Both are black and polished to a shine, but one doorway is a lot bigger and the door has an oversized chrome doorknob that's faceted like a diamond. The other door has a plain ol' doorknob for plain ol' people, probably the kitchen help. I have no business with Sig's kitchen help, so I head for the fancy doorknob.

I don't know what kind of setup is waiting for me on the other side of Sig's door, and without my gun I might as well be wearing a sandwich sign that says SHOOT ME. This burial chamber of a hallway does nothing to improve my sense of well-being, so after I press the door buzzer I pull my cap lower, close my overcoat, and try to get cozy. Soon my skin's heating up and I feel ridiculous shrinking into the protective shell of my clothing as laughably as the old geezer downstairs.

A young woman in a housemaid's uniform opens the door, which surprises me. A thug would be more in line with Loreale's choice of household help. Maybe the maid was one of Opal Shaw's civilizing ideas, like Sig buying art and archeological treasure. Before he met Opal, Sig didn't know the difference between a coloring book and Corot. He probably still doesn't.

The maid gets pushed out of the way by a brawny guy in a dark suit that's in better taste and tailoring than his cauliflower mug would suggest. If the suit is also one of Miss Shaw's remodeling flourishes, she didn't entirely succeed. The guy's still a thug.

The maid scrams. The thug growls, "You must be Gold. The boss is outside on the terrace. Know where it is?" He jerks his thumb behind him, directing me through the living room.

"I'll find it." An aroma of flowers floats toward me as I walk in.

"Don't keep him waitin'."

Wouldn't dream of it.

The living room is a jungle of flowers, big bouquets in gaudy arrangements all over the place. Quite a splashy welcome for the homecoming mobster. I get a laugh picturing Sig's gang of vicious killers picking out posies in honor of their boss's return. Maybe the thug at the door selected that spray of pink roses on the mantel. Frankly, he didn't strike me as the pink type.

Or maybe as news got around tonight about the death

of Sig's ladylove, his jittery crowd of indebted clients and terrified potential targets bought all these flowers, ponied up real fast to arrange costly late-night deliveries as a better-safe-than-sorry strategy to make sure Sig's aware of their heartfelt respect and sincere condolences. No doubt they'll send even showier flowers to Opal's funeral.

Then again, maybe it was Opal who bought the flowers to welcome her Papa Bear back to their big bed and silk sheets. Some women have a taste for showy displays, though if I had to judge by all those pictures of Opal in the papers and what the gossip meisters wrote about her in the columns, I'd peg Opal Shaw as a classier type of dame. But I've noticed that when a woman is in love with a man, taste sometimes flies out the window. As for Opal's taste in men—a Mr. Loreale, for instance—well, you get my drift.

Underneath all the foliage, the living room is a luxe place, homier than I'd expect from a guy who exudes all the warmth of a meat freezer filled with body parts. The rust-colored sofa and chairs are the invitingly overstuffed sort you'd be happy to doze off in while watching Milton Berle do his Uncle Miltie shtick on the television set that's in a big mahogany console, or after you've had your fill of the eighteenth- and nineteenth-century English landscape paintings around the room. Funny thing about English landscape paintings: they tend to show up on the walls of rich Americans whose immediate ancestors could barely *speak* English.

A handsome John Constable oil from the 1820s, a rural scene in the Suffolk countryside, hangs over Sig's fireplace. He paid a fortune for it at one of the big-name galleries in the Fuller Building on Madison. I understand Sig's affection for the painting. In a vast landscape presumably controlled by powerful, baronial people, Constable depicted peasants dwarfed nearly to insignificance. It's an accurate accounting of Sig's view of the social order. The Constable is the last piece Sig bought legally after I saved him a bundle on a late-eighteenth-century Gainsborough: more tiny peasants, this time herding sheep in a mountain landscape. It hangs on the opposite wall.

I've gotten him a few other bargains, too, if you're in the bracket that considers anything under fifty G's a bargain. Over on the mantel in a glass display case next to the pink roses is a twelfth-century Romanesque chalice of jeweled gold that was supposed to go to the Louvre but never made it. On the coffee table is a small granite Egyptian Eighteenth Dynasty statuette of Osiris, God of the Underworld, King of the Dead, who I swear looks a little like Sig. And in a case near the couch is a two-foot-tall seventeenth-century embossed silver vase from Venice that I slipped past General Eisenhower's cultural watchdogs during the Allied occupation of Europe after the war. Sig wanted it as a birthday present for Opal.

I can't spend any more time reminiscing over Sig's collection. He didn't summon me here for a professional appraisal. If he ever wants one, he'll send someone to find me. He's been sending someone to find me since I was a little kid.

And now he's waiting. I open the French doors to the terrace, step outside, and feel the same twist in my belly I felt long ago in that gritty room in Coney Island.

The fresh air helps settle me, and the fantastic view of the city through all those gilded arches around the terrace is a stunner. But the view puts me in my place: I'm as small as the peasants in the Constable painting, insignificant in the colossal skyscraper universe of Sig Loreale's power.

The wind is nippy out here. It blows through the collar of my coat as I walk around toward the uptown side of the terrace. Rockefeller Center glows golden ten blocks ahead, directly across the street from the spires of Saint Patrick's Cathedral. Talk about your Power meeting your Glory.

I don't see Sig so I keep walking. The light rising from nearby streets grows stronger as I walk west along the uptown side of the terrace, the glow brighter, full of color. They're the lights of Broadway, the Theater District, the jewel-box radiance of Times Square three blocks away. Down there, people are still laughing it up at nightspots that won't close until three in the morning, if they close at all. Lots of dreamers are having boozy visions of their names spelled in lights on the marquees of Broadway's theaters and supper clubs. But none of the laughers and dreamers have the faintest idea that there's a silhouetted figure of a man in an overcoat and homburg standing against the ledge at the northwest corner of the terrace, looking down on them as if they were ants.

"Sig," I say.

A thin line of cigar smoke curls around his head and gathers under the brim of his homburg as he turns to face me. After a last pull on the cigar, he tosses the butt over the ledge. The burning tip traces a red arc in the air before the cigar falls out of sight.

There's just enough light coming through a living room window for me to see the exhaustion in his heavy face and in his baggy, bloodshot eyes. The set of his shoulders, usually straight as a general's, is rounder now under his black overcoat. I guess the grind of Sing Sing prison can humble even a boogeyman. Then I see his nostrils flare like an enraged bull's.

All I want is to get this meeting over with, drive home with Rosie, have a stiff drink, and let Rosie and the whiskey soothe away any remnant thought of the killer who's staring at me like I'm a bug he could squash with his foot.

But I don't move. I just stand and wait for Loreale to talk, tell me why he's commanded me here. All I can do is watch and wait, and wonder why he's wearing a tuxedo under his open overcoat.

A tuxedo. An hour after peeling off scratchy prison garb, the man isn't wearing something soothing to the skin like flannel pajamas or a silk robe. No, he's decked out in a tuxedo.

He says, "What is it you are staring at, Cantor? You want the name of my tailor?" He says this, as always, slowly and with precision, his voice a nerve-racking grind of ice shards. He's the only guy I know who can make a conversation about suits sound threatening. "And here I thought that the famously sharp dresser Cantor Gold would know the work of all the better tailors in town."

"Sig, you didn't bring me up here to discuss the art of cutting cloth."

I don't like the way his nostrils are flaring again while he looks at me, or the way his mouth turns down while he inhales a deep breath, then lets it out as if he's breathing the fires of destruction on the world.

"I have a job for you, Cantor."

"A job? Tonight? I figured you brought me up here to ask about what happened to Miss Shaw on the river. My condolences, by the way. Seems like an odd time to hire me to get you some fancy goods."

"It's not that kind of job. I am asking you to find out who killed Opal. That's all."

Those last two little words, *That's all*, drop with the whispery force of a guillotine rushing down to chop off an unfortunate head. He wants me to find the owner of that head.

In the absence of a badly needed slug of whiskey, I take my pack of Chesterfields and matches from my pocket instead, fire up a smoke, and hope the brim of my cap hides my shaking hands. "Sig, I'm not a detective."

"You are the person who must do the job, Cantor."

"But I wouldn't know where to start. Except for what I've read in the papers, I don't know which circles you and Miss Shaw ran around in. I don't know who she palled around with while you were upstate, or who might have had it in for her. And maybe, just maybe, it was a terrible accident. Have you thought about that?"

"I don't believe in accidents."

He should know. He's staged plenty of 'em. Ask the widows.

A long drag on my smoke gives me a few seconds to think, find a direction Sig may go for, a direction away from me. "What about having some of your own people nose around? They know your territory and the people in it. They'd know right away who to keep an eye on. Or better yet, give the job to one of the cops on your payroll. They have the resources for this sort of—"

"No." The word comes at me like a bullet to the gut.

Sig turns his back to me, but I know the conversation's not over. He just wants me to shut up.

He's leaning against the ledge again, pointing toward Times Square. "You see those lights down there, Cantor?" he says. "I always did like those lights, especially when I would take Opal to a show. We used to go out a lot before I went upstate. I took Opal to see that cowboy show, that *Annie Get Your Gun*, with that dame with the loud voice—you know, that Merman woman. I took Opal to all the best nightclubs. Saw all the big names. When we walked into a theater or into a supper club, those lights would splash all over her. It wasn't that the lights made Opal look nice—she made the lights look good. You understand what I'm saying, Cantor."

I don't want to touch that last remark. No good ever comes of sharing opinions about a beautiful woman with the man who sleeps with her. I let the remark hang in the air, let it blow away on the night breeze.

Sig keeps looking out to Broadway. "And it was not only because Opal was a knockout. She had something… something…"

If I wasn't standing right here, you'd never convince me that Sig Loreale could have a lump in his throat. But it's there, and then it isn't. Sig squelched the nasty little emotional threat before it did him in.

"Look," he says, still nostalgic but in command of it, "you remember how her face lit up the room when I gave her that silver vase at her birthday party? I tell you, she was crazy about that vase, Cantor. You could tell, right?"

"I wasn't invited to her birthday party, Sig." If I'm lucky, I won't be invited to her funeral, either.

"No? Well, maybe you should have been. You could have seen that look in her eyes. Happy as a little kid. You did good work on that one, Cantor. I should have invited you to the party. As a token of my appreciation, you understand."

"Don't worry about it, Sig. That satchel of cash your boy gave me at the handoff was all the appreciation I needed."

He takes a deep breath, lets it out slowly, as if he's hoarding it. When he turns around, the brim of his hat shadows his eyes but I feel them on me, bearing down with the crushing force of an oncoming truck. "Listen to me, Cantor. You are part of what took place on the river tonight. You are part of Opal's death. And you are the only person who can get to the truth of what happened to her. You are the only person I trust to do it because not one word can get back to anybody in my organization about what I am asking you to do. We will let them think you are doing your usual work for me, maybe protecting my interests in the purchase of some fancy item. They are not to know anything else for the time being."

The first part of what he said, about being the only one who can get to the truth, is crap. But the second part hits me like bad weather: in Sig Loreale's dangerous world of vengeance and murder, where rivals and treachery nip at him every day, he can never be seen as sentimental or weak. For hard men like Sig and his army of thugs, love from a woman is one thing; love *for* a woman is something else. It's personal, it makes a soft spot in the heart. Rivals, or the Law, could get to you through your woman. Your urge to protect her would be taken for a sign of weakness. Love for a woman could get an outlaw killed. Ask John Dillinger's ghost.

So whaddya know: New York's boogeyman, the Gutter God of Death, was truly and dangerously in love with Opal Shaw. If anyone, even those most loyal, knew the truth of it, fear of the man would dry up. Sig's business runs on fear. Without it, vultures would peck at his business until there was nothing left but Sig's carcass.

He takes another cigar from his inside pocket, lights it, leans back against the ledge, a silhouette again, the glow of Times Square behind him. He says, "You know the only things I missed in prison? Elbow room and Opal. I was looking forward to both when I got out. Did you know, Cantor, that Opal came up to visit me every weekend? She drove up on Saturdays, then stayed at some spot nearby so she could come back to the joint to see me on Sunday."

"That's the part I don't understand, Sig."

"What, you don't think Opal was sincere?" He's looking at me again, I can feel it, even though he's still a silhouette hidden in a shadow.

"No, I mean the prison part," I say. "I don't understand how you were cornered into that penny-ante embezzling charge. Ten thousand they said you skimmed from some low-end garbage-hauling outfit. That's pocket change to you, Sig."

"And to you, too, Cantor."

"What? I'm not in your league. And now I'll have to spend an arm and a leg to replace my sunken b—" I shut up because I see the silhouette of his head tilt back, light from the window catching Sig's mouth and chin. His mouth is open in the shape of a laugh, his teeth glinting in the light, but there's no sound coming out. It's that soundless laugh of his. After all these years it still gives me the creeps.

So it's a relief to hear his voice again, his cold humor. "I am surprised at you, Cantor. You don't recognize a vacation? My chance to get away from all the hoopla of New York?"

He takes a long pull on his cigar. The burning tip throws a red glow under the brim of his hat and around his eyes. He gives me a steady, amused stare, a devilish professor poking a student's brain. So I think fast about the time he left for prison, remember the trial that sent him there. The daily papers ran a picture of the judge, Hizzoner Ezra Marsh, after he sentenced Sig to eighteen months—an easy ride for a pro—and then I remember Sig telling me years ago how he dealt with judges: *You buy 'em by the pound, like any other meat,* he'd said, and now I think maybe the trial was a fixed deal for a light sentence, and Judge Marsh must have been pricey because he's a fat slob, but other than all that, I have only a memory of that crisp early autumn, when everyone in town was enjoying those perfect September days before the yearly onslaught of winter's cold and snow.

Cold and snow. Autumn and winter 1947. That's it.

I look straight at Sig, watch his eyes widen as he realizes I get the drift of what he'd hinted, what started in the autumn of '47, not long after Sig went to prison, and ran through the winter and into early '48. It was like Coney Island all over again but on a much grander scale, the stakes not just a neighborhood or a city, but a major shift in the forces of power and money across the whole damn country. Murder-for-hire, like the rest of American business after the war, was organizing into giant corporations that swallowed puny competitors, and there was only one way to rid the murder business of any independent small-time operators and gangs. Guys, their women, their families, were found dead in New York, Chicago, New Orleans, Los Angeles, in cities and towns and in the middle of nowhere, from the Canadian border to the Rio Grande. And all during that season of organized killing, when all Sig had to do was give coded instructions during his permitted weekly phone call, he had the tightest alibi there is: prison.

I am in the presence of the man who now holds the nationwide monopoly on murder. He can have anyone killed, anywhere. He can reach us all.

A wave of nausea rolls through me. Sig, though, seems to be enjoying himself for the first time tonight. "And I told them what they could do with their parole. I told Judge Marsh I would do the whole eighteen months and then walk out a completely free man. I wouldn't tolerate a parole officer who is out for glory looking over my shoulder and up my ass."

"Is that what you were going to celebrate tonight? Slipping the Law's leash?"

"What are you talking about, Cantor?"

"The tux. You're all dressed up for a party."

He takes a deep breath again. But this time, looking at the windows of his apartment, he seems to be trying to suck the aroma of all those flowers out of the living room and into his lungs. "A party," he says, letting the words out slowly. "A party. It was…it was supposed to be a wedding party. Opal and I, we were going to be married tonight, Cantor. That is why all those flowers are in the living room. That is why I'm dressed in this monkey suit. I had my driver bring it along when he came upstate to fetch me, so I could change clothes before I walked out of prison. I'd promised Opal I would be ready as soon as I arrived home. She was going to be here already, all dressed up in her wedding gown." The words fall out of his mouth with the thud of dead dreams. But his eyes burn.

If I was scared of Sig before, I'm terrified of him now. There's no brew more murderous than sadness mixed with vengeance, and Sig's drunk with it. The longer he talks, the longer he spills his misery, the more my skin crawls.

So I'm grateful when he takes a long pull on his cigar, giving us both a calming break from his brutal agony. But the break doesn't last long. "That fat Judge Marsh was waiting here to perform the marriage rites. A photographer was here to take wedding pictures. Even Opal's mother was here. Opal was close to her mother, you know. The boys in my outfit figured I was just…that my marrying Opal was just to put my tag on her, have a wife around to make dinner and spread her legs when I told her to, the way the other boys do with their women." He lifts his cigar for another pull but interrupts himself, says instead, "Whoever did this terrible thing to Opal, whoever killed her, they *hurt* me." He tosses the unfinished cigar over the ledge as if it's simply too heavy to hold anymore. "What the hell was Opal doing on the Brooklyn Bridge at that hour?"

"I couldn't say, Sig."

"Something is wrong there, Cantor. Something I have to find out. And I am depending on you to do it."

"Sig, please, I have aggravation of my own that's chasing me tonight."

"Yes, I know all about Mr. Ortine. His line's the clip-joint rackets."

There it is again, that reach of his, that web he has all over town, snagging everybody.

"I don't know why you do business with him, Cantor. The

guy's nothing but a fancy pimp. No muscle in his belly, but that's the kind that's moving in on things these days," he says with annoyance. "The world is changing, Cantor, changed a lot since the war. If you listen to all those experts, those guys with the lab coats and the PhDs, they say modern life is about to get plenty exciting. You know the guys I'm talking about, Cantor?"

"I guess so."

"Yeah, plenty exciting, the smart guys say, what with that atomic energy and new electric appliances for the housewife. So you know what *my* smart guys are investing my money in now?" He gives me a snide laugh, then says, "Real estate," as if the two words have a bad odor. "I used to clean up my money through my warehouse operations or labor unions, things with a little muscle. Now I own a lot of ugly little plots of scrubland out on Long Island for all those bungalows the ex-GIs want for their new families. Everybody wants a lawn to mow, everybody wants a charcoal grill on the lawn, and a television set to entertain them instead of going out dancing or to a movie. I ask you, Cantor, does that sound exciting to you?"

Before I have a chance to answer, he gets rid of the subject as efficiently as he gets rid of a corpse and brings everything back to business. "Listen, you will find out who killed Opal. You will do this job for me, Cantor."

If I keep saying no, he'll only press me harder. But I can't say yes, I don't dare just say yes. "What's in it for me?"

"You know I always pay my debts. Listen, you will start on this right away. Opal's mother is waiting to talk to you. She can help you. She wants to help you. She trusts you, Cantor."

"Trusts me? She doesn't even know me."

"Yes, she does, and you know her, too, only you never knew her whole story. The old lady is very good at keeping secrets, let me tell you. You know what? Even *I* never knew she was Opal's mother until we decided to get married. Cantor, Opal's mother is Esther Sheinbaum."

I almost swallow my cigarette, and if I did the burn in my gullet wouldn't jolt me as much as what Sig just said. Esther "Mom" Sheinbaum: for over fifty years the most successful fence in New York.

When I was a kid, Mom was one of the peddlers of secondhand goods who bought my Coney Island loot. She took a liking to me, called me her little American savage. Later on, when I was in my teens, she taught me the fine points of the treasure racket, told me to get educated about the authentic stuff, the real McCoy items that the big shots pay fistfuls of cash for. But she kept her private life to herself. I knew she had a husband—Isaac Sheinbaum, the guy died years ago—but I had no idea she had any kids. I wonder if Opal's the only one.

So, *Sheinbaum* to *Shaw*—Opal's grab for the American Dream. Well, we all have our ways.

"Mrs. Sheinbaum is waiting for you, Cantor."

I can't tell if the night air is getting colder or if this dance of death I'm being invited to join with Sig and Mom and Opal is what's chilling me through to the bone. Either way, I pull up the collar of my overcoat, try to find refuge inside my clothes again. "What's the deal if I fail, Sig?"

"You will not fail. Good night, Cantor." He lights another cigar. The flame illuminates his eyes again, more tired and more bloodshot now, red as Satan's. He turns around toward the lights of Broadway. The conversation's over.

There's nothing I can do except walk back along the terrace to the living room. The walk feels like a forced march into a nightmare.

The smell of all those flowers almost smothers me when

I step inside. The aroma cloys now, the way joy and sadness cloy when they start to rot. Joy, sadness, and the memory of Opal Shaw all hang in this room, rotting together.

❖

The ride down in the elevator feels claustrophobic, my world wrapping around me too tight, releasing chaos in my brain. I've got to put some sense back into things.

Mom Sheinbaum is a sensible woman. I've got to make her see how crazy Sig's idea is. He obviously respects her, he'll listen to her. That's the line I've got to follow.

Boy, do I need that drink. And I want my gun back from Pep Green. Maybe I'll use the gun to shoot Green, get rid of one murderer in the world. Then maybe I'll go back upstairs and shoot Sig. I'd do it if I thought I could get out of this lousy squeeze. But all I'd get is dead. Sig's goons would track me down, scatter my hacked-up remains from here to Canarsie. Then they'd kill Rosie, too, for insurance. She deserves better than that from me.

Pep's standing near the door to the street when I walk out of the elevator. He's smiling that too friendly salesman's smile.

"My gun, Green," I say. My words echo around the lobby.

"As soon as we're outside," he says, giving me his grin. He even opens the door, ushers me through to the street.

I'm anxious to get back into Rosie's cab. I hear the purr of its engine. I bet Rosie's kept it idling all this time, ready for a fast break the minute my foot's in the door. "Okay, Pep, we're outside," I say. "Hand it over."

"What's your hurry?"

But I'm not looking at Pep Green. I'm looking at a guy in

a black coat and gray fedora suddenly sitting up in the backseat of Rosie's cab, the barrel of the gun in his hand moving to the back of Rosie's head.

I know I'm running to the curb, stretching myself forward, the soles of my shoes coming down hard on the pavement, but time itself seems to be made of goo that slows me to a crawl even as I hear the squeal of tires, see the cab pull away from the curb and disappear down Fortieth Street. Rosie's gone.

I barely hear Pep say, "You can have your gun now, Cantor," but when he slaps my .38 into my hand, I snap back to the here and now.

I grab the lapel of his jacket, pull it so hard I nearly rip the seams. "What's going on, Green? She's not involved in anything!"

Pep's doing his best to pull my hand from his lapel. He's angry because he can't pry me off and he doesn't understand why he can't, why a tough guy like him can't overpower a dame, even a dame like me. He doesn't get it that my rage is stronger than his biceps.

He squeals like a scared pig. "Loreale phoned down, says to tell you that you'll see your cabbie again after you've completed his business. For cryin' out loud, Cantor, get off me! Just do what Loreale says, okay? Have a heart, will ya? The guy just lost his chippie!"

Chippie? I feel my mouth move, feel my lips and tongue say, "Shut up, Green," but I don't hear those words in my head. I hear Loreale saying, *You will do this job for me, Cantor.*

CHAPTER SIX

I run up the stoop of Mom's Second Avenue brownstone two steps at a time, then press my finger against the doorbell, press hard again and again, impatient for her to answer the goddamn door. The doorbell isn't getting me anywhere, so I quit its irritatingly cheery ding-dong and pound on the door instead. I don't care if it's almost two in the morning. I don't care if the old lady's gathered up her sorrow and taken it to bed. My rage against Loreale and fear for Rosie's life rush through my arm and push into my fist until my hand opens into a hard and insistent slap against the front door.

The door finally opens, but I'm stopped cold by the unexpected presence of a pasty-faced kid in a blue uniform standing in the doorway. A cop. A young cop I don't recognize. A rookie by the look of him, peach faced and jittery.

I've been so tied up worrying about Rosie and trying to figure what to do about Sig that I forgot to figure the cops into the picture. And now it sticks in my craw that the cops knew to come here, they knew but I didn't that Opal Shaw is connected to Mom Sheinbaum.

I wonder how the hell they found out. Cops have been buzzing like gnats around Mom for years, but they've never been able to get a bite, never been able to penetrate her inner circle or catch her fencing goods. She's too clever, and she has friends and customers in very high places. Since the days when electric streetcars and crank-start autos terrified the last of the city's horse-and-carriage trade, some of the highest hats in New York have made their way to the parlor of Mom's brownstone for a cup of tea, a piece of honey cake, and to buy a diamond bracelet or some other jeweled trinket as a discreetly purchased present for the gent's wife as an apology for having a mistress, or for the mistress as an apology for having a wife. These well-connected gentlemen—and now their sons—have been more than happy to swat away any nosy officers of the Law who ask questions about Mom Sheinbaum's doings. So if the cops think Mom's grief will weaken her play tonight, they are badly mistaken.

The rookie looks me over. The lad's peachy cheeks turn red and his pale eyebrows rise almost into the brim of his cap. I guess his studies at the Police Academy didn't cover the likes of me. He stammers, "Um, what's…what's your business here?"

"I'm paying a condolence call."

"You sayin' you're family?"

In this house I'm family, ever since I was a kid and Mom used to pinch my cheek and give me honey cake. *Eat*, she'd say, *you shouldn't be so skinny*, and give me a smile as sweet as a Mother's Day card.

So I give the rookie the song and dance that'll get me past him. "You think a stranger would pay a condolence call in the middle of the night, kid? Listen, in the end you can only rely on family. So thanks for asking, and keep up the good work of keeping the riffraff out." I walk by him into the vestibule before he has a chance to think things over.

The aroma of honey cake welcomes me into the house, rouses memories of afternoons at the dining room table, my

Coney Island loot laid out on a piece of black velvet spread across the lace tablecloth. Mom would look over my goods, separate the good stuff from the junk, then we'd talk price, and Mom would seal the deal by pouring tea from a pink floral teapot and slice us each a slab of warm cake from the loaf on a silver tray.

My nostalgia's invaded by a wrong note, a man's raspy, insistent voice drifting from the dining room. The voice belongs to a plainclothes cop who doesn't see or hear me when I walk in, my footsteps silenced by the thick Chinese silk carpet.

The dining room's a cozy, old-fashioned place where amber light through silk lampshades mingles with shadows tinted a rich brown by fussy mahogany furniture polished to a luster. The room's looked like this as long as I can remember. The only addition is the cop, a stick of a guy whose brown fedora is grease stained at the pinches, his brown overcoat hanging on him like dead leaves. He's eating a slice of honey cake, his hat pushed back on his long, skinny head as he looks down at Mom through hooded eyes that long ago stopped believing anything anyone told him. His sharp cheekbones and long nose keep bobbing in and out of a shadow while he eats the cake, pushing forkfuls into his mouth between his questions. "So, why was your daughter on the bridge at that hour?" And, "C'mon, Mrs. Sheinbaum, was she on her way to do business for you?" Another piece of cake goes into his mouth, then, "Or for Sig Loreale?" His fork scrapes the plate. My teeth grind.

Mom's sitting at the dining table, silent, stout, immobile in a frilly black lace robe, her fleshy body as upright as a national monument. Her wavy silver hair catches the room's soft patina, creates a lustrous aura of grandeur around her broad, wrinkled face.

The cop keeps grilling her. "Why the hell does everyone

call you Mom when no one even knew you had a kid?" But he's not getting anywhere. He's no match for her. And I certainly won't do him the honor of letting him in on the story of how Mom got her nickname, which—except for me—has nothing to do with motherly affection but was a corruption of *ma'am* by her original gang, a bunch of *lantzmen* immigrant toughs who mangled English.

When the cop doesn't get an answer, he slams his plate and fork onto the dining table. "Wise up, Mrs. Sheinbaum! Your daughter's dive from the bridge is police business, which makes *you* police business. How long do you think you can stonewall us?" The guy's an ignoramus who can't see what's inside the stare coming at him from Mom's small green eyes. But I can see she's marshaling every ounce of her strength to hold back tears. Mom Sheinbaum has never—*will* never—let a cop see her cry, not even tonight, when she's grieving.

I say, "Hey, watch your tone there, bucko. The woman's just lost her daughter. Show a little respect. Or isn't that written into the police manual?"

The guy turns his bony face to me. There's no humanity in that face, just the dry stare of a career cop whose emotions have been pummeled to dust. "And who are you?"

"Cantor Gold."

"Well now, how about that. So you're the character whose boat caught the Shaw dame. I got the report from Feek over in Harbor Division. He says we should keep an eye on you." He gives me the once-over, takes a good look at my getup from my cap to my shoes. It's clear he's annoyed by what he sees, but I can't tell if he's annoyed because my suit and overcoat are better tailored than his or because I'm dressed this way in the first place. His annoyance curls into a sneer, the cop sneer, the kind I saw that night in the city lockup, the kind I got tonight from Feek. I'm beginning to wonder if all cops have dirty minds. If people could get arrested for what they're thinking, the whole damn police force might wind up in jail. Fine by me.

Mom turns to me now, too. The grief in her eyes is so bleak it could snuff out the light in the room. She extends her arm, a silent request for me to take her hand. When I do, she's able to face the cop again despite the misery eating through every wrinkle on her old face.

I say to the cop, "You have a name, Detective?"

"Huber, *Lieutenant* Huber."

"What's the Law's interest in Mrs. Sheinbaum, *Lieutenant* Huber? Can't you let her grieve in peace?"

"Funny you should ask," he says, without any humor at all. "The woman has been holding the best kept secret in town— that Opal Shaw, sweetheart of Sig Loreale, was her kid—and then whaddya know: the girl takes a dive just as you show up on the river. Now here you are again, showing up on the mother's doorstep. Is this just a once-in-a-lifetime coincidence or are you simply a pest, Gold?"

"It couldn't have been such a hot secret if the *cops* knew Miss Shaw was Mrs. Sheinbaum's daughter," I say, playing Huber to take the bait.

"Oh, the old lady can keep a secret, all right. We didn't know she was Shaw's momma until the coroner was strong-armed by Mrs. Sheinbaum's friends at City Hall to release the girl's body to Gottlieb's Funeral Parlor over on Delancey. When we staked out the funeral parlor, who shows up but New York's most famous mover of stolen goods, Esther *Mom* Sheinbaum."

"But why are you grilling Mrs. Sheinbaum like she's a suspect, Huber? Or is that the way you generally talk to grieving mothers?"

Huber gives me a smirk so sour I can almost smell it. He

says, "I talk to you bums like the lowlifes you are, grieving or not. And I have my doubts that criminals even bother to grieve, anyway. You need a conscience for that. Ever grieve for anyone, Gold? Do you feel it like regular people?"

My right hand's twitching inside Mom's, ready to slip from her grip and put my knuckles into Huber's face. The pleasure of blackening his eyes and bloodying his mouth would be worth whatever crap I'd have to endure in the city lockup. But Mom's hold on my hand tightens. The wisdom conveyed in her grip calms me down.

I say, "Why don't you leave us alone, Lieutenant, so I can help Mrs. Sheinbaum arrange for her daughter's funeral. Show a little heart, if you've got one left."

The nastiness in those hooded eyes boils up from where Huber's soul might've been before it rotted away. "Go ahead," he says, "plan your funeral." He can't resist sneering at me again as he walks out of the dining room, passing so close to me his bared teeth nearly scrape my face.

Mom and I don't move a muscle until we hear Huber say to the rookie, "We're finished here," followed by the slam of the front door.

Mom takes both my hands between hers. She lowers her head, her silver hair tumbles forward, her shoulders fall slowly as if she's exhaling a lifetime's worth of breath. A thin wail seeps out of her.

She's still holding my hands when I sit down at the table, but I slip my left hand away to stroke her cheek. The muscles in her face feel loose, exhausted, her flesh clammy and limp. But its Mom's tears sliding down her cheek and seeping between my fingers that get me, warning me of her breaking spirit.

"Cantor…" She struggles to raise her head. "Cantor, how could this happen? *Tell me.*" Mom's singsong English of the old-time Lower East Side is the music of heartbreak, every word a note from an aching soul. "My Opal was…so…so full of *life*. And she grew up so beautiful. And smart! She was so smart! She had the high life of New York at her feet. She—" Making a fist of her right hand, Mom presses it between her teeth to stop from choking on her despair.

I'm scared she'll bite down so hard she'll make her knuckles bleed, so I try to take her fist from her mouth. She fights me, but I hold on until she finally lets go. "Cantor," she says between sobs as heavy as boulders, "Opal was my precious girl."

"I never knew you even had a daughter, Mom. I never saw her around the house. Where was she? Why didn't you tell anyone?"

"What, so she could be a target for the cops, those Cossacks? Harassing a little girl just so they could get to me? Or maybe she'd be picked off by one of my bloodthirsty competitors so I'd give up my business? No, we wanted Opal safe, we wanted her to get an education, so we sent her away to a fancy school upstate. A first-rate establishment. My sister and her husband looked in on her. They have a place a few towns over, in Kerhonkson. They moved up there to open a little tourist business in the mountains, Blick's Cottages. A *kochalain*. You know such places?"

"Sure. One of those cheap vacation joints where guests cook their own meals in the hotel's kitchen."

"Yop, that's it. My sister Ida looked in on Opal while she was at that fancy-shmancy school. We had to enroll her as Opal *Shaw*. Somethin', huh, this country? A child grows up with a name that's not hers just so she can get ahead in life." Mom punctuates her resentment of this arrangement by yanking her hands from mine and wiping her tears with her knuckles, digging deep.

I take my cap off, start to put it on the table, but remember

Mom never allows anyone the bad manners of putting a hat on the dining table, not even the mayor. I shove my cap into my coat pocket.

Mom takes a handkerchief from a pocket of her robe, wipes her eyes, then winces when she looks at me. "That hair of yours," she says. "Like an old broom. You're still a savage, Cantor, an American-born savage. Even Isaac thought so. My Isaac," she sighs, looking idly at the hankie. "He died of the pneumonia when Opal was maybe nine years old, away at school already. You were a kid yourself, a teenager. Thank God Isaac didn't live to see this night. He only wanted Opal should grow up and be happy!"

"Maybe she was happy, Mom. Tonight was going to be her wedding night. Sig adored her."

"*Him?* I didn't want her to wind up with a man like that. A killer. A murderer!" She shakes her head and dabs her eyes again. "Isaac and I waited a long time to make a baby, until we had the money to bring it up right, pay for a high-class education, buy her nice things. I wanted Opal to have the big American Dream, mingle with the first-rate people, not with hoodlums like you."

"You didn't seem to think this particular hoodlum was so bad," I say, stroking her cheek again.

She bats my hand from her cheek and with a *tsk* says, "Don't kid yourself, Cantor. You're just a mug, no better than all the other mugs I've had to deal with. What?" she says, addressing what must be a peculiar look on my face. "You think just because you're in the fancy art business you're not a mug? Heh, I remember when you still had Coney Island sand on your shoes, tracked it all over my carpets. I didn't want my Opal anywhere near a schlepper like you."

"Even after I got cleaned up?" I try to make it funny,

opening my coat to show off my expensive, well-tailored silk duds, but I feel like a circus clown with a painted-on smile. "*Especially* after you got all cleaned up. First with the men's suits, then all those girls you were always running after. You think I liked seeing stuff like that? You think I'd let you go sniffing around my precious girl? I wanted Opal should grow up *normal.*"

Now even the painted smile can't help me, can't shield me from the ax Mom just used to split me open, spill my entrails all over the rug. The wild, mischief-making kid I'd been and the outlaw I grew up to be have just been disassembled, bone by bone, by this woman, this mentor, this teacher, this *Mom* who used to pour me tea and serve me honey cake, who used to let me pour my teenage heart out about my butchy ways and unrequited high school crushes that my own tradition-haunted mom and pop would never understand; this woman who, right now, in that frilly black lace robe, looks as hard-hearted as a black widow spider who just might eat her adopted young.

It takes me a minute to rally, to take my breath back, put the pieces of me back into place. Some parts don't hook together anymore, no matter where in my memories I try to fit them.

I finally give up trying, pulled back by the singsong drone of Mom still talking. "But what could I do? The minute Opal and that murderer laid eyes on each other at that nightclub I took her to so she'd meet the right people, that club with those blue-and-white zebra-skin booths, the whaddya call it, the El Morocco, so who does she meet? *Him,* that's who, another big shot from the gutter." I squelch a bitter laugh, wondering how Sig would take to Mom's low opinion of him.

Mom doesn't notice, just keeps talking. "He was in a booth, schmoozing it up but good with some dolled-up floozie.

Well, he forgot all about the floozie when he saw Opal. He knew class when he saw it, believe me. And when she saw him, oh boy, I could tell she'd made up her mind there and then that Loreale was for her. All that fancy schooling with all those top-drawer people, and she breaks her mother's heart." The old lady shakes her head with the memory, lets out a sigh, then looks at me and smiles as if she just remembered that I'm here. "Have some honey cake, Cantor. It's from Weinstein's on Rivington Street."

"I don't want any cake. Look, you know why I'm here. Let's stick to business. Do you have any idea why Opal was on the bridge an hour before she was supposed to get married?"

"No, I can't figure it at all. Cantor, I know she didn't jump and I know it wasn't any accident. I *know* she was murdered. They told me!"

"Who told you, the cops?"

"No, the woman. At the funeral parlor, the washer. One of the women who washes the dead and says the blessings. She called me up a little while ago, before the cops showed up here. She called because she saw a hole, a hole in Opal's neck where blood had come out."

"Opal was pretty banged up from her crash landing on my boat. She was bleeding all over the place, not just her neck. It could've happened from the crash."

"No, Cantor, *no*. The woman, the washer, she knows her business," Mom says, wagging her finger at me like I have some nerve contradicting her. "The woman knows what's what when it comes to preparing the dead for the grave. She knows the difference between bruises and stabs. Cantor, I tell you, Opal was murdered tonight!" Mom brings the balled-up hankie back to her eyes, takes a few quick breaths to steady herself before she can talk again. "I can't figure why, but I'm sure the whole thing was a setup. I'm sure of it."

"You sound like Sig. And it doesn't sound any better from your mouth than it did from his."

"But it's the truth. So you've got to do what we ask. You've got to find out what happened to my Opal, who hurt her, who killed her. Otherwise, who will be for my daughter, Cantor? The cops? You think they'll be for her just because they come here with their questions? No, no, they will not be. *You* must be for Opal, Cantor." Her tiny green eyes make their powerful demand behind their desperate pleading. But I don't see warmth for me in her eyes. I wonder now if I ever did, or if I was just a lonely little tomboy all those years ago, picking up warmth wherever I'd imagined it should be.

I've got to get this deal back onto steadier ground, where my feelings mean nothing, just do the job so I can get Rosie back—

Rosie...Rosie...my beautiful soldier.

—so I talk to Esther Sheinbaum now with the only truth that's always been ours: outlaw to outlaw. "Then it's got to be a square deal," I say. "You've got to do something for *me*, understand? You have some of the best contacts in the city, people high and low. Use those contacts to find out where Sig stashed a friend of mine."

"You mean the cabbie?"

"You know about that?"

"Sure. Sig called after you left his place, said he'd given you a...an *incentive* to do our job. But don't ask me where he's got her, Cantor. He didn't tell me. He wouldn't even if I asked. Sig keeps his plays to himself."

My mind spins a daydream, a fantasy of being a little kid again with Esther Sheinbaum and Sig Loreale standing side by side in front of me, and I erase them both with my brand-new rubber eraser. I even smile a little. "You know, I have friends in high and low places, too," I say. "Maybe not as many as you do, maybe not as high, but sooner or later, while I'm going through the motions of looking for Opal's killer, someone I know, maybe someone who owes me a favor, will find Rosie—that's her name, Rosie Bliss—and finding Rosie, getting her back, is all I care about. I'll drop your problem like a hot potato, let you make do with the cops, let Sig get eaten alive by the vultures who'll surely come after their lovesick boss. Now, a major player like you can get a line on where Sig's got Rosie a lot faster than I can. Are you getting the picture, *Mom*?"

After she blows her nose into the damp, wrinkled hankie, she looks at me straight, says, "Well, well, we taught you good, growing up, Cantor. Taught you when to make the good play. Okay, you just made the good play. So yeah, sure, you got yourself a deal. I'll make some calls."

"*Some* calls?"

"All right, Cantor, all right, I'll make a lotta calls."

"That's better. Okay, let's get things going. Sig thought you might have some ideas about where I should start, where to get some information about what happened on the bridge."

The old woman's tough hide is pierced again by grief for her daughter. Tears flood her eyes but she wills them back, takes a deep breath, and speaks slowly, trying not to choke on every word. "I hoped to have a little supper with Opal before Sig got home from the prison. But Opal said that she had plans right up to the last minute, that she'd be running around."

"At that hour? Since when does a bride go running around just before her wedding?"

"Yeah, I thought it was meshuga, too, running around on her wedding night, but she sounded so happy about whatever the hell she had planned. She said I shouldn't worry, just a bride's high spirits is what she called it. So you see, Cantor,

Opal was already away from the penthouse. If someone grabbed her, it was while she was running around."

"And that's it? That's all you have?"

"And a name—Celeste. Celeste Copley. Opal talked about her, said they were good friends, that she and this Celeste sometimes took in a movie while Sig was away in the prison. I think Opal might've been running around with this Copley woman tonight."

"Did you get in touch with this Copley and get her story?"

"She's not in the book, I checked before the cops came. But I think Opal might've said something about an apartment somewhere on the West Side."

"That's a lot of somewhere."

"It's the best I can do, Cantor. I was gonna call up one of my operatives to put a trace on this Copley when the cops showed up here. But I don't have time now anymore. I got a lot to do before I bury Opal. The funeral's in the morning. You'll have to trace the Copley woman yourself. Have that clever young man of yours handle it. He's good with these things."

"All right, I'll call him now." I start for the phone in the hall.

"No, you gotta go now, Cantor. I'm tired, and I got plenty of stuff to do before the morning. Now go." A quick wave of her hand makes her point. I'm dismissed.

That's it, then. I'm finished here. On my way out of the dining room I start to turn around for a last look, but I change my mind. I just walk out.

Halfway through the living room I call over my shoulder, "Make those phone calls. Have something to tell me later, you understand?"

I don't get an answer by the time I'm in the vestibule. Maybe I didn't hear her or maybe Mom didn't answer me at all. It doesn't matter anymore as I walk out the door.

I take my cap out of my coat pocket and put it on, figure I'll walk over to an all-night deli I know in the neighborhood. The place has a row of phone booths where I can call Judson, get him started on finding an address for Celeste Copley.

I start down the front stairs. Memories I no longer want grab hold of me, memories of Mom Sheinbaum watching from a window, eating a slice of honey cake, while I played stoopball on these stairs with the neighborhood kids, and how the ball would hit the edge of a step and go careening into traffic. Drivers honked their horns and cursed at us kids while we laughed our heads off. I laugh about it now, whether I want to or not, until my breath catches in my throat and I forget about the past and smile from ear to ear about the here and now that's right in front of me: a Checker Cab is pulling up.

CHAPTER SEVEN

I've never bought the idea of miracles, and maybe what I'm seeing is no miracle anyway. Rosie Bliss is one smart article with the brains and the guts to slip Loreale's rope. She also has the knack to track my scent in order to find me. Tonight wouldn't be the first time. She even tracked me to an all-night poker game in a Bronx basement and got me outta there five minutes before an irate husband and his wife's two equally irate brothers arrived to rip my guts out. But in order for Rosie to track me here, she'd have to sniff out that Mom Sheinbaum and Opal Shaw are family. Has it hit the streets already or did Rosie's kidnapper slip his lip?

Plenty of time to get the story from her later. Right now, I catch only a glimpse of blond hair under the familiar cabbie's cap, but it's enough to make my heart dance like it's New Year's Eve. By the time the driver's door opens my heart's doing high-stepping kicks, which is why it's a hard crash when a young blond-haired guy wearing a cap like Rosie's gets out from behind the wheel.

Yeah, sure, I remind myself, choking on it. A lot of cabbies wear that sort of cap.

Meantime, an old sourpuss of a guy built like a fireplug gets out of the backseat of the cab. His black-and-green checkered lumber jacket and gray fedora are as rumpled and worn out as the rest of him. The guy's one of those thick-necked, stoop-shouldered old lugs with a face full of lumpy folds carved by suspicion of everything. For a guy of his bulk he has a mousey way about him, like he's been caught hitching up his pants.

After the cabbie pulls two valises from the trunk, the old sourpuss guy takes his time about paying the fare, performing a Rube-from-the-Sticks ritual that drives New Yorkers nuts. He's so slow about pulling a roll of bills from his pocket that George Washington's picture has time to grow a beard; then he has to carefully take off the rubber band that's wrapped around the roll of bills; after that, he unfolds the roll and straightens out the bills like he's trying to iron out wrinkles from wet laundry; then he wets his thumb against the tip of his tongue before he finally peels off a bill from the wad.

The cabbie's getting edgy. He thrusts his hand right up against the old guy's wad of bills, says, "C'mon, c'mon, snap it up, fella. You're in New York now. Even our grass grows faster than how you're peelin' them bills."

While the guy fiddles and the cabbie stews, a frowsy old dame in a shapeless gray wool coat slides out of the backseat. One look at her face and I've got her nailed as sure as a mug shot. Her hair's not as silver, more the color of cold ashes, and her face, though plump, isn't as broad, but she has the same chin-in-the-air, nothing-gets-past-me, small-eyed arrogance as Esther Sheinbaum. Despite the frumpy coat and the lumpy black handbag, this woman could only be Esther's sister, Ida Blick, which makes the schlemiel paying the cabbie Ida's husband. They must've taken a night train down from the Catskills, caught a cab from Grand Central.

Ida sees me standing on the stoop. She nudges her husband, says, "Look, Morris."

Morris, a valise in each hand, looks me over. My effect

on him causes his face to move in various directions: his eyebrows up, his chin down, his mouth open.

The cabbie looks up to see what the old guy and frowsy dame are gawking at, but he quickly loses interest because he can't make money standing around sizing up the citizenry. As far as he's concerned I'm just another one of the city's nighthawks, one who he figures real quick doesn't want a cab, and now that he thinks about it maybe he doesn't want the likes of me in his cab anyway. He gets back behind the wheel and drives off.

Ida and Morris Blick keep staring at me, examining, calculating: Ida, her button eyes on me like she's trying to figure if maybe she should alert the Vice squad; Morris, like he's worried I'll show up at his mom-and-pop cabins in the hills.

So we're all eyeballing each other as I put on my cap and walk down the stairs. No one says a word, even though it's on the tip of my tongue to ask Mr. and Mrs. Blick about Opal, about how the little girl they shepherded through a fancy boarding school grew up to be a gangster's dolly. And I'd like to know if Mr. and Mrs. Blick's arrival at Mom Sheinbaum's brownstone in the dead of night is early for Opal's funeral or late for Opal's wedding. But the looks they give me are as blunt as the No Trespassing signs I'm sure they've nailed up around the property of their boondocks hotel. I'd get nowhere with these two.

So I step down to the sidewalk, pass close enough to Ida and Morris to give their suspicious looks back at 'em before I walk down Second Avenue. I hear Ida say, in that same immigrants' singsong as her sister, starting high, curling low, sliding around, "Let's go, Morris. Esther's waiting."

❖

Fein's Delicatessen has been squeezed into a sliver of Ludlow Street since the days when gas lamps flickered along the skin of fat salamis hanging above the marble counter. Nowadays, fluorescent light wraps around the salamis and gives everybody in the place that dried-out look like they haven't slept in days. Well, maybe they haven't; it's the middle of the night and the downtown night owls—the hipsters, grifters, philosophers, and streetwalkers—keep the joint hopping while they slurp their borscht, chomp their salami or corned beef sandwiches, argue with the waiters about the service, and argue with each other about everything else, especially politics. If a good argument is part of the moxie of New York, in our delis it's the seasoning of our meals, a condiment as satisfying and tasty as sour pickles.

I get a mug of coffee from the counter guy, take it with me into one of the phone booths along the back wall. I need the jolt of strong black coffee not because I'm sleepy but to kick the sentimentality out of my gut, the false nostalgia for an affection from Mom Sheinbaum that was never real. The hot coffee burns that sappy nonsense out of me while I dial Judson.

He answers on the first ring. "Yeah?"

"It's me, Judson."

"Dammit, I've been trying to reach you and Rosie on her cab radio for the last half hour. All I get is a lot of weird noise, like water splashing and a grinding sound. Where the hell are you two? Catching the night shift at a machine shop?"

"Listen, Judson, they've got her. Sig's got her. They grabbed Rosie—"

"What? What are you talking about, *got her*?"

"Sig had one of his thugs sneak into the backseat of Rosie's cab while I was up in his penthouse. When I came back down to the street, the guy put a gun to the back of Rosie's head and forced her to drive off. Sig wanted me to see it. Esther Sheinbaum's in on it, too. Now they're holding Rosie as insurance that I'll do what they want me to do."

"What the hell does old lady Sheinbaum have to do with it?"

"Opal Shaw was her daughter. They want me to find out who killed her."

There's a gagged silence on Judson's end of the line before he's able to say, "Damn."

"Yeah. Damn. Damn them both to hell. Look, what about the noise through Rosie's radio. Water and a grinding noise?"

"Yeah, like water lapping around in a bowl. And that grinding noise. I can't make it out. It's just a grinding noise. Sounds like metal grinding. It comes and goes, loud and soft. That's why I figured some sort of machine shop or maybe a factory."

"Any voices? Did you hear anyone talking?"

"Uh-uh, just the water and that grinding metal noise. You make anything from it?"

"I think Rosie opened the radio so we'd hear something if we tried to contact her, Judson, something to lead us to where they've got her. She's counting on us trying to contact her." My soldier. My smart, beautiful soldier. "Keep monitoring her radio, Judson. See if you can hear anyone talking, or hear any other noise that'll give us a line on where they've stashed her. Stay on that radio, Judson."

"It'll be on my ear all night, bet on it."

"And there's something else. I need you to track down an address for a Celeste Copley, probably on the West Side. She was a friend of Opal Shaw's, around the same age, so don't waste time tracing old ladies and babies."

"I'll get on it now."

"Good. Okay, what's up? Why were you trying to reach me?"

"I've got a line on Ortine."

"Yeah? How bad's my trouble?"

"Bad. I reached Red Drogan. He said Ortine is on the warpath, that Ortine was going to your apartment to get his dough back, even have his boys rough you up if he has to."

"Ortine wants to rough me up? Tell him to get in line behind the cops, Pep Green, Sig Loreale, and my ex-girlfriends."

"Get serious, Cantor. And watch yourself out there. Between Loreale and Ortine…"

"Yeah, I know. Just get me Celeste Copley's address fast. I'll call you back."

❖

A quick hop on the Third Avenue El takes me down to the Brooklyn Bridge. The great bridge, the grande dame of the East River, looms out the window of the elevated train, her stone towers and steel cables shimmering in the moonlight.

I'm all alone when I get off the train and go downstairs to the street. The area's cleared out since I was here earlier. The cops are gone, the coroner's wagon is gone, the reporters and photographers are all sniffing up someone else's pants leg by now. Even traffic has thinned to a trickle. Only the docks are still lit up and noisy.

The pedestrian walkway on the Brooklyn Bridge is a broad boardwalk straight up the middle. The walkway takes you above the roadways and the trolley tracks and the abandoned tracks for the old subway line.

If I go up the walkway, I'll have a breathtaking view of the city. The bridge's towers will loom overhead in a thrilling show of gothic grace, but I won't learn a damn thing about Opal Shaw's death because a person can't jump or fall or be thrown off the Brooklyn Bridge from the center walkway. They'd either land on the steel beams above the old subway tracks or bump over the edge to the trolley line. The only way anyone could fall from the Brooklyn Bridge and land in the river is from the automobile lanes at the sides of the bridge. And in order for Opal to land on my boat after I'd cleared the Manhattan tower, she had to drop from the ledge outside the traffic lane that comes into Manhattan from Brooklyn.

I start walking up that roadway. The trickle of traffic is so thin by this hour that only one car has come over from Brooklyn since I arrived at the bridge. Another is just now approaching me. Its driver honks and gives me the business about walking in the traffic lane. Probably thinks I'm drunk.

I have no idea what I'm looking for on the bridge, what trace of Opal Shaw I hope to find here, what I expect to learn. But it's where Opal's death and my life crossed paths, so it's where I have to start.

The roadway arcs upward, the river drops farther and farther below. The light of the full moon slides along the stone towers and through their cathedral-like arches. It shines along the steel cables. The bridge glows, lights my way. The wind moves through the filigree of cables like a bow across violin strings, making them vibrate, hum. I wonder if Opal heard the hum. I wonder if she heard the bridge's melody as her requiem.

A few feet beyond the Manhattan tower, I look down at the river. The lights of the city and the harbor sparkle all over the water, like diamonds on black silk, too beautiful to be disfigured by murder. I try to get a fix on the angle of Opal's fall relative to the location of my boat. The crisscross of lattice-like steel slats along the edge of the roadway doesn't leave much of an opening for a person to slip through, but it's been enough over years since the bridge opened in 1883 for all the stunt jumpers who've dared death and lost in their bid for glory. There's certainly enough space between the slats for someone as lithe and supple as Opal Shaw.

So what the hell was she doing up here on the night of her wedding? I hope the Copley woman can give me the story, otherwise I'm on a road with no end, trying to figure a mystery that has no beginning. I don't want to be stuck in that hell again, the hell I was in after Sophie disappeared. I can't let Opal Shaw's death cause Rosie to disappear, too, or I'll go crazy again.

The wind is turning colder, wetter, the mist hitting my face like a sharp spray of ice. Did Opal feel the wind's bite? Was she still alive to feel the cold scrape of the slats along her skin as she slid through?

That fat sergeant Feek had toyed with the idea that maybe Opal was a jumper, but I don't buy it, not if the washer at the funeral parlor was right about a hole in Opal's neck. Suicides don't stab themselves before jumping off a bridge. And besides, Opal was going to be a bride any minute. Why would she kill herself? And why would someone who wants to commit suicide make the complicated effort to slip through the latticework on the Brooklyn Bridge? Why not just make the easier jump from the more accessible edges of the Manhattan Bridge a few blocks from here? Or from that uptown giant, the George Washington Bridge? Why not just blow your brains out?

What the hell happened here?

I look around, look along the roadway, searching for what, I don't know. There's over sixty years of secrets drifting around up here in the moonlight. Maybe some of those secrets are better left dead, but if I want to get Rosie back, one of those secrets can't be Opal Shaw's.

Another car is coming over from Brooklyn, its headlights sparkling on the dew on the black roadway. A beam catches a small glimmer of red.

The red draws me like a magnet, and as I kneel down to it, reach down to touch it, an hysterical voice from inside the car shouts, "Get the hell outta the way! Are ya nuts?" and I smash myself against the side of the bridge at the last minute before the big sedan can run over me.

I'm breathing so hard I'm actually yelping. It takes me a minute to calm down, slow my breathing, finally peel away from the steel lattice. But without the car's headlights, I can't see the blotch of red, so I get down on my hands and knees to try and spot it by shafts of moonlight coming through the steel beams. My fingers find a sticky spot. I bring my fingers to my nose, get the unmistakable smell of blood.

I pull the book of matches out from my inside jacket pocket, strike one up. The flame finds a line of small red drips. I follow the line to the edge of the roadbed.

Dammit! The burning match singes my fingertips. I leap up like a burned puppy, light another match, and follow its small glow along a slat in the steel lattice where it catches a tiny smear of red along the edge. It's got to be Opal's blood.

The washer at the funeral parlor was right: a hole in Opal's neck, Mom called it. Opal Shaw was stabbed in the neck. The wound dripped blood along the roadway when she was pulled from a car. Maybe she was stabbed on the bridge, maybe even before that. But she was definitely cut before she went through the lattice and over the bridge.

I look down at the river, try to get a fix on the path of Opal's long fall. If she was still alive, even barely alive when she went over, maybe the horror finally killed her, stopped her heart, spared her the crunching pain of crashing onto my boat.

There's another glimmer of red below me, but this one's

sending a small shimmer outward from the side of the bridge. It's a sparkling rag of red, a sight that breaks my heart: a scrap of sequined fabric from Opal's dress, snagged on the bridge as she went over.

I can't leave it there, flapping miserably in the night wind, a ragged remnant of violence against a woman.

I slip my arm through the lattice and down to the scrap caught in a steel joint below. It's a tough stretch; my armpit feels like it's being sawed in half by the edge of the steel crossbeam. But the wind, the cold wet wind that's eating at the flesh on my hand, does me a favor and blows the scrap of fabric upward. My fingers grab it.

CHAPTER EIGHT

The lightbulb's still busted in the phone booth at the corner of Cliff and Ferry Streets where I'd called Judson after my go-round with the cops on the pier. At least now, though, I have the satisfaction of having more than a dime in my pocket, my clothes aren't soaking wet, and my fingers aren't freezing while I dial.

But I'm in a bigger hurry now. I step all over Judson's hello when he answers, don't even bother with a hello of my own, just get down to business. "Have you figured those noises on Rosie's radio? Did you get a line on where she is?"

"I'm working on it, Cantor," he says like he's answering an insult. "I promise, I'm working on it."

"I know you are, kid," I say, letting my breath out. "Okay, how about the Copley woman. Any luck there?"

"Yeah, I got her, and it wasn't all that hard. A few phone calls below street level was all it took. It seems Miss Copley has a reputation."

"Yeah? What kind? Classy or sassy?"

"She won't make it into the society columns anytime soon, though she keeps trying. Looks like her latest relapse into hard times was about a month ago when she moved into a dump on the West Side."

"Any idea how she fell from grace?"

"Nope. I stopped asking questions when I got the address, didn't want to press my sources too hard, risk wearing out our welcome."

The address Judson gives me is on a crummy street in a down-at-the-heel neighborhood.

Ordinarily, I'd wonder why the pampered Opal Shaw would run with someone currently at the shabby end of the social order, except that Opal's apparent taste in friends fits nicely with her low taste in bridegrooms. It seems Mom Sheinbaum's carefully tended boarding school rosebud blossomed into a wildflower who liked the company of weeds.

I ask Judson, "Anything new on Ortine I should worry about?"

"Nah, nothing new. But I'll keep hunting and pecking."

❖

New York has plenty of tough neighborhoods with bleak and dirty streets you wouldn't drive through, and if you did you wouldn't dare get out of your car. But if the city held a contest to determine which neighborhood has been the toughest longest, Celeste Copley's neighborhood, Hell's Kitchen—from the West Thirties northward to the West Fifties, from Eighth Avenue to the Hudson River's midtown docks—would take the crown. This raw-nerve chunk of town, home to slaughterhouses that make the air stink and sooty factories that make your eyes burn, has been grinding out gang wars and dead bodies for nearly a century. Old-time hard-as-nails gang bosses with beat-'em-over-the-head names like Mallet Murphy, One Lung Curran, and my favorite, Battle Annie Walsh, known as the Queen of Hell's Kitchen—a brick thrower of uncanny aim, it was said—ruled the local trade in murder and mayhem.

The Irish have held sway here since those early days when they were crammed into teetering wooden shacks. For the past fifty years or so they've been crammed into four- or five-story brick or brownstone tenements that sag like exhausted washerwomen.

The neighborhood can boast moments of glamour, too. During Prohibition, so much whiskey sloshed through these streets you'd think the Hudson River burst its banks with straight alcohol. Low dives dotted every block, but fancier speakeasies lined the avenues, drawing customers from the nearby Theater District. Actors and Broadway swells in tuxedos, their women studded with diamonds, swilled illegal booze at tables shared with gangland tough guys. Those were Hell's Kitchen's glory days.

The glamour's gone now, but the Irish are still here, clinging to the rough jobs on the docks and in the slaughterhouses and factories while they look over their shoulders with suspicion at the city's newest immigrants, the Puerto Ricans, who've been trickling into the tenements. The old-time Irish are determined to hold on to their turf. The Spanish, like all the other waves of immigrants who've washed over this city, are just as determined to own a piece of America. Fists have started swinging on the neighborhood's streets, switchblades are flashing in the schoolyards. Bodies are piling up again in Hell's Kitchen.

Celeste Copley's place is on Forty-Fourth Street off Ninth Avenue. The street's dark and quiet, but four teenage toughs in a beat-up prewar Dodge coupe parked halfway up the block— Irish kids by the glimpse I get of 'em as I walk by—are drinking beers and cursing the Puerto Ricans. They keep it out of earshot of three young Spanish guys sitting and smoking on a stoop across the street from Celeste's brownstone. Hard, suspicious stares from both camps crawl all over me like tightening snakes.

According to Judson's information, Celeste lives on the first floor of the run-down five-floor walkup. The building, like a lot of other tenement fleabags all over town, sports a bit of dilapidated dignity with its arched cornices above the entry door and windows. Funny thing about old New York, even our tenements were tricked out in architectural pizzazz, familiar old-world details for the old-world masses who crammed their lives and their American Dreams inside. For the lucky ones, the fancy bits of architecture were harbingers of dreams that would come true. For the losers in the game, it was their first taste of the American racket of false advertising.

The tenants in Celeste's brownstone whose windows face the street must be either asleep, hiding, or dead. There's no light in any of the windows. Only a weak yellowish glimmer from the hallway seeps through the smeared glass pane in the front door. It's too dark to see the tenants' names on the buzzers next to the door, so I strike a match, run the flame down the list. Most of the buzzers have no names, or the names have worn off. There's no Copley listed, but it doesn't matter; Judson gave me the apartment number, 1-D. And I wouldn't ring, anyway, can't take a chance that Celeste won't ring me in, or that she'd run out the building's back door while I cool my heels at the front.

Getting into the building won't be a problem, my penknife should do the trick. The locks on the doors of these dumps are the cheap kind, as easy to slide as a shower curtain, but I have to make it fast. The Spanish kids across the street are still giving me the eye, smoking their cigarettes a little faster than they were a minute ago.

The teenage thugs from the Dodge swagger by, too, pumped up and confident that they're hip and dangerous in their cuffed dungarees and two-tone gang jackets, their cigarettes dangling from the sides of their mouths. I stand close to the door while I work the lock with the penknife, try to look like someone simply turning the key in the front door. But let's face it, I'm not fooling these kids. I don't look like anyone who lives in this neighborhood.

The lock slides. I open the door but make a last sweep of the street. The Spanish guys are still looking me up and down while they also keep an eye on the Irish gang boys strutting past Celeste's brownstone. One punk, a blond kid with a mashed-potato face, looks back at me, which starts a trend. One by one, the other boys look back at me, too, their suspicious expressions bleached pale in the light of street lamps. The Spanish toughs across the street abandon their stoop and go inside their tenement, deciding that whatever trouble the white kids might have in mind for me is no concern of theirs.

I step inside and close the door.

The hallway of Celeste's brownstone has a sour smell, that hard-luck smell from the sweat of crummy lives. The odor clings to the faded striped wallpaper, rises from the threadbare carpet on the stairs. Even the drab yellow glow from the single overhead bulb seems to add to the stink.

Apartment 1-D is at the end of the hall, at the back of the building. A slit of dim light slides under the door. I guess Miss Copley is finding it tough to sleep tonight. I'm about to make her night even tougher.

I press the door buzzer, but before my finger's even off the button the door swings open and a woman luscious enough to be a calendar pinup stands in the doorway. Her wavy brunette hair, still damp from a fresh washing, frames big brown eyes that have the look of a dirty-minded puppy. Every breath she takes draws my attention to the floral robe that clings to a body juicy as summer peaches. Her every inhale and exhale makes the flowers on her robe sway as if alive. I could be hypnotized by that sway if I wasn't already under the spell of what's going on inside those eyes.

The woman isn't really looking at who's at her door, just blurts, "You were supposed to be here over an hour ago, not—what is it—a quarter to three in the morning! And how did you get into—?" But she suddenly sees that I'm not who she expected. Her eyes go hard while her mouth, so red and tempting it should be arrested on a morals charge, shuts tighter than a bank teller's window at closing time.

But beautiful women make me very friendly. "I'd have come sooner, Miss Copley," I say, "if I'd known you were in such a hurry for company, though I get the feeling I'm not the company you're in a hurry for. Pity, I can be such charming company."

"Who the hell are you?" She looks me over as if I'm a window display in an unfamiliar store.

I push the door open, say, "I'm the company you've got," and walk past her into the dingy living room. To be polite, I take my cap off.

The living room furnishings are well past shabby and just this side of dead. The green sofa looks like one more sitting could kill it. At least, I think the sofa's green. Hard to tell in the meager light of the only lamp in the room, a floor lamp with a painted shade of a corny landscape scene, the sort that sold by the dozen in cut-rate stores twenty years ago. The pictures on the wall of homey scenes and haloed saints look like the same vintage as the lamp. Somehow, none of it seems like it would be the taste of the gutter goddess who took my breath away at the door.

Her voice is less panicky than when she opened the door,

a nice voice, actually, smooth, the way velvet would sound sliding against my ear. "How come you know my name but I don't know yours?"

"My name's Cantor Gold. I know your name because someone told me."

"Who told you? I'm, um, pretty sure you and I don't run in the same crowd. No one I know would sport that haircut of yours. And you'll excuse me for saying so, but those scars on your face mark you as an alley cat who goes looking for trouble."

"That about sums me up."

She stands against the door as she closes it, giving me that once-over again. If she's window-shopping, I wouldn't mind if she decides to buy, even just on layaway. Meantime, I can at least enjoy the way the lamplight settles on her high cheekbones, brushes her black eyelashes and that eat-me-alive mouth, and illuminates two big red flowers on her robe filled out to voluptuous perfection by a pair of breasts so ripe they make my mouth water.

I drag my attention back to her face, which is as dangerously tempting as everything else about her. "I got your name from Opal Shaw's mother, Esther Sheinbaum," I say. "Know her?"

"I never met her."

"But you know who she is. You know she was Opal's mother."

"What is this? You grill like a cop, but honey, you're no cop. So what are you?"

Honey. A sweet word from sweet lips for a sweet me.

I say, "Mind if I sit down?"

"You're asking? The way you pushed your way through the door, you don't strike me as the type who asks for permission for anything."

I sit down on the couch while Celeste gets a cigarette from

a pack of Pall Malls on the battered heap of sticks that still thinks it's a coffee table. As Celeste bends down for the pack of smokes, lamplight finds parts of her body, lovely parts that press through the flowery robe. She bends near enough for me to breathe her scent of bath powder, an intoxication that makes my hands twitch with an urge to pull open the belt of her robe and let all of Celeste Copley spill out for my delectation.

An alley cat looking for trouble, that's me.

But not tonight. I thrust my hands into the pockets of my overcoat to keep them from misbehaving. My right hand slides against the scrap of Opal's dress I'd pulled from the bridge. The sequins scrape my palm, wake me from the dream of a naked Celeste, kick me back into the nightmare of my kidnapped Rosie.

I get back to business. "What do you know about Opal Shaw's death?"

Celeste takes a deep pull on her cigarette, says, "Nothing," through an exhaled cloud of smoke. She's kidding herself if she thinks she can hide behind the smoke and get away with her next lie. "Must've been a rotten accident. I wouldn't know. I only know what I heard through the grapevine. It's starting to get around that she took a dive from the bridge."

"Cut the crap, Celeste. I'm pretty sure you were with Opal tonight, at least for a while, so let's forget about hide-and-seek. Just answer my questions."

"And who appointed you the chief of police?"

"Sig Loreale."

Amazing, the power of a name, Sig's name. It slaps Celeste across the face, stings her with the danger of giving me the clam-up. She plays it careful now. "That monster was really crazy about her," is all she says.

"And he's hot to get to the bottom of how she died. Loreale doesn't believe for a minute that Opal's death was an accident. And I don't believe it, either. And neither do you. So let's get back to where we started. If you give a damn about your friend you'll help me find out what happened to her. Start at the beginning, Celeste. You were with Opal tonight, driving somewhere, according to her mother."

"She told you Opal was a friend of mine?"

"Uh-huh."

"I'm surprised she ever heard of me. I didn't know she was Opal's mother until a week or so before Loreale got out of prison. Opal had to tell me, I suppose, since she'd asked me to be at the wedding. Her mother would be there, too, so the secret would be out anyway."

"Listen to me. If old lady Sheinbaum knows you were with Opal tonight, then Loreale knows it by now, too. If I were you, Miss Copley, I'd count myself lucky that you're talking to me and not to Loreale about Opal's death. A smart girl like you knows he has rather persuasive ways of getting people to talk. So if you don't want me dragging you off to Loreale for him to cut your pretty face to shreds, you've got to make me happy. You can start by telling me who was driving tonight. Were you in Opal's car or yours?"

"I don't have a car. Look, I already told you, I don't know what happened on the bridge. You're wasting your time here."

"But you *do* know what happened. Opal Shaw went over the Brooklyn Bridge. What you mean is maybe you don't know *how* it happened. But we're going to find out, you and I."

"Says who?"

"Says me and—"

"Yeah, yeah, Sig Loreale." She says this like she's talking about some dullard she got stuck with at a boring party. But the deep, tense drag she takes on her smoke tells the real story: she's trapped and she knows it.

If I press too hard too soon, I risk spooking her more than

she already is, which could kill her cooperation. So I keep things as easygoing as I can swing, keep the tone friendly. "Okay, let's take it from the top, Miss Copley. You were in Opal's car. She was driving. You were in the passenger's seat. But where the hell were you two going on the night of her wedding?"

"I need a drink."

"Go ahead if it will help you chatter. And you can pour one for me, too. Scotch, Chivas if you've got it."

She snorts a laugh as she walks across the room to a beat-up breakfront. "Look around, kiddo," she says, cocking her head. "Does it look like I've got dough to spend on Chivas? I've got a bottle of scotch, sure. Plain old rotgut scotch. I don't care if you drink it or not." When she reaches up to open the breakfront cabinet, the sleeve of her robe slides along her right arm to her elbow. What it reveals makes my throat go dry: a bruise on her forearm about three inches from the wrist. The bruise is wide, red as cheap wine, encircling her forearm where a brute gripped her and wouldn't let go.

She pulls a bottle and two glasses from the cabinet. As she puts the bottle down on the coffee table, the sleeve of the flowery robe drops to Celeste's wrist, covers the bad news on her arm. She stubs her cigarette out, then pours the whiskey into the two glasses.

Seeing that bruise changes everything. Much as I'd like to soothe her into cooperating, that red welt tells me she's deeper into Opal's death than she'll ever admit. So it's time to push a little. I say, "Did you get that red souvenir on your arm before or after Opal went over?"

Her brown eyes aren't puppylike anymore, more like the wide eyes of a frantic, cornered rat. "Get lost," she says. "I don't need an alley cat out for trouble. Go on, leave me alone. Get lost!"

"Not until you tell me what you know about Opal's killing." I spring up from the sofa, grab Celeste's arm, lift it and point to the red welt on her flesh like it's an object for show-and-tell at a school for rough trade. "Who gave you that bruise? The same gorilla who tossed Opal? And did you know she was stabbed, too? That's right, took it in the neck." With my free hand, I pull the scrap of Opal's dress from my pocket, hold it up to Celeste's face, wave it in front of her like a bloody shirt. "This is all her mother's gonna have of her, Celeste, a crummy scrap torn from Opal's dress as she went off the bridge."

Seeing the scrap is like seeing a ghost, the ghost of Opal Shaw demanding revenge. But whatever horror Celeste sees in that scrap of Opal's death, it's still not enough to break her fear of whoever branded her arm.

Her fear bores deep into me, finds my tender spot. Before I know what's happening, I'm very close to her. My hand seems to rise of its own accord to stroke her cheek. "Listen, Celeste, if you need a safe place to stay, I can get you to one. Just tell me what you know, tell me who hurt you, who you're afraid of."

She yanks her arm out of my grip. "You *still* don't get it! Look, sport, my life may not be worth much but I'm not ready to trade it in. Talking to you would be my death sentence. So please, just get out of here."

"I can't. Not until I get the information I came for. Remember who sent me, if it'll help you talk. Maybe the scotch will help, too. Here. You look like you need it." I hand her a glass of whiskey, take the other glass for myself. "Your continued health," I say, then take a swig.

The sight and sound of me gagging on the cheap firewater must be a real corker. At any rate, it makes Celeste laugh. It's a surprisingly sweet laugh, charming, even girlish. "Well, my fancy friend," she says, "how long has it been since you lived on the cheap side of the street? Even your throat's gone soft."

"It's been a while," I say, still trying to cough out the rotten scotch. "Where'd you get this stuff? Mrs. McGillicuddy's bathtub? Doesn't she know Prohibition's been over for sixteen years? She can buy real whiskey now."

"Oh, don't make fun of sweet ol' Mrs. McGillicuddy," Celeste teases. "She's been quenching the thirst of the sorry souls around here since the potato famine brought 'em over from the auld sod." Celeste's smile is wide and warm, a real winner once the shackles of fear are off it.

So my comedy's been useful. Okay, now I've got to keep Celeste friendly. "You don't seem like the type to live in a dump like this," I say as if just tossing an easy, tenderhearted line of curiosity.

"I grew up in this dump. I kept paying the rent after both my folks were gone. It's a place to come back to when the mugs I always wind up with do me dirty, leave me stranded, which they do with predictable regularity. You'd think I'd finally learn."

"So why don't you?"

"Never had anyone teach me how to walk away from a good-looking face, a wad of cash, and the good times that came with the face and the cash. And if he's a danger boy, which he usually is, I'm like metal to a magnet."

"Yeah," slips out under my breath. I know about women who like to play with danger, adventurous women like Rosie, who's paying for her preference right now.

Celeste looks at me in a way that makes me feel caught in a searchlight. I take a drink of the rotgut scotch to put a barrier between me and her probing gaze, hiding behind the glass of liquor as surely as she hid from me behind cigarette smoke. We make quite a pair.

But the burn of the firewater does its job, kicks me back to business. "Is the danger boy who did you dirty this time around the same guy who tortured your arm?"

Celeste may be down on her luck, but she still knows how to work all the angles. She looks right through my little ruse with the glass of whiskey. A smile even curls at the corners of her mouth.

If she's trying to make me feel naked, she's succeeding. I start to hide behind another drink, then lower the glass. It's time for this seesaw of power to tilt me back on top. "That's a fresh mark on your arm, Celeste. He gave you that mark tonight. The guy's mixed up in Opal's death, am I right? And now you're scared he's going to come after you. You know too much."

Her smile shrinks—fear finally kills it. There's no expression on her beautiful face at all.

"Who is he, Celeste?"

She takes a deep breath, the kind that's supposed to cleanse the body, refresh the mind, but the name that rides on the breath just seems to foul it. "Green. Leon Green. They call him Pep."

CHAPTER NINE

You're telling me Pep Green killed Opal? That's not something you spit out like chewing gum, Celeste, just to see if it sticks to my face. You're talking about a guy who's as loyal to Loreale as a seeing-eye dog."

"You know Pep?"

"We're acquainted." She didn't expect that. She shrinks from the news, her shoulders fluttering like the weakened wings of an exhausted bird.

She doesn't fight me when I lead her to the couch, but she doesn't help, either. She doesn't seem to care if she's led to safety or ruin as long as someone else makes the decision.

I sit down beside her, hand her her glass of scotch. "Drink this. Take it slow, let it work." She sips the whiskey, her face so pale she could pass for dead. "Talk to me, Celeste."

Maybe I'm impatient, or maybe the earth really has turned a dozen times until she says anything. "When I was a little girl, my mother always told me to shut up." She sounds as dead as she looks, all dried up and hollowed out. "The way she said it, raspy, and full of hate…it was like she cut my throat with a jagged knife and all I could do afterward was whisper. It feels like I've been whispering ever since. No one ever really hears me."

"I'll hear."

"You?" The word comes out on a strangled little laugh that's more sad than sneering. "If I tell you everything I know"—she's turned to me, her eyes desperate and pleading, full of cold fear that's digging into me, trying to find a warm place to hide—"can you protect me? I need a guarantee."

"I told you, I can get you to a safe place. No one will know where you are. Pep won't be able to find you. Is that who you were waiting for tonight?"

"No, no, not Pep, that louse." She drowns his name in a deep swallow of her drink, closing her eyes, shutting out the sight of the latest danger boy who hurt her. "He called it quits with me a month ago. He had his fill of me, and well…"

"He stopped paying the bills?"

That opens her eyes again, but not to look at me. She doesn't see me, she doesn't see anything except her bitter memories. "Then tonight, he promised…" She can't finish it.

But she has to finish it. I need every scrap of information I can get. "He promised *what*, Celeste? C'mon, you're not alone in this anymore. I'm with you. I can help you."

Her eyes flash with a sudden awareness of me, as if she just woke up. "You're here to help Sig Loreale."

"Sure, but it doesn't mean I can't help you, too. Look, you're nobody's fool, kiddo. You know as well as I do that Loreale won't stop until he has Opal's killer. Then he'll deliver a death sentence same as a judge and jury, and a lot quicker, too." I'm getting to her, and she doesn't like it, fidgeting under the grim story I've just tossed in her lap. But I don't dare ease up, not yet. "So if you've got something on Pep, Celeste, something to prove that he killed Opal, let me have it. It's the only way we'll both be free of Loreale. But it has to be airtight, understand?" I'm really pushing now, tearing down the rickety defenses she hopes will hold me off while she escapes into another drink, but I push the drink away. "Are you listening to me, Celeste? Pep is Sig's right-hand guy. I can't sell just any old bill of goods. I'll need every detail you can give me, starting with who you were waiting for when I showed up, and what's it got to do with Opal's killing."

She looks down at the glass in her hand, then around the room in a frantic search for a way out of the hell she's trapped in other than the risky ride I'm offering. But there aren't any other ways out for her. She finally knows it, sees it, and gives in. "It's got to do with money," she says, exhausted by all the disappointments and dangers that are chasing her tonight. "Pep said a pal of his would come by tonight with money. Pep didn't even tell me the guy's name, just that he was supposed to show up with ten thousand, cash."

"You think he stiffed you?"

"Looks that way, doesn't it? The guy was supposed to be here over an hour ago." She shakes her head in disgust. Disgust at getting stiffed out of the cash. Disgust at getting stiffed one way or another all of her life. "I wanted that dough so I could get away, start over somewhere else, Miami maybe, or California, someplace where the sun always shines, where the sun could bleach me clean."

Ten thousand dollars is a lot of cash for a cleanup. It's the kind of money you shell out for someone to shut up. And if you really want to make sure the party in question doesn't talk, you don't bother with money. You pay them off with a bullet.

Celeste isn't ten grand richer and she isn't dead. The cash-payoff deal looks like a phony, which means the bullet could still be coming for her.

When I was a kid, I used to daydream about being a knight in shining armor, saving damsels in distress. Then I grew up and I couldn't even save the one damsel who mattered more to me than silk suits and money. I couldn't save Sophie. Now

I'm faced with two more damsels whose lives are in my lap: Celeste and Rosie. If I screw up, one or both of them will wind up dead. This is no daydream. It's a nightmare.

I keep coming down hard on Celeste and I wish I didn't have to, but I don't know how else to pry information out of her scared little heart. "You're going to tell me what's going on, Celeste, because without me you're dead. You're already so scared your body's ready to fold up. How long do you think you'd survive on your own with that target Pep's painted on your back? Yeah, that's right. He's marked you. You're prey."

I've got her attention now. She turns and looks at me with those big brown eyes like a puppy begging to be allowed in from the cold. "Please, take me away from here now," she says. "I'll tell you everything after you get me to that safe place, okay? Look, I can be dressed and ready in five minutes!" She gets up from the couch, starts for the bedroom.

I grab her arm, ready to tell her that if she's just stringing me along she can pack up her dreams about living life in the sunshine. But the sleeve of her robe slides along her arm when I grab her, reveals that ugly bruise. My throat closes up. I don't say a damn thing, just release my grip.

Celeste doesn't say anything, either, just stares at me as she lets her arm drop, a stare so full of hurt it accuses me of being as much of a brute as the gorilla who bruised her arm. Her stare shrinks me to a mere mote of dust, and there's no getting myself back until she walks away and into her bedroom.

I work on my glass of scotch while Celeste is dressing. The whiskey may be lousy but it clears my head, gets me out from under how crummy Celeste just made me feel. Instead, I think about my dealings tonight with Pep Green, look for anything to indicate he'd just stabbed a woman and tossed her off a bridge. All I remember is that he was his usual slick self when he greeted me, all smiles and salesmanship, but that's no surprise. Pep can be a cool customer when it comes to killing. That's how he climbed so high in Loreale's outfit. Pep can slit a guy's throat one minute and ask the guy's widow for a date the next.

I go over everything Pep said from the time I showed up at Sig's tower to the moment I grabbed Pep by his lapels after Sig's gunman forced Rosie to drive away. I hear Pep say, *The guy just lost his chippie!* Chippie. That's a pretty cheesy way to talk about his boss's bride. I guess Pep didn't like Opal. Maybe didn't like her enough to kill her? Kill his powerful boss's sweetie pie? He'd have to be nuts.

Unless Opal gave him a reason. Hate's a reason. So is love or jealousy. So is money. If there's money in the mix, for a guy like Pep Green there's no better reason.

I'm trying to piece all this together, make it jive with Celeste's connection to Opal and Pep, when Celeste walks back into the living room. She's dressed like she's on her way to a society luncheon, decked out in a classy navy-blue pinstripe suit that clings to her curves the way curves should be clung to. Below the slim skirt, a shapely set of legs flow into a pair of blue high-heeled shoes. The net veil of her little blue hat casts a tantalizing web of shadows across her face. She's carrying a tan valise in each hand, a blue leather handbag on her wrist, and a pair of red leather gloves draped over the handbag. A mink coat is over her arm. I wonder if Pep gave her the mink before he ditched her. Then I wonder why he ditched her. A woman whose moving parts are as finely crafted as Celeste's is not a woman I'd want to get rid of.

She puts down the valises, her handbag, and the mink, then slides her hands into the red leather gloves. That's when she notices me looking at her, but it doesn't stop her from doing what she's doing; after Celeste finishes pulling on her gloves, she slides her hands slowly down her skirt, smoothing out creases that aren't there, the red leather gloves rippling like snakes in the lamplight. The performance is the opposite of a striptease, and twice as sexy.

But the invitation's canceled when Celeste drops the femme fatale act and picks up the valises and the mink as though she's ready to board a train. Looking at the mink, she says, "I'll sell the coat or hock it. Pelts this good will fetch at least a couple of grand."

"Sure," I say, wondering who the hell *is* this Celeste Copley and why is she trying to make me dizzy? "It's too hot for mink in sunny California anyway."

"Tell that to the movie stars," she kids me.

"You can tell 'em yourself, by the pool."

I put my cap on as we walk out of the apartment. The dreary yellow light in the dilapidated hallway wraps around us like a dirty shroud.

Celeste walks ahead of me toward the front door of the building. She has a smooth, sinuous stride, the sort of I-own-the-floor stride of some high-class strippers whose acts I like to catch now and then. I'm getting a nice view of the rolling rhythm of Celeste's hips as we near the front door, but what I glimpse through the glass pane breaks the spell between me and those hips: the teenage thugs I'd seen earlier, the kid with the mashed-potato face and the rest of the gang, are loitering in front of the building.

I pull Celeste's arm so hard I practically fling her behind me. "Go back to your apartment, now," I say.

"But—"

"We've got bad company on the street. Get going." She's about to give me an argument, so I just shove her in the direction of her door. I shove her hard, again and again, until she finally gives up arguing and walks back to her apartment.

I follow Celeste inside, close the door, and lock it. Celeste starts in on me, "Next time you lay a hand on me—Jesus Christ, you're no better—!"

"Keep your voice down, dammit. Those kids, you know them?"

"The Kavanagh boys and their friends? Is that who you're worried about? They're just a crummy bunch of neighborhood toughs. Hell, I can tell them to shoo and they'll—"

"They'll shoo for two minutes, then show up at our backs. They cased me when I came here. Now they're outside your door. I don't like the coincidence. Do you?"

She doesn't. She looks scared again.

I say, "You think Pep might've sent them?"

"I…maybe…I don't know. How would they know him?"

"They don't have to know him. He only has to know about *them*. Trust me, everyone in Loreale's outfit has a line to every street gang in town. Pep can have instructions and payoff money make their way down the line to those kids outside." I don't mention another bloodcurdling twist, that maybe it's Sig who has the kids in his employ. Maybe it's *me* they're keeping an eye on, with Celeste a by-product of my activities. I wouldn't put it past Sig to keep a tail on me, make sure I'm representing his interests and not my own. The sonuvabitch has been tagging me since Coney Island. "Listen, Celeste, is there a back door out of the building?"

"There's a basement door that leads to a garbage area in the back. But there's a wall around the garbage area."

"How high a wall?"

"Eight feet, I guess, maybe ten."

"Where's your phone?"

"Over there, next to the breakfront."

I dial Judson. He picks up after one ring, says, "Yeah?" fast and anxious.

"It's me, Judson."

"Oh. I thought you might be a sound expert pal of mine. He does surveillance jobs. Plants bugs, that sorta thing. I rang him a little while ago and played him the sounds from Rosie's cab radio over the phone, that grinding metal sound and that watery noise. It's dicey, having him record the sounds secondhand through the phone, but he said he'd try to pick them apart with his equipment, try to figure what they are. I'm still waiting to hear back. What's up?"

"I need your chauffeur services again, Judson. We're not far from the office. Pick us up on Forty-Third between Ninth and Tenth, middle of the block, right away."

"Us?"

"I'm traveling with a lady. A well-dressed lady who needs a ride." I look over at Celeste. Good, I've made her smile again. I've got to keep her spirits up and her trust high.

Judson says, "Copley?"

"Yeah."

"Okay, figure about ten minutes."

I hang up. Celeste tosses the mink over her arm and picks up the valises.

"Leave 'em," I say.

"What? They're all I have! This coat will pay several months' rent!"

"Take only your handbag. We've got a wall to scale. The mink and the luggage will slow us down."

"You're leaving me without clothes? What will I wear? How will I live?"

I want to laugh out loud, but I'm afraid that'll sour Celeste's cooperation, so I hold my amusement to a grin. "Trust me, baby, you'll have no trouble finding someone who'll take care of both."

She puts the valises down but puts the mink coat on, making it clear she's not budging without that coat. She's putting on one helluva show of stubbornness, an alluring show, all in all, exposing a spice in her personality I'd love to get to know in, say, a hotel bedroom.

Well okay, she's made a hit with tonight's audience of one, so I give in about the coat. "All right, take the mink, but leave the damned valises. Judson will be on his way."

"Who's Judson?"

"An associate. Let's go."

"You trust this Judson?"

"You ask too many questions. Questions make trouble. That's why your danger boys always turn on you. Now c'mon, we're getting out of here." I grab Celeste's hand, pull her along and walk us out the door.

Celeste leads me along the back end of the hallway to the basement stairs. She reaches up and pulls the cord on an overhead light, a naked bulb that sways on a fraying electric cord. The swaying bulb creates the dizzying effect of tossing our shadows around in several directions all at the same time while we walk down the narrow, winding stairs. I pull the brim of my cap down a little lower to block the crazy swirling of our shadows on the bare brick walls. All I see now is the back of Celeste's mink coat. The fur has its own gentle sway, moving in rhythm with the undulating body inside it, causing my equilibrium to be as wobbly now as it was when I was surrounded by the crazy shadows.

We finally get to the basement, a below-ground pit of heat, darkness, and dust, and where I find out that hearing rats scurry is much worse than seeing them.

Celeste says, "The light's busted down here, has been for weeks. So watch your step."

You bet I'll watch my step.

When she opens the back door, a welcome breeze brings relief. A shaft of light shows us the way out of the basement.

The light's from a bulb outside, above the door. It's helpful but dangerous, could expose us to nosy neighbors. I don't see a light switch, but a step outside and quick look up to the bulb shows me the ragged end of a ripped-out cord, too little of it left to grab and shut the light. The bulb's out of reach. I'll need to get some height on it.

Moving quietly, I carry a garbage can to the door, stand up on the lid, and using my pocket handkerchief to protect my fingertips I unscrew the bulb. The light dies, the night gathers around me with tender familiarity.

But we're not in pitch darkness; it's never pitch dark in New York. There's always a glow from somewhere, from headlights, streetlights, advertising signs, theaters, windows of apartments where someone's still awake, offices where someone's still working. The glow settles along the cement wall that encloses the entire yard. The wall is maybe eight feet high.

I jump down from the garbage can, carry it to the back end of the yard, then climb up onto the can again. The top of the wall is still about six inches or so above my head, no problem for me to pull myself up and make it over the top if I put a little spring into my knees. But I don't think Celeste is going to have the same bounce in those high-heeled shoes.

A quick look around shows me something that could be useful. "Celeste," I say, my voice low so I don't provoke the neighbors, "see that milk crate? Bring it over here."

She brings it over, then I take the crate from her, place it on top of the garbage can, and step up onto the crate. "Yeah, this oughta do it. Okay, I'll go over, then you follow. I'll catch you and help you down the other side."

"Yes, okay."

The top of the wall's an easy pull from the crate. By the

time I get a leg over I'm satisfied Celeste won't have any trouble.

"Cantor, wait!"

"What is it?"

"I can't climb up, not in this skirt."

This ridiculous obstacle to our getting the hell out of here would annoy me except I remember how damn good Celeste looks in that skirt.

I unhook my leg from the top of the wall, step down to the milk crate, and extend my hand to help her up, but she's not there.

She's at the other side of the yard, lifting what looks like a discarded vegetable crate from the area near the garbage cans. She carries the crate in one hand and pulls a garbage can with the other as she walks back across the yard, a trash picker in a mink coat.

I like a woman who's inventive. Celeste sure makes the grade with her bit of construction work. She puts her garbage can next to mine, puts the vegetable crate next to the can, then steps onto the crate and up to the garbage can, graceful as royalty climbing the stairs to her box at the opera. She even extends her hand for me to assist her, her red leather glove dark as smoldering embers in the night's glow.

She says, "Well, why are you still standing there? I thought we were in a hurry." Her breath drifts along my face. Her breath is warm and moist, like summer air promising a storm. I bet there are plenty of storms inside Celeste, wild, beautiful storms that could sweep me up in their ferocity.

I get my leg over the top of the wall again, hoist myself over to the other side, and hope I don't land on something noisy or break an ankle when I make the drop to the ground.

Hallelujah, there's nothing on the ground but dirt.

Garbage cans are in this yard, too. I carry one to the wall, climb up on it. Above me, the silhouette of Celeste is coming over the wall. I reach up, slide my hands along her legs as she edges down. The hem of the mink tickles my face. Her nylon stockings and satin slip are smooth along my hands. The metal loops of her garter belt are warm against her thighs. All these sensations slide into me, wriggle under my skin. If I let them bore any deeper, I'm a goner.

"I've got you," I say. I guide Celeste down to the top of the garbage can, then jump to the ground and help her down from the can. "C'mon, let's get you to that safe place," I say and start across the yard.

"Cantor?"

"Yeah?" I turn around, thinking, *For chrissake, what now?*

"Thank you."

"Yeah, sure," tumbles out of my mouth like a couple of loose teeth. I take Celeste's hand and lead her toward the tenement across the yard.

There's no space between this building and its neighbors, so we'll have to go through the back door and basement. I'll pick the lock if I have to, but a quick turn of the knob opens the door. The lock's busted.

What a swell neighborhood. Safe as a shooting gallery.

It's hot in the basement, and dark as a subway tunnel. The only light is from the flame in the tiny round window of the boiler in the corner, giving a hellish blue tint to the gloom. I lead Celeste carefully through the basement, trying not to bump into stuff that'll make noise and alert suspicious tenants. By the time I find the bottom of a stairway, my back's streaming sweat like Niagara Falls.

The stairway's even darker than the basement, the steps nearly invisible. I have no idea where to find the light switch, and feeling around on the walls gets me nowhere. But there's a slit of light visible at the top of the stairs, probably the light sliding under the door from the hallway. With my left arm behind me to hold Celeste's hand, I keep my eyes on that slit of light while my feet find the way up the stairs.

The door at the top of the stairs is locked. I let go of Celeste's hand, whisper over my shoulder, "Give me a sec," then take out my penknife and pick the lock. The door snaps open.

Air from the hallway hits me with a welcome change of weather. I reach behind me for Celeste's hand. Not that I need to; there's enough light in the hallway to see where we're going. I just want to hold her hand. She takes it.

We walk through the hallway, then out the door to Forty-Third Street. As we walk down the front stoop, Judson is pulling up in his Chevy.

Celeste gets into the backseat, I slide in beside her. "Stay low," I tell her, "keep your head below the window."

"You think we're being watched?" She sounds scared, not all the way to panic but in spitting distance. "You think anybody saw us?"

"We'll be okay," I tell her. "It's just a precaution."

Judson pulls away from the curb. Celeste grabs my hand. She holds tight all the way to Twelfth Avenue, a few blocks' ride. Her hand is warm through her gloves, the leather supple and seductive along my fingers. I wish the ride was longer.

"Pull into Louie's garage," I tell Judson. I toss the key over the seat. "After you park the car, walk out the front door of the garage. I'll take Celeste out through the back. We'll meet you at the office."

We stay low in the backseat while Judson pulls into the driveway. He gets out of the Chevy, unlocks the garage's big wooden doors, and swings them open. The whole operation's over in seconds, but Judson's efficiency doesn't make a dent in Celeste's fear. She says, "What the hell's taking him so long?"

"Take it easy. We'll be inside in a minute." The words are barely out of my mouth when Judson's back in the Chevy and driving into the garage. He parks across from my Buick. Celeste moves to get out of the car, but I pull her back, say, "Wait until he shuts the garage doors behind him."

Judson saunters out of the garage. Celeste says, "Can't he put a fire under it?"

"Quiet. He knows what he's doing." And what he's doing is keeping the scene low-key in case anyone's passing by. He's just a fella parking his heap in a garage, then walking to his destination, not the sort of fella to attract anyone's attention.

He shuts the garage doors. I say, "Okay, Celeste, we can move."

We slide out of the Chevy. The delicate tap of Celeste's high-heeled shoes against the cement floor echoes around the garage. The ceiling light finds the fear on her face, even as the fear tries to hide in the shadows cast by the veil of her hat. I can't take my eyes off of her. She has the kind of beauty that wears brutal emotions like fear or ferocity as elegantly as a fashion model wears lipstick.

I slide my fingers under the veil of her hat and stroke her cheek, wondering if she'll let me get away with it again or if she'll push my hand away this time. She wouldn't be the first woman to sting me for taking liberties. She could slap my face, maybe even kick me. Let me tell you how much damage a high heel can do. But she doesn't push my hand away, slap my face or anything else. My touch seems to steady her. She unsteadies me.

Celeste looks around the garage, takes stock of her surroundings, eventually settles on my Buick convertible, a pearly yellow '48 Roadmaster with a black top and white sidewall tires. Even in the dingy light of the garage, yesterday's wax job shows off the body's patina.

"You like that car," I say.

"That's quite a house pet. I'd sure like to get to know its master. That kind of cash and taste, my troubles would be over."

It never fails: beautiful women rip your good sense to shreds. Celeste's life may be in danger, but that doesn't stop her from looking for any profitable angle. My good sense tells me to get what I need to know from this woman of dubious intentions and slick charms, then send her packing to fend for herself.

Fat chance. Her big brown eyes and the temptations that live inside them have shredded my good sense to a pulp.

I don't tell her the Buick is mine, or that I'm thinking about trading it in for a newer, even more expensive model. There's no sense in letting Celeste's hooks bite deeper into me than they already have. All I say is, "Let's go."

We walk out the back door into the zigzag of alleys behind the garage. The bellow of ships' horns and the clang of buoy bells drift over from the docks. To an outsider, the sounds of the docks are nothing but noise from the rough side of town, where these dark alleyways seem impenetrable and threatening. To me, the dockside noises are the music of my life, and these alleys are a cozy path to my private Eden.

CHAPTER TEN

I'm taking the one risk I swore I'd never take: letting an outsider into my smuggler's lair. Bringing Celeste to my office is a dangerous risk to my business, but I can't guarantee her safety anywhere else, not even at Sophie's apartment. And I can't bring Celeste to Sophie's apartment anyway. The place has too many memories. Memories of nights with Sophie and memories of crazy nights without her, nights I'd pace around the living room drowning in a bottle of scotch, trying to figure out what the hell happened to her, not knowing if she's alive or dead.

There's no place for Celeste in those memories.

So there's no other choice. I have to risk Celeste stumbling across the basement door to my vault of treasures, or the more likely possibility that she'll blab my secret some night to the next danger boy who promises her the high life. At least she'll be alive to blab.

Judson's on the phone at his desk when we walk in. From the snatch of conversation I hear, I figure he's talking to his pal the sound expert. "Right, just that watery sound and that grinding metal…Look, I know it's secondhand from a cab radio through a phone but it's all I got…Yeah, uh-huh…Okay, get back to me when you know something." He hangs up and dials another number as Celeste and I walk by and into my private office, leaving Judson to his finaglings. He's got his hands full, keeping tabs on Gregory Ortine and pulling every string in town to find out where Loreale's stashed Rosie.

But it's Celeste who's got me by the pants leg right now, and she won't let go until she gets what she wants: safe passage out of town and the sweet taste of a scorned woman's vengeance against Pep Green. I'm her best bet to get both, but it won't come for free. She'll have to give if she wants to get, and my price is the truth about Opal Shaw's murder.

I turn my desk lamp on. Light and shadow settle on Celeste as beautifully as a moonlit night settles on the river, and with the same mystery. I look her over as I take my coat and cap off and toss them over the back of the big green club chair. I search Celeste's eyes, shadowed behind her hat veil, but I'm not just admiring the pretty picture. I'm trying to get the goods on what's inside this woman's soul, get an answer to my question, "Can I trust you?"

"Isn't it me who's supposed to do the trusting?" she answers back.

"Listen, you can't tell anyone you've been here, Celeste, understand? Not even the movie stars lounging at that pool three thousand miles away in California. You're safe here because no one on the outside knows about this place. Not Pep. Not even Loreale. And you're going to keep it that way." My tough-sounding finish with its implied threat gets through to her, and after staring at me for a minute, she just nods her head. I give her a nod back and say, "Okay, make yourself comfortable. I'll pour us a drink." I pour two glasses of scotch, then turn around to see Celeste seated on the couch, looking at me. She lingers over my dark green suit and the blue handkerchief in the breast pocket before her eyes travel down the rest of me all the way to my brown oxfords. I realize this is the first time all evening she's seen me without my overcoat. She's assessing my full regalia.

She doesn't say whether or not she likes what she sees. She just keeps looking at me as she puts her handbag down beside her, then removes her gloves and the mink, but leaves the veil down on her hat. Maybe the veil is her shield against what she decides is unsavory or otherwise iffy about me, but I doubt it when she crosses her legs, the hem of her skirt brushing just below her knee as she leans back against the couch, graceful as a feral animal. The woman knows what she's doing, and she's doing it all over me.

"I hope you like Chivas," I say, handing her a glass.

"What's not to like?"

There's nothing not to like. The whiskey is smooth, the woman sharing it with me is gorgeous, and the way the light from the desk lamp slides along her leg is picturesque. I wouldn't mind taking my own ride along Celeste's shapely calves. Best I can do is let my imagination make the trip, so after I take the scenic route along her leg and continue up the rest of her, I finally arrive at her face, where on the other side of that hat veil her eyes accuse me of doing exactly what I am doing: undressing her mentally and having my way with her. I feel a little guilty about my peep-show imaginings as Celeste uncrosses her legs, until she crosses them again in the opposite direction, showing off the other half of the matched set.

Judson's knock at the door interrupts whatever's jelling between me and Celeste. I grab a badly needed swallow of scotch before I tell him to come in.

Judson starts to say something as he walks into my office, but after a glance at Celeste he changes his mind and says instead, "Uh, Cantor, I need to see you a minute."

I excuse myself to Celeste and follow Judson to the outer office. He closes the door.

He gives me back the key to Louie's garage, then says, "I got another line on Ortine. He's got people looking all over town for you, asking questions. A few of his thugs are even shadowing your apartment building. You'd better stay clear of your place tonight."

"All right. I don't know when I'll get back there anyway. Look, stay on Ortine. Find out if he starts calling in too many favors, especially police favors. Between Opal crashing on my boat and the Ortine business, I don't want cops squeezing me from both sides. Keep me informed."

I turn to go back into my office but Judson grabs my arm. Behind his wire rims his eyes are wide with accusation. He says, "You brought her here. You trust this Copley dame?"

I don't have an answer, only a shrug and an uneasy smile.

Judson lets go of my arm but hangs on to my attention. "It's just a feeling," he says, "but—look, whatever chased her to a dump in Hell's Kitchen, well, stuff like that usually comes with trouble. Did she tell you what caused the nosedive?"

"A broken heart resulting in an abrupt loss of income."

"Oh, it's like that," he says, laughing.

"Yeah, it's like that." I'm not laughing. If Judson knew Celeste was cashed out by the guy she's now accusing of murdering Loreale's ladylove, a guy who may have played her for the murder—and made her the target of the two deadliest killers in New York—he wouldn't be laughing, either. But he doesn't know. He doesn't know anything about Celeste Copley except what his senses tell him, and his senses don't like what they're telling him.

He says, "She's not Sophie," ambushing me with her name.

"What?" Judson's put himself between me and my door, blocking me from going back into my office, back to Celeste.

"Listen to me, Cantor," he says, "I remember the hell you went through looking for Sophie, okay? I remember all those lousy tips that sent you scraping your knees along all those blind alleys, and I remember cleaning you up after you beat the crap outta that doorman for information you thought he was holding out on you. So I know why you're doing this, why you're risking your neck for this Copley dame."

"Get out of my way. You don't know what you're talking about."

"No? I know you look at every woman now like you don't dare lose track of them. You're scared they'll be stolen off the street the way Sophie was stolen, the way Loreale stole Rosie. And now you want to make sure the same thing doesn't happen to this Copley, but you're doing it scared, and working scared opens you up to making mistakes. You'd better make sure Celeste Copley isn't a big mistake, Cantor. You'd better make sure for Rosie's sake." Having said his piece, Judson steps away from the door. But behind his glasses he gives me a no-nonsense look, a potent mix of worry and warning.

I go back into my office. Celeste is standing at my desk, looking things over. Her head snaps up when she sees me. She flashes a smile as sincere as a shyster lawyer's and sits back down on the couch.

"Been looking around?" I say, wondering if Judson is right, if the risk of bringing Celeste here is a mistake that will sink me after all.

"Well, I...I was just stretching my legs."

"See anything interesting in your travels?"

"I wasn't really looking. Like I said, I was just stretching my legs."

"Uh-huh. It doesn't matter, anyway. There's nothing in my desk drawers you could hock for rent money."

"You're a suspicious sort of alley cat."

"You can't be too careful these days. The papers say the crime rate is up."

"Afraid of being robbed?"

"You see anything around here worth stealing?"

"Well, I don't know. I have a feeling you've got more than you're showing me."

"You've seen enough." I sit down in the club chair opposite the couch, finish my Chivas, and think about what Celeste would do if she knew she's sitting above a roomful of treasures, any one of which—say, the 2,800-year-old Greek vase with the scene of a Trojan War hero's funeral—could pay for a hundred swimming pools in sunny California. I tell myself to wise up and pay attention to Judson's queasy feelings about Celeste. His senses about these things are usually right on the money. But those flickers of fear and sadness in Celeste's naughty eyes keep getting in my way.

I say, "I made you a promise to keep you safe and I don't welch on my promises. So now it's your turn to make good on your end of the bargain. Let's have it. Tell me all you know about what happened to Opal Shaw."

"You don't waste any time," she says.

"I don't have it to waste."

"I didn't know Loreale kept his people on a time clock. When does he let you punch out?"

"You think I'm an employee?"

"Aren't you? Then why—? Oh, I see."

I don't know what Celeste sees, but whatever it is shows up as a sly smile behind that hat veil.

She settles herself more deeply into the couch and takes a long, lingering look around the room. Finally finished with her assessment of the place, she says, "What kind of office is this, anyway? What kind of business do you do here?"

Damn her. "The kind of business, Celeste, where I don't waste time with unnecessary questions. The kind of business where I know how to keep secrets and how to keep you safe. Enough questions. Now you'll give me answers."

I may as well be talking to a pampered pet kitten who only pays attention if she feels like getting around to it. She closes her eyes, takes a leisurely swallow of scotch and purrs, "Mmmmm, I like your whiskey. Smooth, the way whiskey should be. The way life should be."

"And if you want it that way again," I say, leaning forward, taking her chin in my hand and giving it a shake to open her eyes, "you'll tell me what I want to know. You hold out on me"—I take her glass of scotch away—"there'll be no more smooth scotch, no smooth ride out of town, no chance to get back that smooth life Pep took away from you. You understand?"

She curls toward me with that feral grace of hers, takes back the glass of scotch, knocks back a deep swallow, then leans back again, triumphant. She's not a kitten now, she's a lioness, confident that her claws are lethal.

Anyone who says that females are the weaker sex hasn't felt the power of Celeste Copley simply sitting on a couch, smiling a teasing smile. That smile's trained to conquer.

So it comes across all wrong when her smile slowly withers, her power crumbling like old bones. "I was tricked," she says, almost choking on it. "You have to believe me, Cantor, I was tricked. Opal is—*was*—my best friend."

"What do you mean, *tricked*? Who tricked you? Pep?"

"Yeah, that bastard. He tricked me, promised he'd give me ten grand just to get Opal away from Loreale's penthouse, keep her away so Loreale would think she'd skipped out on the wedding. Pep told me how Loreale hates to be crossed, that he'd never forgive her. The way he said it, I was scared that Loreale would even kill Opal himself."

"Must've been a helluva trick to get Opal away from the penthouse on her wedding night."

"Yeah, some trick," she says. "As rotten as the trick Pep played on me about the ten grand. But getting Opal to take a ride with me really wasn't hard. She'd already had a few drinks and was feeling pretty jazzed up. And besides, we'd been friends for some time. We'd met at a party, hit it off, ran around together. Shopping, nightclubs, men. You name it, we did it, and laughed about it, too. After a while I knew Opal inside out, I knew what kind of girl she was. And what she was was a real good-time cutie, if you know what I mean. She liked her men expensive and her thrills cheap."

"You saying she wasn't in love with Loreale?"

"Oh, she loved him, all right, in her way. She knew she had Loreale wrapped around her little finger. If she wanted diamonds, he'd buy her a mine. If she wanted furs, he'd empty a jungle. But that didn't stop her from having a good time. So tonight I promised her a good time. One last fling before tying the knot." Uh-huh, good ol' Celeste Copely, the naughty bridesmaid. "But Opal knew she'd have to be a good girl after Loreale came home from prison and married her, so a final blowout suited her just fine. I promised we'd get back in plenty of time for the wedding."

So much for my fantasy of the classy dame in the society columns.

After another slug of the scotch, Celeste says, "And Pep knew I was the only one who could pull it off. I was the only person Opal would run with. That's why he called me. How do ya like that sonuvabitch? He tosses me into the gutter, then calls me up tonight and makes a lot of sweet talk about money and *needing* me. I knew I should've just hung up and not listened to him, but I was a sucker for his line about…needing me." Her knuckles have gone white around the glass of scotch. She's holding the glass so tight I'm afraid she'll break it.

"Yeah, you should've hung up," I say. "That was a rotten gag to play on a friend. Did you really think that by selling Opal out you'd win Pep back?" And why would she want Pep back after he'd treated her like an old suitcase? But I leave that alone. Love can twist anybody up.

"I hoped…" she says, struggling to finish it. "Why should Opal have everything and all I have is heartbreak?! Why should Opal always get the sweet deal?" What flows out of Celeste is so bitter I expect her throat to pinch tight and her tongue turn black. "The fancy boarding school, the money, the penthouse? For a lousy ten G's I'd have some dough of my own for a change instead of always living off the sugar daddies who take the sugar away if they're tired of the way you stir their coffee." She turns away from me when she starts to cry, soft sobs she tries to conceal, almost like she's hiding from me, maybe afraid I'll judge her.

Judge her? First I'd have to get past the other phony affections being thrown around tonight: first from Mom Sheinbaum, now from Celeste, whose affection and loyalty to Opal Shaw were no better than a scam.

Celeste takes a small white handkerchief from her handbag, slides the hankie under the net veil of her hat, and dabs the tears from her eyes. She has plenty to cry about. Could be her betrayal of Opal is eating her alive. Could be she has a conscience after all.

I slide next to her on the couch, take her glass of scotch and put it down on a side table, then take the handkerchief from her hand and wipe the smudged mascara from under her eyes. "Listen, you can't bring Opal back but you can square it. Tell me what happened. I promise I'll keep you safe."

"Nobody is ever safe from Loreale," she insists. "Or from Pep, either. I knew Opal wasn't going to be safe when I saw Pep in that basement in Brooklyn where he had me take her. We drove out in Opal's car. When I saw Pep, when I saw his eyes, I knew he'd lied to me. And I knew I'd been a fool for him *again*. A stupid fool! I should have known he'd had something worse in mind than just making Opal miss her wedding. Cantor, you should have seen his eyes!"

"What place in Brooklyn? What's the address?"

"I don't know the address. Pep gave me directions to an alley behind a poultry butcher's joint in Brownsville, near where Pep grew up. Oh God—and then I saw Opal's eyes. I couldn't bear to see Opal's eyes once she knew, once she'd figured it out…"

"Celeste, did you see Pep kill Opal? Was she already dead when she went off the bridge? Did Pep toss her over after he stabbed her neck?"

"I didn't see what he did on the bridge. I wasn't on the bridge. He told me to get lost once I got Opal to Brooklyn." Her bitterness is so strong it almost eats through my skin. "The bastard nearly broke my arm when he ordered me to drive Opal's car as far away as I could and ditch it, then go home and wait for his pal to bring me the ten thousand. Only there was never going to be any pal. And now Pep will come after me to shut me up as soon as he can slip some time from Loreale. Cantor, I have to get away!"

Dammit, it's not enough. It's only half a story, and it's told by the woman who was ready to sell Opal's wedded bliss and wound up selling Opal's life. If I go to Sig with this ragged tale, he may or may not believe that his right-hand guy killed his bride-to-be, but it's a sure thing he'll take vengeance on the woman who lured Opal to her death.

I can never let him find her.

If I'm going to keep Sig from picking up Celeste's scent, I have to turn his nose in another direction. I have to get something on Pep Green, something that stinks so much it'll clog Sig's nostrils.

But first I have to calm Celeste down. "Soon, Celeste, I'll get you away soon. Trust me. I told you, I keep my promises. In the meantime, we have to tie up Pep nice and tight, take away his ability to hurt you, and take away Loreale's reason to kill you. So I have to know about Pep's scam. Why did he want to scrap Sig's wedding? Did he think Sig was going soft?"

"Uh-uh, that wasn't it," she says, sniffling but calm enough to talk. "He didn't want Loreale to marry Opal because of the deal with Opal's mother, with Esther Sheinbaum."

"What kind of deal?"

"An expensive one, believe me. Opal said she'd marry Loreale on the condition that he cut Mrs. Sheinbaum in for a percentage, and not a little one, either. A yearly percentage for her mother's old age, Opal said. As if the old bat didn't already have millions. But Opal was afraid that the Law could finally catch up to her mother. She was afraid the old lady was losing her edge, still doing business the old-fashioned way, that she wasn't sharp to the new tricks the Law's learned, like maybe the tax man would find a loophole and take Mrs. Sheinbaum's millions away."

The idea of Esther Sheinbaum losing her edge, slipping up, has a wrong ring to it. I doubt Esther Sheinbaum ever had a weak or clumsy thought in her life.

Something else is wrong, too. Why would Pep give a damn about Sig's financial arrangements with his future mother-in-law? Unless… "Celeste, did Pep say where Mrs. Sheinbaum's cut was coming from? From Sig's personal cash, or from the operation?"

"Yeah, from the operation. Right off the top. Before Pep and the other boys got their cut. Pep was not tickled pink with *that*, let me tell you, but Loreale told him that he had plans for the outfit to increase business anyway. But that wasn't good enough for Pep."

I get a chill thinking of how many dead bodies it might take for Pep to be happy with the size of his profit.

"The other boys went along with it," Celeste says. "You know how it is, if you work for Loreale you go along with what he wants or you wind up dead."

Or people you care about wind up dead, people like Rosie.

Celeste says, "But Pep—always the smart guy. He was having none of that. As far as he was concerned, Opal was picking his pocket. Oh God, Cantor, *please*. I'm too scared to keep going like this. I don't care how safe you say this place is. I want to get away from here. *Now*."

"Just a little bit more, Celeste. You've got to give me a little bit more."

"How much more? Can't you see I'm worn out?"

"You're the only lead I've got. Look, it won't be much longer."

"But I can't…" Then she drops whatever argument she was ready to make and puts me under her microscope again instead, looks at me like she's examining every eyelash, every pore of skin, every scar on my face, searching for I don't know what, but she seems to find it. The sadness in her eyes fades, replaced by a glint of satisfaction as she leans toward me, strokes the scar on my cheek, then the knifelike scar above my lip with the tip of her finger. She says, "This is a dangerous game you're asking me to play, Cantor. If I go along with it, if

I help you deliver Pep to Loreale, you'll need to do more than just get me away. I'll need some dough to start that new life. Can you get it for me? Say—"

"Ten thousand?" I say it with a smile. Why not? This gorgeous creature is not only stroking my mouth with a touch that makes the rest of me shiver, she strokes my outlaw soul. "You'll have to work for it," I say. "You can start by telling me where you ditched Opal's car. We have to make sure it can't be traced to you."

She takes her fingers from my lips, to my disappointment, then leans back on the couch and gives me a sly little grin that says we understand each other. "It's in an empty lot in the Bronx. I took the license plates off and took the registration out of the glove compartment. Tossed it all down a sewer in case the cops find the car."

"Fingerprints?"

"I wiped it down, inside and out. Then I went home and waited for the so-called guy who was supposed to show up with my so-called dough. What a dope I've been to believe a liar like Pep. And if that's not humiliating enough, let me tell you, riding the D train from the middle of nowhere in a never heard of rump end of the Bronx is no picnic."

"Drink up," I say and get up from the couch. "We've got traveling to do."

"To the Bronx? Oh no, I don't think I could bear looking at Opal's car. Please, no."

"We're going to Brooklyn, to the place you took Opal."

"That's just as bad! No, please, I don't want to go there."

"I need to look it over, see if there's any scrap of evidence connecting Pep to Opal's death, maybe figure how and where and *if* he killed her."

She's up from the couch, fast. "Of course he killed her!"

"I need evidence, Celeste. Sig won't buy it otherwise."

"What if there isn't any evidence, no trace of what happened there? You know how good Pep is at killing. He isn't sloppy. Listen to me"—she's standing in front of me, close, daring me to make her back off—"we have to come up with something even if it's not there. The only way we can get Pep is to frame him."

"That's a dirty game."

"Are you telling me you're a stranger to dirty games? If that's what you're saying, you're a liar."

If our faces were any closer we'd be inside each other's mouths. I'd love to taste hers, suck the lipstick right off those full pouty lips. "You're goddamn gorgeous when you're angry," I say. "You're goddamn gorgeous all the time. I'll have a fine time keeping my eyes on you tonight, and I'll miss you when you're safe and sound in the sunshine. May I help you on with your coat?"

"Don't let me stop you."

"You couldn't." I take the mink from the couch. It's my first chance for a good look at it. It's a stunner, all right, perfectly matched pelts all around. The sugar daddies may walk out on Celeste, but before they do they sure pay up for the pleasure of her company.

I help her on with the coat, take her arm, and walk out with her into the outer office. "Um, wait here," I say. "I won't be long. Judson, entertain the lady for a minute. Sorry, folks, nature calls."

Celeste's not crazy about killing time with Judson, and he's not happy about babysitting Celeste, but they're not about to argue with me over a trip to the can.

I go back into my office, close the door behind me, but I don't go to the can; I open the wall safe behind my desk. I move the photo of me and Sophie aside to get to the strongbox, take out Ortine's ten thousand, put it into an envelope, and put the envelope into my inside jacket pocket.

What the hell. Celeste is going to earn it tonight but good, and I wasn't planning on giving it back to Ortine anyway.

❖

Celeste and I arrive back at Louie's garage and go in through the alley door. Inside, she walks toward Judson's Chevy. I take her arm and lead her to my Buick. When I open the passenger door, Celeste catches her breath at the sight of the custom interior's dark brown leather seats and burled-maple steering wheel and dash.

Celeste gives me a slow appreciative smile with plenty of calculation behind it, figuring the possibility that if she plays me right she may yet have it all.

I help her into the car, thinking, *You can't have it all, baby. I don't give it all to anyone anymore. But you sure could've had a lot of it.*

CHAPTER ELEVEN

Brownsville may not be as boisterous as the Lower East Side, or as tough as Hell's Kitchen where just about everyone's a brawler, but you couldn't have picked a better spot for a kid like Leon "Pep" Green to get a first-rate education in murder. Since the wild days of the bootleggers' shootouts during Prohibition, through the tommy-gun years of the Depression, and into the years just before the war, a bunch of Brownsville gents were engaged in activities that still give everyone nightmares. Maybe you've heard of those gents, contract killers known as Murder, Incorporated; at least, that's the moniker that stuck, a flashy name dreamed up by the newspapers. But among the killers themselves, and to everyone in the underworld, they were known as The Combination. Just hearing the word *combination*, even in casual chitchat, still makes a lot of people wish they had eyes in back of their heads.

Pep must've been a young tough on Brownsville's streets when Combination big shots Abe "Kid Twist" Reles, Jacob "Gurrah" Shapiro, Frank "Dasher" Abbandando, and their cadre of murderers killed everyone marked for death by the higher-ups in the New York rackets. If Charlie Lucky or Meyer Lansky whispered your name into the ear of boss Lepke Buchalter, you didn't stand a chance. Lepke would make a phone call to the back room of a Livonia Avenue candy store, pass your name along to the boys, and they'd hunt you down. The boys loved their work, turned it into a frolic of bloodletting that scattered burned, swollen, or chopped-up remains in vacant lots as far away as the swamps of South Jersey.

No doubt Sig Loreale studied the Combination's methods, and then—as is Sig's methodical way—he improved upon them. The end result? Dasher Abbandando got the chair in Sing Sing's death house. Lepke fried in the same chair. Gurrah died of a heart attack in Sing Sing, serving fifteen to life. Reles turned state's evidence and sang like a canary in a deal to avoid the death house, then fell out of a Coney Island hotel window while his police protectors weren't looking. But Sig Loreale sits pretty in a golden penthouse.

Guess whose ear Lansky whispers names into now?

Celeste's wrapped snug in her mink as we drive along Pitkin Avenue, Brownsville's main thoroughfare of mom-and-pop shops that sell everything from salami to scissors. A movie palace dolled up in red Moorish tile is down the block. Seems no matter how rough the neighborhood, there's always a movie palace, a place to go to escape the dull reality of your rotten life and get lost in the make-believe of someone else's more interesting rotten life. The movie palace and the shops are shut up tight for the night, except for a saloon where a drunk in a ratty gray coat and a crumpled fedora stumbles out as we drive by. The drunk makes Celeste fidgety. "Relax," I say. "You're just spooked from your rough night."

But the drunk makes me a little queasy, too. For all I know, Sig's planted a drunk in all of New York's five boroughs to eyeball me. Or maybe Gregory Ortine's trying something fancy to get a line on me. I've always thought Ortine too simple a thinker to organize anything as cute as planting eyeballs around town, but I suppose a botched $35,000 smuggling deal can wise up even a simpleton.

Celeste directs me to an alley behind a row of shops. "Park here," she says when we're behind a poultry butcher's place.

The shop has a pull-up type basement door set into the ground. "Some spot for a bridal party," I say as we get out of the car. "I wouldn't figure Opal to go along with a gag like this. Isn't the joint a bit low class for her taste?"

Celeste waves that away. "Didn't I tell you she liked cheap thrills? Anyway, a slick article like you oughta know that some of the most interesting parties in town are in basements."

True. I've fox-trotted with some very classy women at clandestine basement soirees, especially since the war ended and the ladies have been telling their now home-front husbands they'll be out at a card party playing canasta. In basements across the city, dames in gowns dance with dykes in suits, hidden from the hissing eyes of a vindictive world and the bare-knuckled fists of husbands and the Law. "How long before Opal figured out there wasn't any party in this particular basement?"

Celeste doesn't look at me when she answers, just pulls the mink around her, shivering as if feeling a chill. "She had it figured as soon as we started downstairs."

"Yeah, and I bet you walked behind Opal, blocked her escape back *up* the stairs. You're a real pal, Celeste."

She starts to say something, but the disgust on my face tells her not to bother.

I pull the basement door open.

The wooden steps creak like bones cracking as we walk downstairs. I find the light switch at the bottom of the stairway. When I flip it on, an ugly yellow glare lands on butchering tools and general hardware stacked around the room: empty egg crates, gizzard shears, boning knives, shovels, buckets, hammers and saws, their jagged shadows rising on the dirty brick walls like hell's skyline. The basement smells like hell, too, the stench of chlorine and old chicken feet clogging my nose and throat. The whole setup reeks with the rotten stink of killing.

Bloody chicken feathers are on the dirt floor. Spots of dried blood, some the size of nickels and dimes, are visible on the butcher block. I don't know if it's chicken blood, Opal's blood, or even human blood, but the sight of it gives me a prickly feeling, hints that murder's been done down here, and not just of chickens, and not just tonight.

Celeste's standing behind me. I take her arm and pull her next to me, show her the blood. "Were those bloodstains on the butcher block when you and Opal arrived?"

She shrugs, says, "I don't know. I wasn't looking at the butcher block."

"What about Pep? What was he doing when you and Opal got here? Did you see a weapon? A knife or maybe an ice pick? Word's out that Pep's expanding his skills to include quietly killing by ice pick. Maybe he practiced on Opal's neck."

"No. I didn't see anything like that. Pep grabbed her, then he hollered at me to scram, which is exactly what I want to do right now. So hurry up and look for whatever it is you're looking for, please? This place is giving me the heebie-jeebies." If she taps her foot any faster I'll have to buy her a pair of tap-dance shoes.

"Patience, dearie," I say. "I have to find something that'll tell me whether Opal took a stab here in the basement or someplace else."

"Maybe there's nothing here," she insists. "Or maybe Pep killed her on the bridge, before he tossed her over."

"Maybe." I run my fingers along the surface of the butcher

block. The blood spots are soaked into the wood, dry now, too dry to have been spilled tonight. If Opal was killed here, I'll have to find some other remnant of it. "What kind of coat was Opal wearing over her dress? If she tried to fight Pep off, maybe the coat was torn in the struggle and I'll find a scrap, something Loreale will recognize. What color was the coat?"

"Black, as I recall. Black wool."

Wool doesn't usually make me itch, but the way Celeste describes Opal's coat, like she's trying hard to picture it, I'm starting to itch as bad as if the black wool is scratching the back of my neck.

Celeste closes the mink more tightly around her. I don't like the way she's doing that, either, as if she's afraid that if she lets go, the coat will run away.

"Celeste, lying to me is a very bad idea. Remember who I'm working for tonight, and that he wants me to find out what happened to Opal no matter what it takes. You got that? *No matter what it takes*, no matter what I have to do or who I have to do it to. Now, you can talk to me, or I can take you to Loreale and you can talk face-to-face to the most dangerous guy in town. Do you want the most dangerous guy in town to see you in that mink?"

She answers with the nervous smile of someone caught naked in the wrong bedroom.

"You're a ghoul, Celeste. A gorgeous ghoul. That's Opal's mink, am I right? Probably a gift from Loreale. No wonder you're in such a hurry to leave town."

Her forced smile hardens into a leer, her body goes rigid, a trapped animal caught hiding in a dead animal's skin.

"Aw, c'mon, honey," I say. "Haven't you figured it yet, that I don't want to see your pretty face cut up or your delicious body chopped to bits? Play it right with me and I can make sure that doesn't happen. Keep lying and I'll throw you to Loreale, though it'll break my heart, and we have better things to do than break my heart."

There's a slight twitch of her nostrils, the cornered animal sensing a shift in the wind. Carefully, she says, "Do we, Cantor?"

"You know we do, but if I have to use a chisel to dig information out of you, there might not be enough of you left for me to play with. So do us both a favor and tell me how and when you got your hands on Opal's mink. Was it before or after her death?"

It's probably been a long time since Celeste reminded anyone of a sweet and innocent little girl, but right now, with her chin tilted up, she could almost pass, except for the spiderweb shadow across her eyes from her hat veil. She says, "Does it matter when I got it? The coat wasn't going to be of any use to Opal anymore. It may as well do me some good. I still have to lead life somehow, and this coat could bring me a nice few bucks." By the time she's finished there's no more little girl. The lioness is back, claws out.

"You'll need the cash for a good lawyer to get you off from an accessory-to-murder rap," I say, moving close to her. "That is, if you're still alive to face trial. Loreale will kill you for vengeance, and you know Pep is already planning to shut you up. So here's how it works." I crowd her against the butcher block, lift that net veil from her face. There's nothing between us now but the mink, its hairs swaying under my breath, writhing like damned souls. "Promising you safety wasn't enough for you," I say. "You just kept stringing me along, and then you even held me up for cash. But I told you you'd have to work for your getaway money, so okay, start earning it. You give me the truth or I don't come up with the cash."

The mention of money warms her up, puts the color back in her cheeks and a little smile on her face, awakens the slick operator in her heart, the one who looks for ways to work me over. She retracts her lion's claws and uses her other reliable weapon: that soft, curving body that's supple as a snake. She moves against me and I let her. She slides her hand up the front of my coat, and I let her do that, too. I don't want to stop her, I want to take her, press myself all over her until she sucks me dry. We've been stroking that possibility since I arrived at her door, and now it's pawing at us like a rapacious animal as she slides her hands under my overcoat. Celeste's hands understand my nature and my desire, her fingers arousing every muscle, bone, and sinew in my body, bringing me close to a recklessness I'm about to unshackle when her right hand stops at the bulge of my gun.

She suddenly freezes. She's the trapped animal again. "What if you don't like what I say about Opal's death? What if you don't believe me? Are you as dangerous as Pep? Could you kill me, too? Is that what you want?"

"I want what I want, Celeste."

"Are you talking about me, or my story? Which is more important to you, Cantor? Which are you willing to pay for?"

"Ten thousand dollars buys me all of you, honey, your story included. But okay, for starters, I'll take your story." She's afraid of Loreale, she's afraid of Pep Green; maybe it's time for her to be afraid of me, too. "And it better be the truth, Celeste. My hands are at your throat. It's not a caress."

I've brought her face so close, my last word, *caress*, slides along her lower lip when her lipstick brushes my mouth. I've wanted to taste this creature from the minute I laid eyes on her. I'm crazy from watching and waiting. I pull her to me, press her mouth fully on mine.

She's delicious, sweet like one of those dangerous flowers

whose fleshy petals drug you with their narcotic nectar, a drug that kills all the hurt in your heart. Celeste Copley is the kind of woman you crave for the rest of your life.

She pulls away, but only slightly, talks fast, breathless. "Come with me, Cantor. Let's get lost together."

"Can't do that." I pull her back to me. I haven't finished enjoying that mouth. We speak between my tasting her.

"Why not? What's there to stop you?"

"Loreale, for one. He'd find us both and kill me as fast as he'd kill you. And by the way, I have to save someone's life."

Celeste tries to pull away again, roughly this time, but I pull her back. I'm stronger than she is and I like it that way. I keep her against me, keep her breasts pressed against my gun and the cash she doesn't know I have in my jacket pocket.

But her eyes are on me like probes, and her smile now isn't forced or nervous. It's triumphant. "I knew I had you pegged," she says. "I realized it back at your office. You don't usually run with Loreale's pack. He's got something on you, doesn't he. What is it? Is he holding a hostage over your head? Is that the life you have to save? A female life, I'm sure. You in love with her?"

I hold her tighter, pin her arms back to force her to stop fighting me. "I don't trust love any more than you do, angel. But her life matters to me. Her life matters a whole lot more than Opal's mattered to you."

"More than mine matters to you?"

I can't help smiling at that one. It's rich. I slide my hands back to her throat. "There's no one around to see what I'll do if you don't come through with the truth. *Now.* Or I'll throw your pretty little corpse at Loreale's feet." My fingers tighten ever so slightly, just enough to make her wince.

"Don't do this," she says.

"You have only one way out, Celeste." I tighten my grip on her throat.

"Take your hands off. *Please.* You're hurting me."

I loosen my grip, but only a bit, finding it useful to let Celeste think I might really be a killer. "This is the best I can do," I say. "My hands will stay right where they are so I can feel it if you lie to me. Start talking."

The muscles and sinew in her neck weaken beneath my fingers. When she speaks, the words grind in her throat, fall out of her mouth in broken bits. "Pep...he...he didn't kill Opal. I did."

CHAPTER TWELVE

Celeste won't be the pretty little murderess I'd imagined sharing a cell with in my old age because she isn't going to live long enough to take up residence in our cozy prison dwelling. Sig Loreale will see to that.

"Well, well," I say, my hands moving from her throat. I can drop my song and dance about killing her. She's dead already. Or at least she will be when I turn her over to Loreale. Sure, she'll try to sell him her tale about Pep's wedding-night scam, and then Loreale will kill them both.

I'll hate turning her over. There's something crummy about sentencing to death a woman I've just held in my arms, a woman whose body and soul I'd wanted to know intimately.

Okay, so it's crummy, but Celeste's a killer and a liar. My heart will heal. And handing her over to Sig is my best play to save Rosie's life.

But it's Celeste's life that's looking me in the eye, reading my lousy thoughts and begging me to get rid of them. "Don't turn me over to Loreale, Cantor. *Please.* You have to let me explain!" But it's a dead-end gamble. She can plead from now 'til doomsday. I've had all I can take of Celeste playing fast and loose with the truth, and I'm tired of the way she yanks me around. And she's still trying. "You know what Sig will do to me. Can you live with that?"

"Save it. You killed a woman, and you want me to help you get away with it. That's not how it works. It's either Sig's justice or the Law's justice for you, sweetie. But I don't do business with the Law, and you wouldn't want me to, anyway. The Law will hold you in a filthy lockup with a dozen scabby sisters. By the time your case comes up for arraignment twenty-four hours later, you'll be just as scabby as they are, inside and out, from the sport the guards will make of you. So believe me, handing you over to Loreale is a mercy. Sig's justice is a lot faster and cleaner. And the best part is it has something in it for me."

It's like I slapped her, stung her fear and jolted it into anger. But her anger curdles into a disappointment so familiar to her it settles into her eyes as easily as a regular guest settles into a comfortable chair. Celeste Copley is disappointed with every single thing in the world, with a life where every road she travels is a dead end and everyone she meets does her dirt.

So she backs off from me, leans against the butcher block, and looks me over, trying to find a way to stop me from handing her to Sig, maybe find a thread that could unravel me if she pulls it. She says, "I suppose the something that's in it for you is the life of the hostage Sig's holding? The dame you're not in love with?"

I answer with a nod. It's not much of a nod, but it's all I'll give her.

Celeste comes back with a sharp, fierce laugh. She's suddenly confident again, wriggling her lioness's claws and eyeing me as if she's found something better than a thread to pull, a way to sting me fast rather than unravel me slowly, finding a scab to pick instead. "You're wrong about me," she says. "You said I don't trust love any more than you do. Well, you're all wrong about that. I loved Pep and maybe I still love him, you hear me? A rotten love for a rotten guy, sure, but love nonetheless. You know what that means, Cantor? It means that I still have something true inside me, even if I have to lie my way through my lousy life just to survive. But you? I don't know what you've got going with this dame Sig's holding hostage, but I bet she's nuts about you and you don't lift a finger to discourage her. Hell, you probably even *encourage* her, which makes *you* the liar. You're a bigger liar than I'll ever be."

Celeste picked that scab right down to the bone.

I could bloody her mouth to shut her up, and I would if I could live with it. But I can't. I'd lie awake nights, hating myself. I might not be able to look another woman in the eye ever again. So I give Celeste the only response I can live with, the only one that matters anyway. "Then the best way for me to make it up to her is to save her life."

"And then you can keep lying to her."

"I don't lie to her. I've never told her—" I choke it back before I get suckered into a conversation I have no business having with Celeste, a conversation that's been tough enough to face with Rosie. "Look, it's *your* lies that get you into trouble. Now you have to pay for 'em."

"So you can have a clear conscience when you hand me over to Loreale, to that murdering monster? I don't deserve this. You said you'd help me."

"That was when you were breaking my heart. Maybe my heart will break again when Sig kills you for Opal's murder."

"But it wasn't murder. It was an accident. An accident, I swear! I was trying to *save* Opal's life, but I…well…it went wrong." The pleading in those big brown eyes could bring the saints to their knees.

I'm no saint, but I'm no sucker, either. This accident routine could be another dodge.

But what if it isn't? If it isn't a dodge and I turn her over to Sig, I'll have blood on my hands. I already have plenty of other stuff on my hands, juggling a lot of people: Ortine, Sig, Mom Sheinbaum, the cops. Blood would only make everyone slippery. "You'll have to work a miracle to convince me, Celeste, and I don't believe in miracles."

"You want to throw me back in the gutter? Fine, be my guest. But don't give me to Loreale. I'm no killer, Cantor. It really was an accident."

"Since when is a stabbing an accident?"

"When it isn't actually a stabbing. When it's more of a cut, a puncture really, sort of a rip. A rotten, clumsy…" She's choking up, crying now, pitiful as an orphaned little kid. But I stopped trusting anything that comes out of her pretty mouth—not her words, not her sobs. Her kiss was probably a lie, too.

Her smudged mascara is real enough, though. Wet black streaks drip down her face. Her tears don't get to me, and neither does her pleading, but those long black streaks, like jailhouse bars shadowing her face, get me good.

I'm torn up by the idea of Celeste in the city lockup, of having to endure the rough stuff she'll take from the guards and from the street-tough sisters who'll bait her as prey. I take my handkerchief from my breast pocket and give it to her. She wipes her eyes and face, smudging the blue silk with black.

She gets her crying under control, settles down, and hands the handkerchief back to me, but I say, "Keep it. You may be doing a lot more crying if I don't buy your story."

Getting past a last weak whimper, she says, "The story would go a whole lot better with a drink, but I'll settle for a smoke. Got one?"

I pull out my pack of Chesterfields, give a cigarette to Celeste, take one for myself, and light our smokes. Celeste takes a deep drag the way you might take a deep breath before you jump off a cliff. Her gaze drifts past me, looks toward the cliff's edge. "You've got to believe me, Cantor, I didn't want any part of Pep's scam," she says, "but Pep gave me no choice. It was either my life or Opal's life."

"Why didn't he just lure Opal out here himself and leave you out of it?"

"Because—listen, Opal wouldn't give Pep the time of day, that's why. He was just one of Sig's hired thugs as far as she was concerned. Pep hated that snotty attitude of hers. I wasn't crazy about it, either, if you want the truth."

"It's all I've ever wanted."

"Yeah, well…anyway, Pep figured Opal would go along with me if I asked. He knew I was her best friend, we had a lot of good times together, and that I kept her company while Sig was in prison."

"And I bet she showed her appreciation," I say. "I bet Opal tossed you a few bucks, or treated you to lunch at the classier places? Your kind of life, right, Celeste?"

"Don't be such a cynic," she says, disgusted with me for always thinking the worst of her, even though she makes it easy. "I didn't need Opal's handouts, not then. Pep was taking real good care of me. We had a nice setup at his place on the East Side." Celeste fingers Opal's mink without realizing it. Then she realizes it. She stops fingering the fur.

"Keep talking," is all I say.

But she needs another drag on the smoke before she can go on, using it to withhold herself from me while she recovers from getting caught in the act with the fur. Finally, she says, "It's like I told you, that louse Pep eventually threw me over. Then tonight he calls me up and asks me to drive Opal out here, before Loreale gets home from upstate. Oh, boy, Pep sure turned on the charm, let me tell you, dripped syrup all over me.

All of a sudden he needs me, he says. He needs *me*." She's smiling at the memory, a weird childlike smile that makes my skin crawl.

Her tiny triumph doesn't last long, though, as lousier memories seep back. "Pep knew I was hard up for cash, really hard up, so he put his hooks into me with that promise of ten grand. But I heard a threat inside that promise." Her eyes darken and her shoulders sag with that scary memory. I'm tempted to offer her a little tenderness, but it doesn't take much to talk myself out of it. Celeste's moods can be as dishonest as her stories.

Pulling up what little confidence she can muster, she says, "I know Pep. I know what his voice sounds like when he's figuring a killing. You don't live with a guy, share his nights, pour his coffee, and not know how he's put together. I knew he'd kill me if I didn't go along. Funny, huh? Now he'll kill me anyway."

Not if Loreale does first. But I don't mention it. "So you brought Opal out here," I say. "And you walked behind her, blocked the stairs. She never had a chance to run."

"She tried, but I grabbed her. She fought me, but Pep came up the stairs and overpowered her. She couldn't fight us both." Celeste's hands rush to cover her face, shield her from the memory. Tears seep between her fingers, leave dark spots on those red leather gloves.

I let her be, let her cry it out, let the story burst from her. "Pep stuffed a rag into Opal's mouth so she wouldn't scream and wake the neighborhood. Then we got her downstairs. Cantor, you should've seen Pep's eyes. They were too bright, too strange."

"And what about Opal's eyes, Celeste? The poor kid must've been scared out of her mind, or didn't you notice your best friend's eyes?"

"I saw, and then I couldn't look at her. I just…couldn't. Especially when Pep tied Opal's hands behind her back. Or he tried to tie her hands," she says, suddenly laughing, a brittle laugh with as much joy in it as a slit throat, "but this fancy fur coat got in the way! With Opal struggling, wiggling like crazy to get free, the fur on the cuffs kept getting tangled in the rope and Pep couldn't tie it up. It annoyed the hell outta him. So he tackled Opal by her neck and told me to take her coat off."

"And you just couldn't resist putting it on."

"No. I did *not* put it on," she says, disgusted with me again. "I put it down on the butcher block. I wasn't thinking about the goddamn coat. All I was thinking was, how the hell did I wind up like this, in this lousy cellar with this rotten guy and mixed up in the murder of my best friend? I begged Pep not to kill her. I tried to convince him that maybe we could pay her off, shanghai her out of town, *anything* to prevent her marriage to Sig and stop the money skim to Opal's mother."

Pep must've laughed her off. Her ridiculous schemes even make me snicker.

"Yeah," she says, "go ahead and laugh. Stupid ideas, I know, but it's all I had." Her shrug is so limp and sad, I'm afraid she'll topple over. For all I know, she's playing me for a fool, giving me the weak little girl act again to get my sympathy, but I can't be sure. So if I want the rest of this tale of death, I'd better play along.

I put my hand on her arm to steady her. She gives me the kind of smile that makes scolding daddies feel guilty. Then she says, "Of course Pep wouldn't go for it, but I kept trying. I was frantic. I didn't know what else to say or do. And those sounds Opal made while Pep tied her hands, shrill, horrible groans through that rag in her mouth, they scared me, Cantor. I felt sick. I started to scream, which made Pep even madder, so he swatted me one! Gave me the back of his hand, real hard and vicious. He tried to land it on my mouth, but what with Opal wriggling against the rope, Pep's arm wasn't steady. My hands were at my face while I was screaming, so Pep's already messed-up aim was blocked again, and his hand landed on the lapel of my coat."

"Black wool?" I say, knowing that a good liar always bases their lies on facts, and Celeste is a helluva good liar.

She looks at me with surprise, then remembers she'd lied to me about Opal wearing the black coat. After a deep breath to clear the lie away, she says, "I wore a big brooch on the lapel of that coat, one of those big silver birds, must be about four inches, I guess, with lots of rhinestones. Pep caught his hand on the brooch when he tried to swat me. It must've pinched him because he cursed like a stuck pig. You should've heard him squeal." This time the laugh's real, a vengeful joy filling her whole body.

I don't laugh with her, but the picture she's painting of Pep in clumsy pain makes me smile, a sneery smile full of swaggering glee.

As her laughter winds down, she says, "It gave me an idea. I pulled the brooch off my coat and used the pin as a weapon. The back of the brooch has a long, heavy pin to hold the weight of all those rhinestones, and I thought if I used it to stab Pep's hands, hurt him enough, he'd have to let go of Opal, and she and I could run away. But I couldn't get to his hands. He was too fast for me. I kept catching the sleeve of his overcoat with the pin," she says, making a stabbing motion over and over with frantic energy. "Then I had this crazy idea that I'd aim for one of his eyes, blind him. Hell, I wanted to kill him! But he was still too fast for me. When I came at his face with the brooch he twisted away and pushed Opal at me, and that's when the pin went into her neck. I tried to pull it out, but she kept…twisting, kept struggling. The more she struggled, the deeper the pin went into her neck and the more it tore her flesh. Oh God, Opal's blood spurted straight at me like a fire hose!"

Celeste covers her face with her hands again, instinctively protecting herself from the memory of Opal's blood rushing at her. She must've caught blood by the bucket load, her face, her black wool coat, soaked in Opal's blood.

No wonder she was freshly showered and her hair washed when I showed up at her apartment.

I say, "Where's the black coat and the brooch now? The brooch wasn't in Opal's neck when they fished her out of the river."

"I ditched the coat when I ditched Opal's car. I pushed the coat into the sewer with the license plates and registration. I don't know about the brooch, though. I wasn't on the bridge when Pep—when he pushed Opal over."

Pep wouldn't be stupid enough to keep the brooch as a souvenir. Either he buried it, threw it into the river, or more likely left it in Opal's neck to sink with her, but it must've slipped out and sank to the bottom of the river on its own. I wonder if it settled anywhere near the other piece of treacherous jewelry that's bookending my night and Opal Shaw's death: the empress's emerald and silver brooch that sent me on the river in the first place.

Celeste is crying again, and I don't like the effect those sobs are having on me, pounding against my heart like a homeless beggar desperate for sanctuary. Before I know what I'm doing, I take Celeste in my arms. Her tears quiet down a little as she puts her face against my shoulder. Her softening sobs make a kind of muffled drumming, its rhythm suddenly pierced by that bone-cracking creak of the stairs and by Pep

Green laughing, "She's snookering you, Gold! If you believe her story you're even more of a sucker for a beautiful dame than I am."

CHAPTER THIRTEEN

Pep's holding a .45 automatic, a big chunk of steel with a five-inch barrel. It's pointed right at my belly. At this range, a .45 slug can rip right through me and take my guts and spine with it out the other side. Even scarier than the gun is Pep himself. His black fedora is pushed to the back of his head, and with his wide schmoozy grin and his pomaded red hair almost orange in the yellow glare of the overhead bulb, he looks like a Halloween pumpkin on a death march.

But the spookiest thing about Pep Green, aside from his enjoyment of killing, is that sales-pitch style yammer of his, especially when he's yammering about murder. "Cantor," he says, sliding my name slowly through his grin, "you make it too easy. This habit you got of following a nice set of legs around gets you into trouble, could even get you killed. Say, whaddya know? You *are* gonna get killed. You and this pair of legs who's been leading you around by the, uh, nose." He slides his eyes and his grin to Celeste. She lowers her hat veil back into place in a useless effort to shield herself from Pep.

He says, "Hello, my sweet. Been playing me a double cross?" No matter what comes out of Pep's mouth, whether he's ordering dinner or ordering a murder, it sounds like *Can I interest you in a nice low-mileage number that just came on the lot?*

"You're one to talk," Celeste answers back. "You double-crossed me out of ten grand. You promised—"

"So what if I promised? I lied. I can be a good liar, you know that. One liar to another, that's us. Only forget about getting away with your crazy lie that you killed Opal by accident. Yeah, yeah, I heard you try and sell that bedtime story to Cantor. Well, Opal's death was no accident, honey. You just wanted it to look like one."

"Says you."

"Right, says me. By the way, you look real nice in Opal's mink. Real nice." He hisses it, like a snake crawling up Celeste's leg.

It makes my skin itch. It makes Celeste's skin itch, too, judging by the way she's fidgeting inside the mink. She looks away from Pep, tries to escape her humiliation, but she can't escape it and she starts to remove the coat. Then she changes her mind, gives Pep a look that tells him to drop dead, and wraps herself more deeply into the coat.

It's a ghoulish performance, flaunting a dead woman's coat. Makes me want to gag. But Celeste's defiance of Pep sure is gutsy. Makes me want to take her to bed.

She's annoying Pep, though, and it's not a good idea to annoy a homicidal nut job who's holding a gun.

I have only one play to keep Pep from pulling the trigger: keep him talking, stretch things out while I keep an eye on that big .45 and try to figure how to get us away from this charnel house alive. "How long you been on to us, Pep?"

"How long did you think it would take me to puzzle out what Loreale wants you to do? Y'know, I'm not his top guy for nothin'. I can usually figure him. And like I said, you made it easy, Gold. It didn't take much to figure that sooner or later you'd find your way to Celeste, and once you found Celeste, I knew you'd find your way here. And see? Here you are!"

"Then you know you're a dead man," I say.

"And who's gonna kill me? You? Or this cheap date you were snuggling with when I came in?"

I'd kill him just for being so smug. "As Sig's top guy," I say, "the guy who says he can usually figure his boss, you should know Sig will put it together that you and Celeste were in cahoots to get Opal and her mother out of the picture, even if it meant you'd have to kill Opal to do it. Too bad Celeste spoiled your fun and did your killing for you, Pep."

"*Me?* Kill Opal? Are you kidding? That dame was money in a dress. She was gonna be my meal ticket. Cash every month, regular as the Bank of New York. Hey, what's wrong with you, Gold? You look like you don't understand a word I'm saying, like I've started blabbing a foreign lingo."

I understand the lingo, all right. I've heard it lots of times before. Every word has two *X*'s and its grammar is based on endless combinations of the double cross. One of its most fluent speakers is standing next to me, motionless behind the veil of her hat, too terrified to say anything in any lingo at all.

She has plenty to be terrified about. And if she expects me to keep sticking my neck out for her, she has plenty of explaining to do, too, if Pep will let her, if he doesn't just take care of his business and go ahead and kill us. There's only one way I can find out. "Let's hear it, Celeste. You know what Pep's talking about?"

"She knows." Pep doesn't even give her a chance to open her mouth before he answers for her. "She knows most of it anyway. Jealous little bitch."

The word *jealous* floats around Celeste like smelly fumes. Maybe that's why she catches her breath. People can choke on their own jealousy.

Pep says, "Okay, you two, I'm tired of looking at your faces. Especially yours, Celeste. I got tired of your face a long time ago. Turn around." He'll put a bullet in the back of our heads.

So I don't turn around, and I practically have to hold Celeste up to keep her from collapsing from fear. "Wait a minute, Pep," I say, making a fast play for more time to save our skins. "I'm the only one in the room who's not up-to-date. So c'mon, give it over. You've got all night to kill us. You can spare a few minutes to tell me why I'll be a corpse. Consider it my last request instead of a cigarette."

He thinks that's funny, gives me a quick laugh. Fine. It's better than shooting me.

Celeste tugs at my sleeve. "Cantor, you don't seriously believe he'll tell you the truth?"

I don't seriously believe either one of them knows how to tell the truth, but I shut up about it. I've got to keep Pep calm if I want him to talk to me instead of kill me. So I say, "Why shouldn't he tell the truth? He's on the winning end of it."

"You bet I am," he says, taking the bait. "There's only one truth that's worth anything anyway—money. That's what this is all about. Money. Money that should've been mine in the first place, money that was gonna come outta my pocket."

"You're talking about the percentage Sig was planning to skim for Esther Sheinbaum," I say.

"You know about that? Yeah, well, I found a way to get it back, and then some. A nice little scam fell right into my lap. And you know who tossed me that scam?"

"No, but I'm all ears, Pep." The more conversation that passes between us, the more time I have to watch him, watch his eyes, the twitch of his hands, look for the tiniest break I can sneak into, and jump him.

Pep fires back with a laugh, the short, smug kind that's meant to put me in my place because he knows something and I don't. "Hah! It was the Queen of Diamonds herself, Opal

Sheinbaum Shaw, that's who, and she didn't even know it. Let me tell you, Cantor, leave it to a dame to forget what's good for her. You know as well as I do that even the smartest of 'em have no brains."

This happens sometimes, a guy will talk to me like we share the same locker room. I don't usually bother to correct him. I pick up a lot of useful information that way, even when what comes out of the guy's mouth makes me want to smash his teeth. "Maybe you meet the wrong women, Pep," is all I say.

"They're *all* wrong, but we can't live without 'em, eh, Gold? And they know it! It's how they pry the cash from our pockets. Well, I saw my chance to turn the tables on Miss Opal Shaw. Know what the dizzy dame did?"

"Enlighten me, Pep. I'm still listening."

"Yeah, and you're gonna be surprised at what you hear. She made a play for me, that's what she did. Can you believe it? Her man's in Sing Sing and the tramp doesn't have the decency to wait it out." His eyes narrow into slits that have no light in them, just hate. "If Sig heard about it, he'd put a contract on her just for breakin' his heart," he says, enjoying it. "End of wedding. End of money flyin' outta my pocket for old lady Sheinbaum. But then I get smart, see? I ask myself, why settle for just the same old cash when I could milk the cow for a lifetime?"

Blackmail is nothing but murder done slow. Right up Pep's alley. "You cornered her into a shakedown," I say, sure that I sound as disgusted as I feel. If it annoys Pep and he kills me, well, there's not a damn thing I can do about it.

He's annoyed, but not at me. "She had it coming, if you ask me. So I tell her, sure, come on over to my place and we'll have us a time. We set a date for the next night, then I go out and buy two of those wire recorders. I camouflaged 'em on a shelf in my living room, behind some big books. Rigged 'em up so all I'd have to do is flip a switch before I open the door."

The idea of Pep having books, of being curled up on a couch reading anything but the *Daily Racing Form* surprises me. Maybe the books are weapons manuals. They have pictures.

He's warming to his story, though, happy to crow about his prowess with women. I bet he'd strut like a peacock if it wasn't for the nuisance of keeping that gun pointed at my belly. I keep watch on that gun from the corner of my eye while he regales us with the saga of his conquest. "So Opal comes over to my place," he says, "shows up right on time and looking damn fine in a slinky black number that fits like skin. I keep my mouth shut mostly, let Opal do the talking so it's real clear on the wire recordings that this rendezvous is all her doing, and that maybe I don't think it's such a good idea, me being loyal to Sig, you understand. After I have enough on her, a lotta *Come on, baby* and *I've always had a thing for you* and stuff like that, I give her a kiss so I can smear her lipstick, send her off to the bathroom to fix her face while I turn off the wire recorders. Sweet deal, huh?"

Sweet as sewer water. "And of course you were gentlemanly enough to send her home once you had the goods on her."

"And pass up a pair of the juiciest thighs in New York? Would you, Gold? And boy, oh boy, Opal was quite an athlete in—"

"When did you start soaking her for cash?" I can live without an image of Opal and Pep between the sheets, and I really don't want it lurking in my mind's eye the next time—or anytime—I talk to Sig, assuming, of course, I get out of this slaughterhouse alive.

Pep talks through his high-pitched giggle. "What's the

matter, Cantor? You turning into a bluenose biddy? All right, all right, I'll spare you the sordid details." He calms down from his giggling, then resumes his I'm-letting-you-in-on-the-inside-dope style of patter. "Okay, here it is. A week or so before Sig gets outta the joint, I take one of the wire recordings and the machine and go visit Opal in the penthouse. She's all set up in the living room like she owns the place, spread out on the couch reading a magazine. I play her the wire, see, tell her I have a spare hidden offshore so she can't play it cute and think she can pay me off all at once and that's that. I tell her I want five G's up front and a grand every month afterward, otherwise I take the recording to Sig. Well, I gotta say the woman showed backbone. No brains but plenty of backbone."

"And that surprises you? Did you think Sig would go for a dame who crumbles like stale bread? Uh-uh, I figure a guy like him wants a woman with real spirit, the type to put up a fight where it counts, if you know what I mean." I even toss in a knowing wink.

He gives me that high giggle again, only now it sounds even crueler. "Yeah, I know what you mean, Gold! So you know what she does when I play her the wire? She lifts her snooty nose and tells me to get lost, says her mother has connections high up and she'll have that other recording traced and found in no time. The dame played it dangerous. I have to hand it to her. Bold as brass." The compliment comes with a sneer.

"You surprise me, Pep," I say. "Seems like you'd just knock her off after she called your bluff. It gets the wedding off the table and your percentage back in your pocket. Why go through all the fancy planning to lure Opal out here?" I'm walking that dangerous edge between annoying him and flattering him. Annoy him, and he'll pull the trigger. Flatter him, keep him crowing about how clever he is, and I stand a better chance of finding my moment to sink him.

"Weren't you listening, Cantor? I said this is all about money. I wanted the whole gravy train, and I figured I'd have another shot at getting it by scaring Opal into accepting my deal. Bringing her out here to my own turf on her wedding night, getting her away from Sig's other boys and the protection of the penthouse, I'd have control of her. I could scare the bejesus outta her. I can be pretty scary if I have to." He says this so matter-of-factly it takes a minute to catch up with me and chill me through to the bone. "Just ask Celeste here," he says to her. "Right, honey? Like the night I told you we're through? Remember what I did when I told you to get the hell out?" His grin would make mothers grab their children from the playground and hide them indoors.

Slowly, in a whisper so cold the air around her might splinter, Celeste says, "You lying sonuvabitch, you had that gun to Opal's head. You were ready to kill her."

"If I had to, I guess," Pep says, "if she wasn't gonna play ball. But she was. You know she was. That snotty tramp was finally so scared she agreed to the whole setup." Talking to me again, he says, "And you know what made her roll over, Cantor?"

"Opal didn't want her brains sticking to the chicken feathers all over the dirt floor?"

"You don't give her enough credit! Opal Sheinbaum Shaw was one gutsy dame, let me tell you. She held out on me when I said I'd blow her head off, but when I told her I'd go after her sweet old mother, Opal fell apart like a rickety chair."

So the bond between mother and daughter was tight after all.

Pep slides his attention back to Celeste again. But his gun doesn't waver. It's still steady, his finger still on the trigger, my nerves still on edge. "Only that wasn't enough for our Miss Copley here," he says. "Oh no, she wanted Opal dead. She couldn't stand it that her friend had eyes for me. You didn't like that at all, did you, honey. You didn't like me tasting your best friend's dish."

Celeste's face is hard, cold. Only the movement of her red-lipsticked mouth proves she's made of flesh and not soulless stone. "Why should I like it? Why should I like any of it? You throw me out like garbage and then my so-called best friend goes after the guy I'm in love with. But I'm no killer." She turns to me, tugs at my sleeve again, says, "Please, Cantor, listen to me," but I keep my eyes on Pep, stay on every breath he takes, the slightest sway of that gun, while Celeste pleads with me. "Don't believe him, Cantor. He's a murderer and always has been. Why would you take the word of a murderer?"

"Because he was going to get what he wanted from Opal. He had no reason to kill her."

"Yes, he did. He didn't tell you that part. He didn't tell you that even after Opal gave in and said she'd pay him, she spit in his face. He hates that. He hates it when a woman insults him. He goes crazy. Opal spit in his face and that's when his eyes lit up like fire!" Celeste's rant is getting dangerous. If it pushes Pep too far, he'll make that gun go bang, and it's driving me crazy that there's nothing I can do to stop her. If I make a move, yeah, Pep's gun could go bang. "Remember I told you about his eyes?" she says with no letup. "Well, he went crazy. He put the gun to Opal's head again. He was going to blow it off, money or no money. That's when I tried to stop him. That's when I fought him and tried to stab his hand with the pin on my brooch!"

Pep's laugh is so raw it's not really a laugh, it's a growl. "Nice try, honey! But that *Ooo, I tried to save her life* story won't sell. Cantor, tell her she's done for. Actually, you're both done for. I'm done talking."

"But the bridge," I say, throwing it out fast. I need more

time to find a chink in his armor, any little sliver I can slip through and get a drop on him. "Why'd you toss her?"

"Oh yeah." He laughs. "You got stuck with the body, didn't you."

"Uh-huh, and she sank my boat, too. I took a helluva beating tonight, lost a bundle of money on a deal when my boat went down. So come on, Pep, at least tell me how my rotten luck got started. Then you can kill me."

I don't know where I got this knack for making Pep laugh, but I'll do a Borscht Belt comedy routine if it buys me time.

"Sure, sure, okay, Cantor. A minute either way won't matter. You're crackin' me up. Okay, look, with my plan gone sour, I had to get rid of the body. I didn't plan to toss her, but I couldn't take the time to bury her here—"

"In the basement?" That explains all the hardware down here in this chicken coop, all those shovels and saws making those weird shadows on the walls. My toes curl in my shoes just thinking about how many layers of body parts might be inches under my feet.

"Yeah, this basement's one of my good spots for it," Pep says, "but I couldn't linger down here any longer so I figured I'd drive over to a vacant lot I sometimes use just over the bridge, down by the Fulton Fish Market."

"And then you manhandled Celeste into getting rid of Opal's car. That bruise on her arm is as red as cheap jewelry."

He smiles like he just sold me a high-mileage lemon. "Let's just say she needed a little convincing to do as she's told, which I guess you know by now she's not much good at."

I'm tempted to tell him I'm not crazy about women who only do what they're told, but I guess it's not really the time or place. And under the circumstances, I'd rather let Pep do the talking while I just listen, and watch.

"Anyway, after Celeste scrams I carry Opal up the stairs,"

he says. "I'm gonna put her in the trunk of my car, but just my luck, a nosy neighbor's taking his garbage out to the alley. He sees me carrying Opal. Well, with my arms full, I can't get to my gun to knock the guy off and get rid of him, and I can't just put Opal in the trunk like she's dead. He might call the cops. You know what I'm talking about, Gold."

"Yeah, cops can really be a distraction, Pep," I say, friendly-like. Just two outlaws talking shop. Except he's planning to kill me, and I'm twitching for any chance to stop him.

He says, "You said it. Cops always seem to be underfoot. So anyway, with this guy there in the alley I have to put Opal into the car like I'm taking a sick woman to the hospital or something, which the guy figures is none of his business and he walks away. Only thing though, I didn't think about Celeste running off with Opal's mink. And without the mink, Opal was bleeding on my front seat. Not a helluva lot anymore—she spurted plenty when Celeste got her in the neck—but she's bleeding enough, and I shelled out a small fortune for my custom upholstery, a very classy black-and-gray houndstooth. Even paid extra for the black piping across the top. I know you can appreciate that, Gold."

"Sure."

"I was afraid a big bloodstain would never wash outta the weave, so instead of letting her bleed some more, I gave up on the vacant lot at the fish market, and when I was driving across the bridge, I dumped her."

"That's it?"

"Yeah, that's it. You were expecting a big opera?"

The story can't end on an idea so small. The story can't end at all, not yet, or Celeste and I are dead. So I press the conversation. "You took a helluva chance. Didn't you think you'd be seen, maybe someone would call the cops? And you

• 159 •

must've tied up traffic. There's heavy traffic on the bridge at that hour with the late-show supper-club crowd driving in and the after-theater crowd going home."

"Nah. Let me give you a tip. You can shoot a guy in the head in the middle of Times Square, but if you just walk away no one will remember what you look like or that you were even there because they don't want to. Did you know that? Works every time," he says, grinning that syrupy salesman's grin. It's starting to give me an upset stomach. "But who the hell knew you'd be on the goddamn river, Gold, or that the whole thing would turn into a circus? I figured Opal would just drown. Sig would never be the wiser. He might wonder where she was for the rest of his life, but who cares?"

I'd care, because I'd hate having anything as intimate as heartbreak in common with a monster like Sig Loreale. I'd hate knowing exactly what he's going through, the torture of trying to outrun, outdrink, outthink the endless mystery that will drive him crazy. "You know Sig won't rest," I say, "until he finds out what happened to his sweetheart."

"Like I said, who cares? He could look forever. He'll never find an answer. The answer dies with you two."

"Then I guess you're sitting pretty."

"Looks that way." He gives me his best slick salesman's grin. "You know, I always liked you, Cantor, even though you're a pervert, one of those, uh, bull types I suppose is what you call it—"

"It's not what I'd call it."

"—but you have class. You run a classy operation. Too bad you fell into the gutter when you took up with Celeste here." That grin has twisted from slick to stomach turning.

I let Pep's *pervert* remark slide—how far would I get with a belly torn up by a .45 slug?—and throw him a grin of my own instead. We toss grins back and forth. Pep's grin is trying to be smart-alecky, taunting me about seeing me and Celeste in the clutch when he came in. My grin is just my end of the seesaw, another stall to keep Pep from pulling the trigger.

"Listen, Pep," I say, starting another line of chitchat, "you know—"

"I know a lotta things, now shut up. You're done."

I'm still locked on him, looking into his eyes for the slightest lag in his intention to fire that gun. I don't see one. All I see in his eyes is that rising fire that terrified Celeste. That fire's blazing at me as he raises his gun, aims right for my heart. He's grinning like a madman. I have less than a second to make a move.

A red blur flashes in front of me. Celeste's red-gloved hand comes down on Pep's, throwing his aim. "Bitch!" he yells, turning his gun toward Celeste.

But I grab his wrist, twist it to try to shake the gun loose, try to pry his hand open. Celeste's screaming, pulling at Pep's gun. He fights like a rabid dog, tries to lift his gun hand, aim up at Celeste, but I keep pulling his aim off, twisting his wrist. We're all wrestling, struggling for control of the gun, when there's a blast as loud as thunder followed by a shower of blood and brains and bone. Pep's head is blown to bits.

CHAPTER FOURTEEN

I never knew my heart could stop beating but I'd still be alive. If my heart was beating, it would pump blood to my muscles and sinews, allow them to feel, force them to move, which would disturb the air, which is completely still.

My heart's not beating but I'm alive. No doubt about it. Otherwise my face wouldn't sting where flying shards of Pep's skull nicked me. My eyes wouldn't burn from the spray of Pep's blood.

Celeste is alive, too. In the dead quiet of the basement I hear her breath fight its way up her throat, hiss through its tightening cords until it finally bursts out in a long, shrill scream that kick-starts my heart, triggers my muscles to move. My hand rushes up to Celeste's mouth. "Quiet!" I say. "You'll bring the whole goddamn neighborhood down here, and the cops won't be far behind."

Celeste gags on her scream. It congeals into sobs. Her shoulders sag and her spine gives way as she sinks to the floor, kneels beside Pep, her shadow falling across his mutilated head.

The mink coat she'd hoped would give her some class, provide a few bucks for her new life, is sticky with Pep's brains, soaked with his blood. It's the second time tonight that death sprayed itself all over Celeste like a tomcat marking its territory, and ruining two coats to boot. The gore will never come out of the mink. The coat's worth about as much now as Celeste's future in New York: nothing.

So she really loved Pep, just like she said, which might be the only thing she's told me that isn't a lie. Those tears she's crying over Pep's body aren't fake juice for my benefit. I doubt she's even aware I'm standing next to her. Every nerve in Celeste's body is stretched out to Pep. She's alone with him.

They say life isn't fair. Well, neither is death. Just listen to the radio or read the daily papers. They're full of stories of lonely souls who kick the bucket with nobody to give a damn about them. But the vicious killer Leon "Pep" Green, who doesn't deserve a single tear from anybody, leaves this life with a beautiful woman crying for him.

I won't send flowers to the funeral.

I've got to get us away from here. Hanging around while Celeste has her cry could attract nosy neighbors and itchy cops who'll see us with a dead body and won't bother about explanations. Pep is the second dead body around my neck tonight. Cops don't like those kinds of coincidences, and cops don't like me, either.

I pick up Pep's .45 from the floor, then kneel down and rifle through his pockets for any extra clips and rounds. He has one full clip besides the one that's in the gun. The clip and the .45 go into my coat pocket.

Here's a laugh: it was Mom Sheinbaum who taught me years ago to pick up and stow any hardware lying around at a job site. And now I'm cleaning up after the louse of a guy and the lying dame who were responsible for Mom's daughter's death.

The way Celeste is looking at me kills the joke. She glares at me through that blood-spattered hat veil, accusing me of desecrating the dead. I doubt it's possible to desecrate a guy whose soul was rotten to the core, but the accusation twists into me just the same. So I find what's left of Pep's hat, tidy his coat and straighten his arms, make him look a little less broken. I can't do anything about the blood all over him or the frays on his sleeve where powder burns from the gun blast must've singed the fabric.

Celeste is fingering Pep's sleeve, sliding her fingers back and forth along the frays, her red leather glove blurring into the globs of blood. "See?" she says in a whisper that's threadbare and exhausted but with something else under it, too, the tiniest bit of spark, a pinprick of sass. "See these frays? They're from the pin on my brooch. Didn't I tell you I kept trying to jab Pep with the pin? You believe me now, Cantor?"

I don't bother telling her that the frays look like powder burns to me. She might argue and we don't have time. "C'mon," I say. "We have to go."

"We can't…we can't just leave him here."

"We've got to, for now anyway. C'mon, Celeste. Staying here is a sure ticket to the police lockup. Take it from me, you don't want to go there."

She gives me a weak nod, then takes the mink coat off and covers Pep with it, hiding his destroyed face.

That coat sure gets around.

Celeste holds out her hand, says, "Help me up, will you? I'm kind of shaky," so I take her hand and help her to her feet. Her gloves are slippery with Pep's blood, smearing my fingers. "Where are we going?" she says. The question starts out fine but ends up ragged. I guess she's scared about what I might have in mind for her. "Are we going to Loreale's place? You're taking me to Loreale? God, *no*."

"It's a long ride back into town. You'll have lots of time to convince me not to." She's shivering, maybe from fear that

I'll take her to Sig, fear of what Sig will do to her. Or maybe Celeste's just cold, now that she's not wearing the mink. Either way, the sight of her gets to me, this shivering woman whose tears roll through blood spatters on her face. I take off my overcoat—it was mostly spared of Pep's spraying blood—and wrap Celeste in the coat. She almost smiles. Her almost smile shrinks up when I take Pep's gun and extra clip out of the coat pocket.

I say, "You still have my handkerchief?"

She fumbles for it in her handbag, finds it, and hands it over. The handkerchief's smeared with her mascara. I find a clean spot—there aren't many—then I lift her hat veil and wipe the blood from her face. Her eyes almost do me in. She looks at me like she doesn't know whether to cling to me and trust me with her life, or run from me to save it.

I don't have an answer for her except to wipe the blood from my own face, then offer her my arm and walk with her up the stairs and out of the basement.

❖

I'm driving back across Brooklyn. Pep's .45 is stowed in the trunk. Celeste is surprisingly quiet for someone who's supposed to be trying to talk me out of handing her to her executioner, but I suppose the shock of blasting your ex-boyfriend's face to smithereens could put a gag on chatter.

She looks lost inside my overcoat, just a head and a hat and a beautiful face sticking out above the tweed. There's no expression on that face, no clue to what she's feeling. In the light of street lamps sliding by she doesn't even look real. She looks like a painted doll. Painted dolls feel nothing.

What gives with this woman? She tells lies with the ease of a City Hall pol, kisses like she wants to taste everyone who ever loved you and swallow everything you ever did, she was wild for a guy who threw her out like spoiled meat, and to top it all off, she killed her best friend. And now I'm stuck trying to sort out whether she's a murderer who killed in a jealous rage or was just on the wrong end of a dirty scheme and a lousy accident.

Celeste's jealousy over Opal's play for Pep doesn't help her case, but if you ask me, Pep's story that Celeste intentionally jabbed Opal in the neck is about as dicey a murder tale as you get. I can think of easier ways Celeste could've killed Opal than jab a jewelry pin into an artery while Opal thrashed around in terror and struggled with every ounce of strength. But I might buy it as a freakish accident, as freakish as Pep tossing Opal a hundred feet off a bridge and having her land on my boat, which he didn't plan on, either.

My mind's running in goddamn circles. I'm spinning one crummy thought after another about the woman who's sitting next to me and what I'm going to do about her, do *with* her, and wondering how she fits in with getting Rosie free of Loreale's grip. If I take Celeste to Loreale, it won't matter if he buys the accident story or not; he'll kill her. If I don't, and he finds out, which he will, he'll kill me. He'll kill Rosie, too, just because he won't need her anymore.

I'm caught in this crazy, endless loop until Celeste throws a rock into my spinning thoughts and stops them dead. "What did Pep mean when he said you run a classy operation? What's your racket that you can afford that silk suit and a sweet car like this?"

"Is that all that's bothering you? I figured you'd knock yourself out trying to talk me out of taking you to Loreale."

The mention of Loreale tightens her up, though she tries to hide it. "No," she says, "I want to know your racket."

"All right. I'm in import-export." I give it no more

emphasis than a legit operator might say *insurance* or *shoelace manufacturer*.

"Oh, you're a smuggler."

I'd smile at that—women who are wise to my ways tend to make me smile, especially if they're as knockout gorgeous as Celeste—but I don't want her to know any more than she already knows, and she already knows too much for my taste. The woman's as trustworthy as a busted lock.

She goes quiet again, just looks out the window, gazing with no particular interest at Borough Hall and the Brooklyn courthouses as we drive onto the approach ramp to the Brooklyn Bridge. Celeste's silence gives me room to think about my next moves, but it also gives me the creeps. She's not even trying to stop me from taking her to Loreale.

And then she says, "You owe me."

"I *what*?"

"I saved your life, didn't I? As a matter of fact, I saved both our lives. If I hadn't made my move—"

"Your *boyfriend* might still be alive."

"Well la-di-dah, aren't we spiteful."

"Listen, you jumped the gun on me, girlie, did you know that? I'd been keeping my eye on Pep, looking for a chance to get the drop on him and take him alive. He'd be useful to me alive, but then you make a grandstand play and we all wind up dancing a tarantella with a forty-five auto."

"What am I?" she spits at me. "A mind reader? Or maybe you're just rattled because I took away your chance to be a hero. You always gotta be the hero, don't you."

I don't answer. I don't want to talk about it, don't want Celeste rummaging around in my old daydreams. I don't want Celeste to talk, either, not now, not when we're passing the spot on the bridge where Pep Green tossed Opal Shaw and where I remember the miserable sight of that scrap of Opal's red dress flapping in the wind.

My reverence for Opal's memory is snagged by a flash of light in my rearview mirror. Headlights are fifty feet or so behind my Buick but gaining fast. Soon I see the headlights are on the front of a dark sedan, a big DeSoto whose wide chrome grille glitters like a toothy grin. I can't make out the driver, just a silhouette of a guy in a hat. He doesn't try to pass me even though he's got plenty of room.

If Ortine's found me, he's smarter than I thought, which could be trouble. It'll be even more trouble if it's one of Sig's thugs who's behind me. It's a good bet Sig could already know about Celeste and about what happened to Pep, and he's not happy about it. If that DeSoto stays on my tail, it could run me into the East River the minute I drive off the bridge.

Or it could be nothing, just another car on its way back into town.

But it's not just another car. Its mouthful of chrome is still grinning at the back of my head when I drive off the bridge and make a right turn onto Centre Street. The DeSoto lingers behind me as I skirt City Hall Park, stays with me when I make another right onto New Chambers Street. I don't know if the guy driving the DeSoto is an angry Gregory Ortine or an assassin from Sig's outfit, but I know I have to lose that sedan or Celeste and I could end up dead.

"Hold on tight," I tell Celeste.

"What for?"

I floor the accelerator, gun the Buick. Celeste snaps back against the seat. The guy behind me guns the DeSoto, but there's a good chance he doesn't know the waterfront like I do, doesn't know the alleys and hole-in-the-wall slits between the warehouses and flop joints. He's not ready for it when I make a sharp, fast left into the loading bay of a marine-supply place on Oak Street, corkscrew out the other side, hook a right onto Roosevelt Street, then make a near-hairpin left into the sliver of an alley called Batavia Street.

Celeste's stiff as a stick, holding onto the armrest for dear life. She'd better get ready for more rattling because even though I don't see the DeSoto in my rearview mirror, I see the glow of its headlights rake the brick walls of the warehouses behind me. I push the Buick even faster, take a two-wheeled right turn onto James Street then another screeching left onto Water Street, thread my way along the waterfront through Catherine, Market, and Pike Slips, slide under the Manhattan Bridge where I cut my lights, and back the Buick into an alley between two oyster bars that are closed for the night.

There's nothing to do now but wait.

Celeste, breathing fast, tries to talk. "What the…hell was…?"

"Shhh. Stay quiet. I need to listen for anything outside." I hear light traffic and the Brighton Line subway to Coney Island cross the bridge overhead. The familiar music of buoy bells and the groaning horns of ships harmonize on the East River. Car horns honk and police sirens shriek around the city. A fire engine clangs across town. But I don't hear rolling tires or an engine slowing. I don't hear any cars coming to a stop. The only sound in the alley is labored breathing, Celeste's and mine.

CHAPTER FIFTEEN

Waiting is tough on the body. My nerves beat a rat-a-tat-tat under my skin with the force of a million jackhammers. The jackhammers don't stop until I'm sure I've lost the DeSoto.

When my senses are finally quiet, I breathe easy again, let my lungs fill with air.

I take my cap off, open my suit jacket, and roll down my window, let the night breeze coming off the river cool me down. I pull my pack of smokes from my pocket. Celeste jumps at the crackle of the cellophane wrapper. "Hey now," I say and reach for her hand. She's got it balled into a tight fist. "You can relax," I tell her. "We lost him. It's all over." I offer Celeste a cigarette. She ignores it, too tense to move a muscle. I light a smoke for myself.

Celeste's silence has her wrapped so tight it even ties the air around her in knots. I'd talk to her, try to calm her down, but after the way she ignored me and my offer of a smoke, I figure talking to her won't do any good. She's too wound up, my words can't get in. All I can do is pass the time with my smoke and wait her out.

She finally cracks her silence with a sudden deep breath. When she lets it out, she says, "Loreale must be on to us."

"Could be."

Celeste turns to me slowly, almost carefully, then throws my words back at me like they're a handful of sand: "Could be? You mean someone else could be following us?"

"Look, the guy's gone. That's all that matters." I start the car.

Celeste grabs my wrist before I can put the Buick into gear. In the light from the dashboard, her red leather gloves wrap like bloody fingers around my wrist. Her face, still free of her hat veil, is pale as the moon. Her eyes, still smudged from tears, are alert now. She's a cornered animal again, sensing danger. "I don't like that answer," she says. "It's too slick. What aren't you telling me?"

I pull my wrist from her grip, say, "I'm knocking myself out trying to save your life, honey. That's all you need to know." I park my cigarette in the corner of my mouth and start again to put the car in gear.

Celeste grabs my arm, doesn't let me drive. "Save *my* life? Listen, you think I'm stupid? If the guy following us wasn't one of Loreale's apes, then maybe somebody's coming after *you*. Well, that's just great. I'm supposed to put my life in your hands while someone has you in the crosshairs? Some hero I've got protecting me. Dammit, Cantor, I'm not trying to be funny. Why the hell are you smiling?"

The dashboard glow that found Celeste's face betrays my face, too. Yeah, I'm smiling, because the sight of her swaddled like a papoose in my overcoat while she gives me a piece of her mind burrows into my sweet spot. "I already told you back at my office, you're beautiful when you're angry."

"I'm not angry. I'm terrified."

Celeste's fear, that needy gnome who's been pestering me all night, trips me up again. My smile shrinks, scurries away.

"I'll take that smoke now," she says.

I give her a cigarette from my pack. She doesn't look at

me when I hold the match to the tip and light the smoke for her. She even turns her head away before I blow out the match.

I don't mind her giving me the brush off; I just didn't expect it to hurt.

I put my cap back on and drive us out of the alley.

❖

The atmosphere in the car is thick with the bad air of our sour moods by the time I make a left off Lexington Avenue and onto East Thirty-Seventh Street in the Murray Hill section of town. The kicker of it is, Celeste and I are both annoyed at the same goddamn thing: me. I promised Celeste I'd keep her safe, and I'm failing.

Bringing Celeste here isn't going to sweeten her feelings for me. She might even want to scratch my eyes out. I can't blame her; I'm parked in front of the nest she shared with Pep Green before he broke her heart and threw her out, sent her tumbling back to her fleabag in Hell's Kitchen.

Pep's apartment is in a four-story town house that started life as a private residence during the heyday of the Robber Barons. Like a lot of town houses around the city, it was broken up into apartments when the gold flaked off the Gilded Age. The house is typical of the Italianate variety popular in those days, faced in light gray limestone with Classical lintels above all the windows and a lintel and scrollwork above the arched front door: Renaissance Rome in Midtown Manhattan. The old Robber Baron money dressed itself up in the classiest history money could buy.

Celeste may not be happy to be here, but she doesn't ask me why we've come. She's smart enough to figure it. I want those wire recordings before the landlord hears about Pep's death and finds the recordings when he cleans out the apartment. The smartest thing the landlord could do is throw them out, but if he decides to get cute and tries to make a few bucks from them he'll wind up dead, courtesy of Sig Loreale.

One of the recordings, the one Pep played for Opal, is probably still in his apartment, and there might be information, maybe a storage receipt, for the backup copy, the one he told Opal he stashed offshore.

Celeste pipes up and answers a question I didn't ask, at least, not out loud. "No, I don't have a key to the place anymore, in case you're wondering." Smart girl.

I say, "What's Pep's apartment number?"

"You don't know? You drove like you've been here before."

"I know which pile of stones is his, but not the apartment."

"Apartment 2-A. In the front. You're going to break in, I suppose."

"You can wait here if you don't want to be part of it." She hasn't looked at the place since we got here.

"I'd rather not go in there," she says. "Just leave me a cigarette, will you?" I leave her my pack and the book of matches but take the keys to my car. "You think I'd steal it?" she sasses me as I get out.

"I don't know. Would you?" I don't wait around for an answer. It doesn't matter, anyway. For all I know, she knows how to hot-wire a car. Wouldn't surprise me.

Unlike Celeste's claptrap building in Hell's Kitchen, Pep's town house is well tended and well locked. It takes a little finagling with my penknife to open the front door, but it eventually gives.

The thick carpeting on the stairs and along the second-floor hallway muffles my footsteps and the footsteps of the guy coming down from an upper floor. He's as surprised to see me at Pep's door at nearly four thirty in the morning as he expects I am to see him coming down the stairs. He squelches his surprise, then gives me the double take. I get that double take a lot. It comes in two flavors: disgusted, with a hint of looking for trouble; or the mocking chuckle. This guy's the chuckle type. I don't give a damn how much he snickers at me under his breath as long as he just moves along, stays out of my business. I stand at Pep's door like I'm about to ring the buzzer. The guy walks by me and down the stairs, clearing his throat. I guess I not only make the guy chuckle, I also make him gag. Fine, let him choke.

I wait to hear the guy open the front door and go out to the street before I crack the lock on Pep's door.

The door opens into the living room. There's a floor lamp nearby. When I turn it on, it shows me a room all decked out in Contemporary Impersonal, the current rage among that class of interior decorators whose clients' money is so new it's still breast-fed. I don't get much business from that crowd, and when I do it's from the likes of Gregory Ortine, who looks in the mirror and swears he sees an aristocrat who was accidently switched at birth with a pauper's kid.

Pep Green obviously didn't have aristocratic illusions, but he sure as hell hired one of those nouveaux decorators. The living room has lots of expensive blond wood furniture in the latest style of straight lines and black-and-green plaid upholstery, but there isn't a shred of human personality in any of it. It's probably just as well, since the primary feature of Pep's personality was his love of killing. A room reflecting his personal tastes might end up looking like a torture chamber.

The big books Pep said hid the recorders stick out on a wall shelf like two sore thumbs. The books aren't weapons manuals after all—in fact, they're not even books. They're boxes tricked out to look like a set of oversize dictionaries in tooled-leather bindings. Decorator props, as hollow and phony as Pep's romantic invitation to Opal or his loyalty to Sig. The dictionary boxes stick out because one of the two wire recorders is still behind them on the shelf. The recorder's a small portable job with a leather handle. The wire reel is gone. I figure the missing recorder is probably a portable model, too—must've been the one Pep brought with him when he visited Opal and gave her the shakedown.

But Pep wouldn't leave the recorder and wire reel with Opal. That'd be a sloppy play, and though he may have had the heart and soul of a pig, Pep wasn't a sloppy player. I'm sure he brought the goods back to his apartment.

A search of the living room, including a look in closets, inside the television console, under furniture, behind drapes, and in the sideboard in the dining nook, turns up nothing but lost change between the sofa cushions. The wire reel and the recording machine aren't in this part of the apartment, and neither is any information regarding the backup copy.

Same story in the kitchen and bathroom.

I move into Pep's bedroom, turn a lamp on next to the bed. Somebody pinch me, please. The bedroom is even duller than the living room. No plaid upholstery, no patterns at all, and everything is either brown or beige. The beige bedspread is so boring it could put me to sleep, which may be why Pep liked it. Maybe the guy had insomnia. Frankly, I'd rather have insomnia. I can't imagine a more boring place to make love to a woman than on a beige bed.

The only interesting item in the room is on the night table: the other recorder. Yeah, it's a portable job. The wire reel's on it, too, played about halfway through. The machine is plugged in, the dial's turned to *Playback*.

Some people listen to the radio to lull them to sleep, other people read a book until their eyelids droop, but Pep Green, the sick bastard, listened to the cravings of Opal Shaw. It turns my stomach, thinking he got his rocks off listening to her seductive cooing, but it makes me even sicker to think maybe he fell asleep counting the money all that cooing was supposed to bring him, every word another dirty dollar floating down to his pillow.

It must've knocked Pep silly when Opal laughed off his shakedown. I wish I could've been a fly on the wall for that one. I never met Opal Shaw until we were introduced tonight with a crash, but any woman who tells off a thuggish guy like Pep Green is the right stuff in my book. As soon as Celeste spilled it about Opal spitting in Pep's face in that poultry basement tonight, I knew why Sig was nuts for her. It wasn't just her curvy body and pretty face; a big shot like Sig Loreale can buy as many pinup girls as he likes. It was Opal's guts and sass that Sig fell in love with. The combination's irresistible. It'll keep you in love for the rest of your life.

Even Pep couldn't resist her. After playing his hard-to-get act for the microphones, he gave in and brought Opal into his bed. His boring beige bed.

Now there's a vision I don't want to get stuck with.

I just want to pack up this gear, see if I can snag a line on the whereabouts of the other recording, and get the hell out of here.

I park myself on the edge of the bed and start to pack up the recorder, then stop.

I have to hear her. I have to hear the woman who crashed into my life, whose death caused the kidnapping of my beautiful soldier, whose family secret ripped open Mom Sheinbaum's phony affection for me, whose need for kicks found both a friend and doom in Celeste Copley, the woman who killed her, the sassy woman whose guts have been tested over and over tonight and whose life is now in my hands. All of this is in the voice of Opal Shaw.

I flip the *on* switch.

Her voice flows around me, a voice rich, dark, smooth, and tasty as melted chocolate:

Because…you're dangerous. You're dangerous and I like that. I bet you know how to do plenty of dangerous things. Come on, Pep, touch me in dangerous places. I want you to. Come on…
I don't know—

I turn it off. That's Pep talking. I don't want to hear him trick Opal, tangle her up in her own words. I'd wind up wanting to kill him. Too bad he's already dead.

I pack up the reel and the recorder, then make a thorough search of the bedroom for any clue to the whereabouts of the backup recording. I don't find anything in the closet, nothing in the pockets of Pep's clothes. The drawers of his bureau have nothing but shirts and socks, cufflinks and tie clips, until I open the underwear drawer. In the corner, next to Pep's carefully folded silk boxer shorts, is a small metal strongbox. It's locked. I jimmy the lock with my penknife. Inside is a checkbook and a key with H-1102 etched into the brass. Both the checkbook and the key bear the insignia of El Banco de Habana.

Bingo. Pep kept an offshore account and a safe-deposit box in a bank in Cuba. According to the checkbook, Pep hid over a hundred grand from Uncle Sam, or maybe from Uncle Sig. I slip the checkbook and key into my pocket, then pick up the recorder and walk out of the bedroom.

I stop by the phone in the living room, call Judson, hoping he's cracked Rosie's location. I mutter, "Crap," under my breath when all I get is a busy signal. I hang up, then immediately dial another number for one more housekeeping chore. When the number answers, I give the cops the short and sweet. "There's a stiff with his face and part of his head blown off in the cellar of a chicken butcher's joint on Pitkin Avenue in Brooklyn." I hang up before I give them enough time to trace the call but giving them enough information to find Pep's body. His driver's license will identify him. Sig will hear about it seconds later, if he hasn't already, if a neighbor who was rudely awakened by a gun blast got antsy and called the Law. The Law always keeps Sig informed.

I'm done here. Time to get the hell out.

On my way down the stairs I feel a sudden chill, but there's no draft from anywhere and the door to the street is closed. The chill seems to seep from the recorder itself, from its wire reel of conversation between Pep and Opal, a conversation of the dead.

❖

I stash the recorder in the trunk of my car, then get into the driver's seat. Celeste stubs out her cigarette in the ashtray. "Find what you're looking for?" she asks.

"Yeah." I put my key in the ignition.

Trying to sound matter-of-fact but stumbling on her heartbreak, she says, "I guess—I guess you listened to the wire recording?"

I take my hand off the ignition, lean back against the seat. How do I tell her I heard the woman she killed make goo-goo noises to the guy she loved? "Yeah, I listened. I listened to a piece of it, anyway."

Celeste lowers the veil of her hat, takes whatever refuge she can find behind the scanty net, then asks, "Was it bad?"

"The smartest thing you can do, Celeste, is forget about it. What's on that recording is old news. Its scores are all settled."

It takes her a minute to absorb all that, work through the

horror and the hurt. She finally gives me a small nod and a heavy sigh that sinks her more deeply into my overcoat. "What about the backup recording? Did you find out where Pep stashed it?"

"It's in a safe-deposit box in Havana. I found the key."

"What'll you do with it?"

"It might come in handy as a crowbar, or maybe a very sharp knife. C'mon, let's get out of here."

CHAPTER SIXTEEN

Lights are still on in the first-floor windows of Mom Sheinbaum's brownstone when I pull up. Maybe the old lady's grief is keeping her awake. Or maybe the Blicks are busy swilling Mom's expensive liquor while they play a round of canasta. Or maybe everyone just fell asleep in their chairs.

Celeste says, "What is this place?"

"Opal never mentioned it?"

"No. Why?"

"It's her mother's place. Esther Sheinbaum lives here."

"What? Oh no…I can't go in. Why did you bring me here? Opal's mother will want to kill me even more than Loreale does."

"Listen to me, Esther Sheinbaum might be our only way out of this mess."

"*Our* only way out? What makes you think I'm interested in saving your scarred-up skin? Look, you have your charms, sure, but the only skin I'm interested in saving is my own."

"You're referring, of course, to the skin that's staying nice and warm in my coat?"

Celeste slides me a glance that tells me to drop dead, but she gets my point.

"You know the deal," I say. "My protection has a price."

"Yeah, yeah, help you save that other dame's skin, Loreale's hostage. Well, I'm not interested in saving her skin, either."

"You're all heart, Celeste. All right, get out. See if you can outrun Loreale on your own."

"Maybe I should. So far, your protection hasn't protected me all that much."

"You're still alive, aren't you?" I take her chin in my hand and turn her to face me, lift her hat veil so nothing can shield her from me while I hold her pretty little chin tighter than she'd like. "Didn't Pep or Opal ever tell you anything about Loreale? About how he always, *always* connects the dots? He'll be coming after you, Celeste. He'll be coming after both of us because you and I are the only dots connecting Opal's fall from the bridge and Pep's head exploding."

"You're sure Loreale already knows about Pep?"

"Yeah, he knows because I called the cops from Pep's place, gave 'em an anonymous tip about where to find the body. You can bet the word got back to Sig the minute I hung up the phone. He owns eyes and ears in every precinct in town."

If looks could kill, I'd be dead from the poisonous stare Celeste gives me. "Why don't you just leave a trail of breadcrumbs behind us for Loreale to follow? Why don't you just shine a light on them, too? Oh God, how the hell did I wind up with you? Let go of me, dammit!"

I don't let go. I take her face between both my hands and hold even tighter. "Shut up and listen. Sig is the only guy who can clean up the mess in that poultry basement and cut the cops out of the action. There'll be no police investigation, no questions at all. Pep's body will be taken out of that basement without anyone ever hearing a footstep or seeing a shadow. It wouldn't surprise me if Sig even gives Pep a nice funeral."

That line about Pep's funeral knocks Celeste back. Her anger and fear are sandbagged by her sadness over her dead gangster. She whispers his name, though it's nothing more than a weak breath. "He...he was proud of being Sig Loreale's lieutenant. Made him feel like a big man." A sigh seeps through her like a slow breeze through tattered curtains, and when she speaks she sounds just as ragged. "With Pep dead, I guess Loreale will want vengeance."

"You think Sig will give a damn about Pep's death? Pep was Loreale's right-hand guy, sure, but there'll be plenty of talented triggermen lining up to take his place. As far as Loreale is concerned, Pep's killing is just the cost of doing business, and Sig's business tonight is all about what happened to Opal. So, yeah, he'll connect the dots, and we're the dots. Us. The only two dots between Opal and Pep. But Sig knows I didn't kill Opal, which makes *you* the only dot he'll be interested in. You get what I'm saying?"

She doesn't answer but I know I'm getting to her. I see it in the way she's clutching her handbag, holding tight to one of the few safe and familiar things she can still hold on to in a night that's taking everything else away.

"If you try to run, Celeste, Sig will find you. He has ways of finding people. And when he finds you, you're done for. Even if he buys your story that Opal's death was an accident, he'll kill you. Even if you sink that story and try to sell him another one, he'll kill you. One way or another you're part of Opal's death, so he'll kill you. You begged me to keep you safe and help you get away, get out of Sig's reach, and that's what I'm breaking my neck to do. But you have to pay for it, Celeste. You have to pay."

She's been knocked around a lot tonight, and I just knocked her around again. "It seems that's all I ever do, pay for other people's plans," she says. She may be black-and-blue inside and out, but she's not ready to go down for the count. She's crying a little but frowning a lot, the stubborn, beautiful defiance inside her rising like a fist raised against me and a world that's kicked her around. The defiance makes its stand as a barely perceptible but brassy little smile that pulls slightly to the corner of her mouth. Celeste may be keeping warm in my overcoat, but she's busy storing tricks up the sleeves.

I slide my hands from her face. She turns away from me and looks out the window at Esther Sheinbaum's brownstone. "Tell me why we're here."

"It's simple. We stand a better chance of Mrs. Sheinbaum buying your story that Opal's death was an accident th—"

"Don't *you* believe it?" She turns back around to face me, throwing me not just a question but a plea.

"It doesn't matter what I believe. It only matters what we can make old lady Sheinbaum believe, because if she believes it, she's the only one who can convince Sig to believe it. And if Sig believes it—"

"He'll release that girlfriend of yours, the one you're not in love with but who you're putting your life on the line for."

"Don't be cute. I don't have to be in love with someone to want to save their life."

"You're not that decent."

"Fine. I'm just the hooligan who's trying to save *your* life, so lose the tough act, Celeste. It won't get you anywhere with Mrs. Sheinbaum."

My scolding hits its mark. Celeste shrinks away from me and softens her attitude.

"That's better," I say. "Now listen, that old lady's whole life was wrapped around Opal, so you have to milk a mother's heartbreak. You're going to spill your guts, understand? Tell her everything. Tell her you used to be Pep's girl. Tell her he resented the percentage Sig was cutting her in for, resented it so bad he'd do anything to kill the wedding and kill the deal. You can even tell her about the dough Pep promised you to lure Opal to Brooklyn, but make sure she understands that you didn't have a choice, that you were scared of Pep, scared for your life."

"But I *was* scared for my life!"

"And that's how you'll sell it. She'll buy it because she knows how Sig's thugs operate. Tell her the whole rotten story."

"Why don't I just tell her Pep killed Opal when he threw her off the bridge? He threatened to kill her anyway. He even said so. You heard him."

"Because Opal was already dead when she went off the bridge, and Mrs. Sheinbaum knows it. That's right, they found the stab wound at the funeral parlor. And Pep didn't kill Opal, so if you try to push that phony story, you'd have to weave a bunch of lies that could tangle you up. You're a damn good liar, Celeste, a pro, but even a pro would have a hard time fooling Esther Sheinbaum. She's been outsmarting the Law and big-shot politicians since New York read its papers by gaslight, and politicians are the best liars in the business. So just stick to the facts. It's the only story you can get away with."

"You make me sound like a cheap piece of goods," she says, more hurt than angry.

"I never said you were cheap. You're not cheap. Don't think of yourself as cheap."

"I—well, thanks." She gives me what I guess is supposed to be a shy smile, sweet with gratitude and humility, but on Celeste humility is about as natural as the wrong shade of lipstick, and she wipes it away fast. "Okay," she says, looking out the car window to the brownstone, "let's get this over with. Maybe it's time the old bat heard about all the sleazy stuff her darling daughter Opal could do, like spreading her legs for my guy while her lover boy Loreale was cooling his heels in Sing Sing."

"Hey, put your claws back in. We'll only use that if we have to. The wire recording is in the trunk of the car. The safe-deposit box key for the Havana copy is in my pocket. If I need a crowbar to pry the old lady open, I've got it."

"Wow, you really don't like her."

"What?" It's a stupid reply, but your mouth gets stupid when your brain's been stunned.

"You sound like you want to hit her over the head with a real crowbar. You have a beef with Opal's mother?"

Too late to sidestep the shiv Celeste just plunged into me. The best I can do is ignore the wound. "I have a beef with you asking so many questions," I say. "Haven't you learned yet? Now pay attention. You've got to win over old lady Sheinbaum, understand? Turn on the waterworks when you tell your story. Turn 'em on like a rainstorm flooding your soul. Win the old lady's sympathy, and you might win your life. Tell a story different than the one you told me, and I'll throw you to the wolves. Remember, I'm the only one who can back your story."

"What if I'm not a good enough actress?"

"I'm not asking you to be an actress. You're fighting for life. That's as real as it gets."

She opens her mouth but no words come out. Whatever gripe she wants to throw back at me won't survive out in the air anymore, and she knows it.

I say, "You ready?"

She opens her handbag and takes out her lipstick. For some women, dolling up calms their nerves, and Celeste is that kind of woman. She uses the mirror on the window visor to apply the fresh red to her mouth. When she's done, she's herself again, the knockout dame I met at her apartment door, damn sure that her good looks and her know-how to use them will get her what she wants. She puts the lipstick away, gathers her handbag, and opens the car door.

I get out of the car and come around fast to Celeste, take her arm as we go up the front stoop. It's not just chivalry on my part; I'm still not sure she won't bolt. I don't trust Celeste any more than I'd trust any cornered animal.

But she's in my marrow. She seeped in when I held her, when I kissed her. The taste of her mouth, sweet and intoxicating as an exotic drug, is still on my tongue. No amount of her fear or my anger or the bitter residue of gunfire from Pep's .45 will take the taste of her away. In fact, they season it.

She's a liar, though, and liars have venom in their veins instead of blood. But is she a murderer? A killer whose jealousy craved Opal's life? I don't know.

I don't know and it's twisting me up. There's as much about Celeste that's delicious as there is that's rotten. I bounce between her guilt and innocence like a punch-drunk fighter bouncing off the ropes. I don't know whether to feel sorry for her or be scared to death of her, so I'm both. The combination hooks me. Celeste Copley hooks me.

She glances back at my Buick when we're at the top of the stoop and I ring the doorbell. "You didn't bring the recorder," she says.

"I'll save it until I need it."

Celeste gives me a grin so sly, a fox would slink away with envy. "I was right," she says. "You really don't like the old lady. That wire recording's an ace in the hole you'll play when you're good and ready."

I'd like to wipe that sly grin off her face, but I don't get the chance because a light goes on next to the doorpost and shines across Celeste's hat, and what the light picks out makes my skin go prickly: there's a splatter of Pep's blood near the top of the hat. Esther Sheinbaum mustn't see that blood. If Celeste appears like an Angel of Death, it could kill her chances of putting over her sob story. But before I can tell her to take the hat off and stow it or toss it, the door opens.

"Yeah?" It's Ida Blick. Her dull pink housedress makes her look even more like a cut-rate version of her sister than she did when she and her husband arrived in the cab.

She remembers me, all right. She looks me over like maybe she should call a pest control outfit.

I say, "Tell Mom—uh, tell Mrs. Sheinbaum that Cantor Gold is here."

Ida recognizes my name—Mom must've told her to expect me or a phone call from me—but she's not any happier at my present arrival than she was at my earlier departure. Sour as old boiled cabbage, she calls over her shoulder, "Morris! Go on upstairs and tell Esther this Cantor Gold person is here." She steps aside and with a sharp toss of her head motions us to come in.

"We'll wait in the dining room," I tell Ida as we step inside. I take my cap off, hoping my gesture will prompt Celeste to remove her hat, too. When she doesn't, I figure I'll mention it on our way to the dining room, but Ida stays with us like a case of indigestion, so I keep my mouth shut.

Ida turns lamps on as we enter the dining room. The old-fashioned room glows again with that patina I love, or used to. The truth of Mom Sheinbaum's less-than-warm feelings for me poisons my memories. But the polished coziness of the place isn't lost on Celeste. She eyes the room and its old-world antiques, envying the security she imagines this place must've given Opal as a little girl.

I won't be the one to kill Celeste's daydream and tell her that Opal rarely spent time here. Let Celeste have her swoony delusion. It could put her in the right mood to sell her story.

I say to Ida, "We'll be fine here while we wait," but she doesn't leave the dining room. With the gracelessness of a beached whale and the determination of prison guard, Ida sits down at the far end of the dining table.

No sense wasting my breath; she's not going to leave us alone, so I can't tell Celeste to get rid of that hat.

I pull a chair out for Celeste, then start to help her off with my overcoat, but she pulls it more tightly around her as she sits down. The gesture's her way of reminding me to keep my promise and protect her.

"So, Cantor," I hear Mom say behind me. She walks into the dining room with her brother-in-law Morris in tow, a lump of a guy in his wrinkled white shirt and brown pants. He takes a seat at the end of the table, next to his wife. Both of them stare at Celeste like she's merchandise of uncertain quality. I want to spit in their faces, smear their low-rent smugness. These two meat racks wouldn't know quality if it wore a gold crown.

Mom's still wearing that frilly black robe, only now it looks wrinkled and knotted, like she's tossed and turned in it. She sits down next to Celeste, looks at her through her narrowed, red-ringed eyes. She says, "So who is this person?" Mom's looking at Celeste's face, not her hat. I notice that the blood spatter's less visible in the dim glow of lamplight. But less visible isn't the same as not visible, and Mom Sheinbaum isn't one to miss a trick.

Before this party starts, though, I try a play that might scratch the need for it altogether. "First things first," I say to Mom. "Tell me if you've found out where Sig's got Rosie. Did you make those phone calls?"

"Sure, I made phone calls," she says, but she's not looking at me. She's still looking at Celeste. "Why is this girl wearing such a coat? A man's overcoat?"

"It's my coat," I say. "She was cold. Now what about those phone calls?"

"Now nothing," Mom says with a shrug. "I called, but got nothing. What, you think Sig told Mr. Walter Winchell to announce on the radio about where he's stashed your cabbie girl so everybody should know? Listen, mommaleh, Sig didn't even tell *me*, so why should he make announcements?"

"You have other sources. Use 'em."

"Hey!" comes from Morris Blick. "You can't talk to Mrs. Sheinbaum like that."

His wife growls, "Be quiet, Morris." I don't usually feel sorry for husbands. I could almost make an exception for Morris.

Mom says, "Cantor, I swear, I *swear* I called *everybody*, called the big shots, even woke up a judge who owes me but good. But nobody's making a sound, not a peep. Everybody's *sha-shtill*, nobody knows anything, and no sane person would cross Sig even if they do know something, which nobody knows anyhow, so I got no information to give you. Listen, even once since you were a little savage, have I ever lied to you?"

A part of me rages to answer her, expose her years of phony chumminess. But it would be the worst play I could make. The old woman's already peeled raw from the death of her daughter. If I peel away more of her skin, she could soothe that wound by shutting me out completely, and I'd lose the power she wields to get Rosie back. So I keep quiet and find a bit of pleasure in thinking I'll save the skinning for another time, just like Celeste said I would.

"So, Cantor," Mom says to my silence, "tell me already. Who is this person?"

Celeste grabs the moment. "My name is Celeste Copley." She sounds shaky and scared, her voice barely above a whisper.

"I…I know how Opal died, Mrs. Sheinbaum. I was there. I tried to save her life. Please, I need your help." That last bit, asking for Mom's help, is as good as it gets, as good as any leading lady on Broadway.

I must've been loco to doubt Celeste. She's gone right for the tear-jerk play. Her instincts are right on the money, and as she keeps talking, laying out Pep's resentment and deadly schemes, I start to think she just might get her piece of the old mother's broken heart after all.

With Mom and the Blicks hanging on Celeste's every dramatic word, I slip out to the hall to phone Judson.

I dial my office, then brace the receiver between my chin and shoulder while I pull out my smokes and light one up. When I get Judson on the line, he blurts at me, "Dammit! What took you so long to call?"

"Settle down. I called a little while ago but got a busy signal."

"Oh yeah. I was on the phone with my sound guy. Cantor, he thinks he cracked the sounds coming through Rosie's radio. The water, the grinding metal noise—"

"What's he got? Where does he say they've got Rosie?" This could end the nightmare. This could give me the pleasure of telling Loreale and old lady Sheinbaum to go drown their sorrows without me.

Judson says, "It's someplace near water where trains go by. My guy's pretty sure that's what that grinding noise is that comes and goes, *literally* comes and goes. Trains passing by, but rolling slowly. And that lapping water-in-a-drain sound is maybe a river lapping under something and around something, like around pylons under a pier. Cantor, there are dozens of places like that all around the harbor, but—"

The line goes dead because a thick finger, Morris Blick's finger, comes down on the cradle and kills the connection.

"It ain't polite to use a person's telephone without askin' permission," he says, but his hard stare makes it clear he's not talking about my lack of etiquette.

I stub out my smoke in the ashtray next to the phone, then give Blick a stare of my own, look right into his dull-witted gray eyes, and say as politely as I can muster, "I beg your pardon." I start to put my cap on but take it down again and say, "Oh. Sorry. It's not polite to wear a hat in the house. Where *are* my manners?" Then I put my cap on anyway and push past Blick.

He follows me into the dining room. I feel his hatred clinging to my back like a sweaty palm, but the schmo and his stupidity are unimportant, so who cares? My brain is busy with Judson's information. Yeah, there's plenty of riverfront around the harbor, and lots of places where trains roll by. But Judson said the trains roll by slowly, and there's only one place that I know of that's along a river near slowly rolling trains and has a connection to Sig Loreale.

So, my condolences to Mom and Sig. Maybe I'll send flowers to Opal's funeral, but it's time to make my move.

The drama in the dining room has had a bad change of script. Instead of the heartbreaking scene I walked out on a few minutes ago, there's a tableau of menace: Ida Blick standing and sneering, a white-knuckled Esther Sheinbaum clutching at her robe in her lap, and an ashen-faced Celeste, whose voice has turned as thin and brittle as a dead leaf in the wind as she finishes her story. "Please, Mrs. Sheinbaum, please believe me! Opal was my best friend. She…" But her plea dies in the air, the fading cry of someone falling off a cliff.

"Cantor," Mom says, "this girl here killed my Opal. The woman at the funeral parlor, the washer, she was right. I knew it. I knew Opal didn't die by falling off any bridge. She was killed, and this girl—this girl did it. See? There's blood on her." Mom's pointing at the blood on Celeste's hat.

"No," I say, "that's Leon Green's blood. Didn't she tell you she stabbed Opal by accident? A crazy fluke of an accident that happened while she tried to save Opal's life?" But my rant's useless. As far as Esther Sheinbaum's concerned, Celeste Copley is the Angel of Death and that's that.

"Sure," Mom says, the word erupting in a dismissive snort. "She talked all about that accident business. And you believe her? Didn't you learn anything I taught you, Cantor? Didn't I tell you how to spot a liar? But I must've been talkin' to a wall 'cause you're still a sucker for a pretty face. Well, thank you for bringing her to me. You did a service for a grieving mother. I'll call Sig now, let him know you solved his problem. He can send one of his boys over here to pick her up. Once he's got her, you can see about having him release that girl of yours, though I don't know how he'll feel about you killing his man Green."

"What? I didn't kill Pep Green. At least not—" You could spin my head around like a corkscrew and I wouldn't feel as twisted and dizzy as I do right now, looking at Celeste. "Is that what you told her? That I shot Pep?"

"Well, you did. You grabbed his gun after I slammed him."

"Funny, that's not the way I remember it. I remember the three of us dancing around together and Pep's forty-five trying to cut in." Feeling sorry for Celeste is finished. I'd better break free of her lies if I know what's good for me. "I should just leave you to Sig, let him have his revenge on you, break you in two. But I have plans for you, arrangements you have no say in, but I'm not asking your permission. I'm in this to save a life, Rosie Bliss's life, and that's exactly what I'm gonna do, Celeste. You're coming with me."

Morris stands up, whining, "Esther, you gonna just let 'em walk away?"

I don't give the old lady the chance to think it over. I pull my gun, aim it first at Morris, who backs off. Then at Ida, who sits down. Then at Mom, who looks like she's thinking that maybe she should've served me honey cake. "It was you, *Mom*," I say with a smile so cold my teeth hurt, "it was you who taught me never to argue with a gun. This is a good time to practice what you preach. Celeste, get beside me. Make it quick."

Celeste doesn't look at me as she stands up and moves next to me, her red gloves a blur in the lamplight, but there's a tiny smirk of triumph at the corner of her still freshly lipsticked mouth. She's won again. I've saved her life again.

I keep my gun on the trio of geezers staring at us. "If any one of you follows us to the door, I'll use this," I say. "You might wind up crippled, you might wind up blind, or you might wind up dead."

Mom reaches out her hand to me and smiles, the kind of maternal smile she's been giving me for years, the smile I used to believe was real. "You won't kill us, Cantor. I know you better."

"Actually, no, you don't."

With my gun raised in my right hand, I grab Celeste's arm with my left hand and back us out of the dining room. When we're in the hall, I hear Morris whine, "She was on the telephone, Esther, talkin' about where that cabbie girl is stashed! I think she mighta figured it!"

We're out the door before I hear whatever Mom has to say about it.

CHAPTER SEVENTEEN

There's plenty I'd like to tell Celeste about her song and dance that I killed Pep Green. There's plenty I could do to make her pay for her crummy trick. I could throw her to Loreale or dump her on the cops' doorstep and laugh when they send her to fry in the chair, but none of it would matter. Nothing matters now except getting Rosie back.

"Get in the car," I growl at Celeste when I open the door.

But Celeste doesn't get in the car. She just stands at the curb, fierce and stubborn in the halo of a street lamp. "I'm not getting in that car until you tell me where we're going," she says. "I'm sick of being dragged all over the place like a piece of luggage." Celeste folds her arms across her chest, my overcoat bunching at her shoulders like giant epaulets.

"You're in no position to give the orders," I say. "And if you lie to me again or pull any more tricks like the doozy you tried to get away with in there, I'll drop you in Loreale's lap and let him cut you up like a tender steak. *Now get in.*"

"No. Look, I'm sorry, okay? I didn't mean to jam you up with that story about shooting Pep, but when you left the dining room I thought you'd skipped out on me, left me for dead. I was losing the old lady and those two hangers-on and I was scared to death that you'd dumped me, so I grabbed anything that could give me an edge."

"Yeah, so you could cut my throat with it."

"Listen, you told me Sig wouldn't care about Pep's death, so I didn't think it would matter if I said you shot him. So what if we both had our hands on Pep's gun when it went off? I was trying to make points with Opal's mother, appear blameless in her eyes about Opal, about everything. Why can't you believe me?"

"*Believe* you?" I say through a laugh so stinging Celeste puts her hand to her cheek as if I'd slapped it. "I wouldn't believe you if you told me my name is Cantor Gold. I'd have to check my driver's license."

"Very funny."

"You think so? Okay, here's another laugh. If Mrs. Sheinbaum tells Sig that you and I are in some sort of cahoots, he'll think I've double-crossed him. We'll be dead the minute Mrs. Sheinbaum hangs up the phone. Then he'll kill Rosie because he won't need her anymore. Just like that, *bam-bam-bam*—you, me, Rosie, dead. Are you laughing yet? No? Well, maybe you'll get a kick out of this—remind me to go out of my way to save your life tonight, Celeste. Y'know, in case I forget."

"That's not fair." She uncrosses her arms and lets them fall to her sides, the bunched shoulders of my coat collapsing around her. The sleeves nearly cover her gloved hands, leaving just red fingertips sticking out. She looks as abandoned as an orphan in a hand-me-down sack and sounds just as miserable. "Please…I really thought I was on my own, Cantor. I thought you'd skipped. You say I'm a liar. Okay, maybe you're right, maybe sometimes I am a liar. But I'm not a very brave one."

Yeah. There's the catch. Just because she's a liar doesn't mean she's not scared. She *is* scared, crazy scared, scared enough to do wacky things, say wacky things, like Pep's death was murder, or Opal's killing was an accident. Celeste puts truth and lies on a seesaw, and she's stuck me in the middle to slide up and down. Sooner or later I'll lose my balance and fall off, too dizzy to figure this woman out and find my way through her mystery.

I can at least get rid of the haunting souvenir of our dance with death: I take her bloodied hat off, toss it into the gutter.

Celeste tries to grab the hat as it rolls into the sewer, but her gesture's automatic, no real stretch to it. The hat's just another loss, like her luggage, the mink, and the high life she once had with her handsome gunman.

When she turns back to me, there's no more splatter of Pep's blood to advertise his killing. There's no veil between me and Celeste's beautiful face. Her eyes, those big brown naughty-puppy eyes, plead with me to believe in her innocence. Her eyes glisten. But phony diamonds glisten, too. Funny, it was Mom Sheinbaum who taught me how to spot liars and fake jewels.

Celeste says, "Where are we going?"

"I'll tell you along the way. It's too dangerous to hang around here now, so get in the car and let's get out of here."

She doesn't argue with me this time, just gets in the car.

I come around and get into the driver's seat. "It's almost over," I say, trying to calm her a little as I start the car, put it in gear.

Celeste rests her face in her hands, tired to the bone. Can't blame her. It's been a rough night. If she catches a nap while I drive, that's fine by me. I could use the peace and quiet while I figure a way to grab Rosie from her jailers.

"*Almost* over?" comes back at me. Celeste's suddenly wide awake, her exhaustion kicked aside by some new annoyance with me. She's a lioness again. "You mean you know where Loreale's stashed your girl?" My peace and quiet just got clawed.

"I have a pretty good idea, yeah."

"Then why do you still need me? You think you can use me as bait? The hell you are! Now I *am* getting out of here!"

I start to pull away from the curb before Celeste can open the door, but I'm cut off by flashy chrome and glaring headlights that come out of nowhere from the wrong direction along Second Avenue. A big dark Cadillac sedan screeches to a stop in front of me, blocking my Buick.

Before I can give a piece of my mind to the Wrong-Way Corrigan whose driver's license should be stuffed down his throat, a giant thug in a long overcoat and a fedora tears out of the Caddy's backseat. He's at my door fast, yanks it open.

Celeste screams, but that doesn't put a wrinkle in the thug, who's only a little smaller than a Rocky Mountain. He grabs both of my arms and pulls me out of the car, nearly wrenching my arms from my shoulders. While I'm wasting time trying to get an arm free so I can grab my gun, out of the corner of my eye I see Celeste run out of the Buick. I have a glimmer of hope that she'll kick the thug in the shins, do something to distract him so I can get out from his grip, but my stupid hope crumbles to dust when I see her run up the street.

She doesn't get far. Another Rocky Mountain is out of the Caddy, runs after Celeste, and grabs her.

If this is a taste of what Loreale and his thugs have in store for us, the rest of our night will be painful—at least, what little of it Loreale lets us survive. Maybe I can convince Sig to be a gentleman about Celeste and kill her fast and clean, skip the torture.

My Rocky Mountain drags me to the Caddy, throws me on the floor of the backseat. The overhead light is on. I look up and see a guy grinning like the Cheshire cat. It's not Loreale. It's Gregory Ortine.

In his belted camel coat and horn-rimmed tortoiseshell

glasses, Ortine sits with a society swell's poise, something I'm sure he spent hours practicing in front of a mirror. Even the distinguished gray at his temples is probably a put-up job, maybe his blond hair, too. The only reliably real thing about Ortine is the coldness in his eyes, gray and hard as concrete blocks, magnified through his thick glasses.

I'm about to give him a frosty hello when a screaming Celeste is tossed next to me on the floor of the Caddy. Ortine smacks her across the mouth with the back of his hand to shut her up. There's nothing poised about Ortine's smack or the grunt that accompanies it, just the brute vestiges of his real self, the one that grew up in the rough part of a rotten town in the middle of a crummy nowhere. The smack shuts Celeste up but leaves her with a bloody cut at the corner of her mouth.

Guys who beat up women tick me off. And ever since that lousy night in the lockup, with cops smacking women left and right, seeing a woman get hit maddens me like a rabid dog. Ortine just let loose that dog. I make a move to ram my fist into him, ready to smash Ortine's balls and pecker, rip out his guts, but the thug standing at the door slams his foot into my side, kicks me back down. My ribs are on fire.

The blow sends me crashing against Celeste, jolting her. I groan through my aching ribs but manage to sit up, try to steady Celeste. She's shaky, fragile as a teacup that's been glued back together too many times. I wonder how much more of this brutal night she can take.

I don't have my handkerchief anymore, so I put my wrist against Celeste's cut lip as carefully as I can, let the smooth silk of my suit jacket blot the blood away. I think she smiles a little, or maybe her mouth just trembles from the painful cut. I can't tell.

The thug reaches into the car, pulls me away from Celeste so he can frisk me. I force myself not to groan. I won't give him the satisfaction of knowing that my ribs hurt like hell. When he finds my holstered gun under my suit jacket, he takes his paws off me and hands the gun over to Ortine.

Lucky for me, Ortine hires for brawn and not brain. The stupid lug missed the envelope with his boss's ten G's in my jacket pocket. Celeste's getaway cash. Maybe.

Meantime, Ortine's grabbed Celeste's handbag. He rummages through it with phony delicacy. Finding no weapon, he tosses the handbag back into Celeste's lap, then pockets my gun and nods to the thug to get beside him in the backseat. When the big galoot slides in and closes the door, the overhead light goes off, leaving the streetlight the only illumination through the privacy blinds on the rear window. The galoot and Ortine form a striped silhouette that looks silly, but I don't laugh.

The other thug is at the wheel. He drives us away.

"Well, Cantor," Ortine says too slowly, his diction as practiced as his posture, "where is my treasure?"

"At the bottom of the East River. Didn't you see my boat capsize and toss me in the drink?"

"Yes, but I'd hoped you'd secured the brooch. Pity. I already had a display case for it installed in my apartment. You know, I had to special order the velvet lining. You can't buy that sort of quality off the street. Well then, since I've nothing to show for it, I believe you owe me a refund. I want my ten-thousand-dollar deposit returned."

"Deposits are nonrefundable. You know that, Ortine. The cost of doing business."

"*Your* business, maybe. That ten thousand is *my* business and I want it back. I will not take no for an answer."

My ribs threaten to crack when I talk, but I do my best to keep myself chatty. It's my only play to distract Ortine from the cash I don't want to give him. "What brings you to this part of town, Gregory? You should be up to your ears in business at your fancy clip joints at this hour. You know, the ones the liquor board doesn't know about. The private ones that go all night. The society crowd's heavy drinkers usually walk in for their predawn nightcaps right about now. Aren't they your favorite clientele?"

"Don't be naïve, Cantor. As soon as our transaction on the river met with disaster, I made it my business to find out what happened."

"I hope you didn't work too hard, Gregory. All you had to do was turn on the radio." Taunting the slimy snake feels good. Useless, but good.

It stops feeling good, though, when Ortine takes his revenge and kicks me in the stomach. The vicious combination of bruised ribs and smashed guts doubles me over. I'm a dizzy lump of hurt. A grunt and a gag are all I can manage. They don't come anywhere near expressing all the crappy things I feel, but they do the trick and allow air back into my lungs and take just enough edge off the pain so I can unfold and look up at Ortine. His glasses reflect the passing light of street lamps: bright, dark; bright, dark.

Ortine keeps coming at me with his irritating, high-hat tone. "Behave yourself, Cantor. I went to the Sheinbaum house because I was told you were there. It's as simple as that."

"Who told you?" The question chills me. I never told Mom or Celeste about Ortine and our intended business on the river, and though Sig knows about it, he wouldn't give five minutes to a clip-joint Johnny like Ortine. And I know Judson would never spill my whereabouts, so where's the crack in the wall?

"Never mind where I heard it. It came to me about a

half hour ago. You know, word's getting around that the unfortunate Miss Opal Shaw was not only Loreale's fiancée but the secret daughter of Esther Sheinbaum. Let me tell you, Cantor," he says with a gossipy laugh that's as shrill as nails against a blackboard, "that little tidbit is going to keep the town chattering for weeks! It's all I'll hear at my supper clubs, and since people like to lubricate their gossip with liquor, I'll make a fortune in bar tabs."

"Good for you," I say.

He ignores my bit of sarcasm and just goes right on yammering. "Now, I know you do business with old lady Sheinbaum, Cantor. You've been close to her since you were a kid, I understand. I figured you'd show up here sooner or later to offer your condolences, help her through the night, that sort of thing, so I sent a man to watch her house. When he arrived, your car was already here, so my man drove to a delicatessen nearby and called me. And here I am. Just in time, too, it appears."

His mock friendliness nauseates me more than his kick to my gut. But his story clears something up: the guy chasing me in the DeSoto wasn't Ortine's. He was Sig's, checking my movements for his boss. I wonder how many other eyeballs Sig has out for me, and I wonder if the guy in the DeSoto told Sig that I shook him off. If he has, the guy's probably dead. Sig doesn't tolerate mistakes.

Ortine says, "Well, are we going to come to terms?"

"Your man is driving us around in circles, Gregory. Where are we going?"

"You tell me. Where do you have my ten-thousand deposit? In your apartment? Your office? Do you even have an office? All I have for you is a telephone number."

"Look, Gregory, we can deal with this tomorrow. Right now, the lady and I are in a hurry."

"*Yesss*"—if anyone can hiss and leer at the same time, it's Gregory Ortine—"I'd be in a hurry for bed, too, if I was accompanied by such a pretty young lady. By the way, I'm sorry, miss," he says to Celeste, "I hope I didn't hurt you too badly. Your screaming was getting on my nerves, that's all. Oh, and I see Cantor's done the, um, gentlemanly thing on this chilly night and given you her coat." He flashes us a tongue-y smile that makes me want to smash that flapping, fleshy organ between his teeth. "Well, you two," he says, "playtime will have to wait until I get my cash. And, Cantor, it's already tomorrow."

"Sorry, I don't have my checkbook on me."

"Checkbook? You slay me, you really do! Maybe I should feature you as the warm-up comedian at one of my supper clubs." Ortine's laughter tangles up with the snickers of the mountainous thug sitting next to him. Their combined giggling is weirdly repulsive, like lunatics in a horror picture.

"Okay, Cantor," Ortine says, losing his laugh, "you've had your fun. It's time to go get my cash."

"What if I already put it in the bank?"

"What if you did? I'm sure you have that much lying around. Yours is a cash business. Same as mine. Only mine's legal."

"You don't say? When did the State of New York legalize backroom gambling? I must've missed it. And how about your shakedown operations? Or your girlie rackets? Yeah, you run a cash business, a bunch of 'em, the ones the Law and the tax men don't see."

He shrugs that off, says, "I want my ten thousand now, Cantor. Since you and this woman are in such a hurry, we can make the evening short. Give me my cash and I'll be on my way."

"We'll talk about it later."

"Dammit, I paid you to do a job for me. Have you forgotten that in this matter you work for me?"

"No!" cracks from Celeste like a rock crashing through a window. "We're working for Sig Loreale. That's right, *Sig Loreale*. He wants us to find out what happened to Opal Shaw. You want to get in his way?"

The woman sure knows how to knock me silly with surprises. She's making a brilliant play by scolding Ortine like he's a naughty child, and I'd be a dope to spoil it. It's a smart, gutsy move, complete with the magic words: Sig Loreale. The threat behind his name stops Ortine's chatter as if Celeste had ripped out his tongue.

Celeste Copley. Possible murderer. Possible victim. Gorgeous creature, with sass and brains to boot. Not the sort of dame who gets swallowed up by the night. No wonder I'm a sucker for her.

Ortine cringes at the mention of Loreale. He shifts his attention from Celeste to me. He says nothing, but it's obvious he wants me to either corroborate or dismiss Celeste's story, and he hopes to hell it's the latter. I keep my mouth shut, just let Sig's name hang in the air, let it scare Ortine the way it scares Celeste, the way it scares everybody.

But Ortine's no bush leaguer in the rackets. He may be a dull thinker and a social-climbing weasel, but he's risen high by making sure things add up. Right now, something's not adding up. Squinting through his glasses as if he's trying to see a puzzle in the dark, he says, "Loreale has his own outfit, the best anywhere. He doesn't need you two to get the goods on the dead girl."

"Believe me, Gregory," I say, "I didn't want any part of this thing. I have enough aggravation between losing your brooch and the loss of my boat. But Loreale has his reasons, and only an idiot with a death wish argues with Loreale's reasons."

"What reasons?"

"Well, my connection to Esther Sheinbaum for one. You pegged that right." Maybe flattery will get me somewhere, hurry him up. I need to get to Rosie and outrun Sig.

But Ortine drags on, asks more questions. "What about Missy here? What's she got to do with Loreale and his woman?"

Celeste fires back, "I was Opal's best friend, that's what. I know things. Things that could be helpful."

"Is that so? What things?"

"You think I'm stupid enough to talk behind Loreale's back? Huh, Mr. Supper Club? Mr. Clip Joint?" The woman's on a roll, playing the game as good as the best grifters I've seen. I don't know if it's natural talent or years of twisting the truth, but the performance is as dazzling as the woman.

Ortine doesn't answer. The thug beside him coughs, either from boredom or nerves, while his boss mulls things over.

I push deeper into the crack Celeste so expertly pried open in Ortine. "Loreale will come looking if I don't show up, Gregory. And you know how good he is at looking in the right places. He already knows about our botched doings on the river. Oh yeah, he knows, and he'll piece it together that you have something to do with me getting sidetracked from his business. You want Sig Loreale looking for you? He will, unless you turn this heavy heap around and take us back to my car."

Ortine stays quiet, doesn't move a muscle. The Rocky Mountain next to him is getting fidgety. So is Celeste. And if any more sweat rolls down my back I'll flood the car. Between the four of us, there's enough tension in the backseat of the Caddy to explode the windows.

"Shorty," Ortine finally says to the other mountain, the one driving the car, "take us back to the Sheinbaum place." I draw my first full breath since being thrown in the Caddy.

During the quick drive back to Second Avenue, Ortine doesn't bother with conversation, so I don't bother with him, which leaves me free to think about how I'm going to grab Rosie. And I wonder how bad Celeste's smacked lip still hurts.

The Sheinbaum house is dark when we pull up. The old folks must've finally gone to bed. My car is still in one piece even though it's sticking out from the curb and the doors are still open, but if someone inside the house saw me getting hijacked by Ortine and took the opportunity to jack the keys to keep me from going after Rosie, I'll have to hot-wire it. I never got the chance to grab the keys before Ortine's galoot dragged me to the Cadillac.

Ortine says, "You can expect to hear from me later, Cantor. We aren't finished until you hand over my ten thousand."

"First hand over my gun."

"Let's consider it collateral, shall we? You'll get it back when you give me my cash. Good night, Cantor." He nods to the thug beside him to open the door.

I have to crawl over the lug's big feet to get out of the car. He doesn't even budge for Celeste. I help her out.

The guy slams the door. The Caddy takes off.

First thing I do is look in the driver's side of my car, check the ignition. The keys are gone. "I'll have to spark it," I tell Celeste as I back out. "So stay put. It'll only take—" But she grabs my hand and slaps my keys into my palm.

I don't know which rocks me back more: my surprise or the drop-dead-satisfied smile on her face. She says, "In case you got free of that gorilla, I didn't want you coming after me when I tried to make a run for it. So I pulled your car keys."

Now it's me who's smiling. The dame's brains are as gorgeous as the rest of her.

She comes close to me, looks at me like she might start to cry but isn't sure. "I have to tell you something but it's hard for me to say it."

"Yeah, your lip probably stings like hell from that wallop Ortine gave you. Here, let me have a look at it."

"No, that's not it." She laughs and brushes my hand away. "It really doesn't hurt so bad now. What I'm trying to say is, I think…well, maybe I…what I mean is, I think I'm starting to trust you. The way you handled yourself getting us out of there"—she nods toward Mom's brownstone—"and then after Ortine smacked me, and you gave me your sleeve to wipe the blood away. I knew it was tough for you, I saw the pain on your face from that kick to the ribs."

"Anybody would—"

"Shhh," she says, her fingers at my mouth, tracing the scar above my lip. Her gloved fingertip is smooth and warm as it stalks me. Celeste brings her face close, those incredible glistening eyes, her red mouth a blur and then soft when I feel it on mine. Her mouth brushes me, doesn't linger, now it's gone.

Speaking so softly I feel it more than hear it, she says, "I trust you now even though you don't need me anymore. You know where your girl is, you can rescue her yourself. But you said you want me along, so I figure it's for another reason. Must be a good reason. All right, I'll take that ride."

I pull her gently back to me. "Yeah, it's a good reason. You'll like it even more than you like this." I take her in my arms and kiss her, but my kiss isn't a brush-by, it's a search, a probe to find her heart, to find it and explore what's in it, explore what's strong and gutsy, the Celeste Copley who outsmarted Gregory Ortine—and what's rotten, the Celeste who lies to get what she wants. This may be my only chance to know her, this woman I've run through the night with, who I've killed a man with.

I open my eyes to take in more of her, her creamy skin, her hair dark and glowing as a Manhattan night.

A wrong light suddenly glints on Celeste's hair.

A light's been turned on in an upstairs window in the Sheinbaum house. It's Mom Sheinbaum's bedroom window. She's silhouetted against the light.

I pull away from Celeste. "We have to go," I say. "We're being watched from the house. Don't look."

"Oh," is all she says. I walk her around to the passenger's side, help her into the car. On my way back to the driver's side I open the trunk and grab Pep's .45. It's too big for my .38's holster, so I slip it into the waistband of my trousers.

I close the trunk, get into the car, and drive out of Mom Sheinbaum's sight.

"Cantor?" Celeste says. "Don't you think it's time you told me where we're going?"

"Paradise."

CHAPTER EIGHTEEN

I pull over to a phone booth outside an all-night drugstore on Canal Street. A green neon DRUGS sign hangs over the street, throws a spooky glow on the sidewalk, reflects off the plate-glass windows of the spaghetti parlor and chop-suey joint on either side of the drugstore, and creeps up the face of the five-story brick tenement that sits above all three storefronts. The eerie light gives Canal Street's usual mom-and-pop atmosphere a hold-your-breath unease that clashes with my rarin'-to-go mood. Two lives are on the line tonight, and I have to save them both if I hope to make this lousy night right, and I don't want any bad juju screwing me up.

"Sit tight for a minute," I tell Celeste as I get out of the car. If she's wondering why I've interrupted my ride to Rosie's rescue she doesn't say. She just lights a cigarette.

I step into the phone booth, drop a dime into the slot, and dial a number. After two rings, a voice ragged as splintered wood says, "Drogan."

"Red, it's Cantor. How'd you like to make back some of the dough you lost on the Ortine deal?"

"Sure I'd like it, and I hope it's comin' outta Ortine's hide. Believe me, my tug woulda gotten to you before that cop boat showed up if it wasn't for Ortine fussin' around when he gets aboard. And then he tells me in that highfalutin way he's got,

Have to make sure everything's secure and up-and-up with you. Guy's got a helluva nerve."

"Yeah, it'll come out of Ortine's hide," I say. The ten-grand deposit Ortine knocked me around for just became a late fee. A cut of the cash, say two and a half G's, will go to Drogan as a carrying charge. "You'll have your dough soon, Red."

"I know you're good for it. I'm just glad you're okay. I was gonna come pull you outta the water, but that cop boat got there first. Anyway, whaddya got in mind?"

"Get your tug to Paradise Pier fast, Red. Be ready to make one of your special trips with all the trimmings."

"Sure, I got it. Okay, Paradise Pier." He hangs up.

I get back in the car and drive, get the hell away from the bad light on Canal Street.

Celeste says, "Everything all right?" and stubs out her smoke in the ashtray.

"Everything's in place," I say.

"And you're taking me to Paradise?" She's finally able to relax a little bit, now that her ordeal is almost over. There's even a lilt of humor in her voice that tickles the word Paradise.

"Next stop," I say. We're coming up on the toll booths to the Holland Tunnel. In a few minutes we'll be across the river.

"In *New Jersey*?" she says, part laughing, part disappointed.

"You'd be surprised what turns up in Jersey."

"Or who. Your girl's stashed there, isn't she. So what's my part in it?"

I give the toll guy my fifty cents and drive into the tunnel. We're under the Hudson River, alone in the white-tiled tube, talking through the tunnel's muffled, under-the-world drone that wraps around the car and makes everything sound as if Celeste and I are the only two people in the world. There were times tonight when I wished we *were* the only two people in the world, but those moments kept blowing up in my face.

Sometimes Celeste blew them up. Sometimes I did. And sometimes it was everything the night threw at us. "You don't have any part in it," I say. "I'm getting you out of here, away from the Law and Loreale."

"And you think I'll be safe in New Jersey? What are you planning to do? Pass me off as a dairy cow?"

"Don't worry, I'm not dragging you off to farmland. We're only going as far as the border between Jersey City and Hoboken."

"Jersey City and Hoboken? But they're up to their necks in gangsters! Pep said he used to take care of business there." Celeste says "take care of business" like she's afraid the words alone could slash her throat.

"You mean where he'd kill people," I say.

"Yeah, that's what I mean. And you think I'll be safe there? The whole place is a graveyard."

"You said you trust me now, Celeste, so just be quiet and listen. I don't know if you killed Opal by accident or murdered her when you saw your chance, and I'll never know."

"But I told you—"

"I said be quiet and listen. I'm talking about saving your life, understand? I can't turn you over to Loreale and let him kill you. And I don't turn people over to the Law. The Law takes orders from the likes of Loreale and Mom Sheinbaum anyway, so after a flashy trial and a crummy defense, the Law will fire up Ol' Sparky and fry that beautiful body of yours, which would be a great loss to the world of pleasure, not to mention the loss to my imagination. My only out—your only out—is to give you the benefit of the doubt. And believe me, honey, I have enough doubt to sink every goddamn ship in New York Harbor."

She's trying not to twitch inside my coat, trying to squash an anger she knows won't do her any good anymore.

ANN APTAKER

"You look like you could tear my throat out," I say. "Yeah, you've got it in you to kill, Celeste. We both know you do. There's a lioness inside you with great big claws, so don't give me any more poor-weak-little-me stories. But just because you can kill doesn't mean you committed murder, and an iffy death sentence from either the Law or Loreale would keep me awake nights, so I'm getting you to safety. I'm setting you up with a guy named Red Drogan."

"And what's his racket? Another one of your shady acquaintances, like that creep Ortine?"

"Listen, I'm trying to save your life here," I say. "Though with an attitude like yours, I'm starting to wonder why."

She doesn't answer that. Just fidgets inside my coat like a brat tamed by a scolding.

"Drogan's a tug boater with the kind of connections that help people disappear," I say, now that she's behaving herself. "He'll get you a passport with a new name and put you on a ship to Europe or maybe South America, no questions asked. You'll be sailing away by dawn. Loreale and the cops won't even know you're gone. And by the time they do, *if* they ever do, Celeste Copley will have vanished into thin air. No trail, no trace. Look, so it's not a heart-shaped pool in Hollywood. But it's a chance to see the world. You'll like that."

"Yeah, sure."

"Why the cheap enthusiasm? You're getting your second chance, a clean slate and all that. Isn't that what you've been angling for all night?"

"Well, yes, but—Cantor, come with me. We're a natural. We'd make a great team. I've seen the way you handle yourself, better than Pep ever did."

"Uh-huh. And what's your contribution to this great team?"

She's suddenly close to me, pressing against my side, one

gloved hand around my neck, the other moving up my thigh, moving so close to my joy engine it starts to throb, sets off pictures in my mind of a naked Celeste with me all over her. I can even feel myself against her, imagine myself mounting her. I almost lose control of the car, nearly slam us into the wall of the tunnel before I veer the car out of the way.

The smashup could've killed us both, which would've been one way, I guess, to solve everyone's dilemmas. Everyone's except Rosie's. "Celeste, take it easy! This isn't a joyride!"

"But…back there, the way you kissed me, the way you touched me, it was wonderful. I thought you…I mean, I thought maybe *we*—"

"Don't," I cut her off. "Don't stroke that idea. Listen, I'd be a liar if I said running with you didn't cross my mind. It made a nice daydream, rolling around with you on silk sheets in a hotel in Paris or sipping rum under a palm tree in Brazil. Sure, I'm a sucker for you, a sucker for everything you've got, inside and out. Your outside dazzles like a full moon. And inside, what's deep inside that gorgeous, dark place that's your liar's soul could wrap me in blissful oblivion. And that's the problem."

"I don't understand," she says in that baffled way beautiful women have when their charms don't win over their mark.

"It's like this," I say. "I'd get dizzy trying to figure what's real in you and what's an act. Truth and lies change hands with you, Celeste, as easily as a card sharp dealing from the bottom. But even if I could handle that, even if I could let your lies roll off me, I'd go nuts wondering if every bad boy with a sweet smile who comes along is a lick of sugar you can't resist, either because you'd get tired of us not being welcome in places you really want to go, or tired of ducking the Law, or just because you like the male brand of sugar. I'm not good at being sidelined, honey. Makes me cranky. But what would *really* turn me inside out, what I couldn't live with, was knowing that I ran out on Rosie when she needed me. I can't do that, Celeste. Not even for you."

The way she's stroking my neck makes it tough for me to drive. Her hand on my thigh makes it tough for me to think, until she finally unwraps from me, moves away from me to the other end of the seat. I miss her hands on me. I wish I didn't.

She says, "We're even, then."

"Where do you get that?"

Celeste shrugs, says, "You'd be right to wonder about the bad boys. And I guess I'd always wonder about the dame you ran out on. Your Rosie."

"Look, I told you. She's not *my* Rosie."

"That's your opinion. I bet it's not hers. And I bet she's not the first woman to fall in love with you even though you don't have the heart to love anyone back. What's the matter, Cantor? You look like you just got arrested."

I don't give her anything back. Not a sneer, not a sigh, nothing. I just keep driving, keep my eyes straight ahead, but for the first time in my life I feel like I might suffocate in the long white tube of the Holland Tunnel.

We finally cross the line of wall tiles that marks the underwater border of New York and New Jersey. Celeste leans back, turns up the collar of my overcoat, and rests her head against the car seat. Closing her eyes with a sigh, she says, "So who knew that all this time Paradise was waiting for me in New Jersey?"

❖

We come out of the tunnel, out into the darkest time of night, that thick black darkness that pushes back against dawn.

Celeste hasn't said anything since she came dangerously

close to seeing into my soul, seeing all the way to the empty place Sophie left behind. I welcome the lull in conversation. It gives me a chance to run through my moves to nab Rosie, that is, if I'm right about where Sig's stashed her, because if I'm wrong I've wasted precious time. If Mom Sheinbaum made the phone call I think she made, time is something Rosie's running out of fast.

I make it quick through the alleys behind the Jersey City waterfront. Across the river Manhattan glows like Wonderland. Back here, though, it's black and deserted, with ships quietly at anchor, the docks emptied of their freight.

It's not a good idea to look too deep into the shadows around here. Celeste is right about gangland's Jersey death squads, but she doesn't know the half of it. The Jersey waterfront is as tough as the piers in New York. The grafters and labor-racket thugs do plenty of rough business around these docks long after the local longshoremen have gone home to their women and their whiskey.

Celeste says, "Doesn't look much like Paradise."

"We're not there yet. Soon."

A light slices through the darkness up ahead on my left. It's the headlight of a slowly moving train. The train's coming close enough now for us to hear it, that grinding metal sound of steel wheels rolling slowly along steel rails. The grind gets louder and its headlight gets bigger and brighter as the train gets nearer. The glare floods the car, almost blinds me.

Celeste sits up fast, her eyes wide with panic. She's wondering if I'm suicidal, if my idea of Paradise is a smashup death for us both on a railroad track.

"Cantor!" My name's a whisper, a gag, a scream she can't scream as the train heads right for my car. Celeste's mouth is open, but nothing else comes out until she shrieks a laugh as loud and shrill as the locomotive's whistle when the train veers off and crosses a trestle over the narrow channel in front of us, a deep cut of lapping water separating us from the Hoboken Rail Terminal.

"Welcome to Paradise Pier," I say.

Celeste's still laughing, but she slows it down. The terror's gone from it. It's a laugh of relief.

Paradise Pier gets its name from the painted sign on the brick face of the warehouse at the head of the long pier: PARADISE STORAGE AND FREIGHT COMPANY. It's one of Loreale's oldest front operations, a legit business to clean up the cash from his underworld deals. The warehouse sits in front of the railroad track and next to the channel. Anyone inside the warehouse would hear a train grind slowly by as it crosses the channel and pulls into the Hoboken rail yard.

Someone's inside, all right. A line of light is visible under a loading-bay door. It doesn't mean that this is where Sig's stashed Rosie. It only means people are inside. For all I know, it could be the night crew stacking crates of tomatoes.

Finding out will have to wait, even though my nerves are standing up and scratching at me. First I have to get Celeste to safety, get her to Drogan's tugboat at the foot of the pier. Celeste can't be with me when I make my move on the warehouse. There could be gunplay, and I might not be able to defend her if I have to fight my way to Rosie. A choice like that, to protect Celeste or rescue Rosie, could jam me up, leave me with sleepless nights for the rest of my life.

I drive down the pier toward the river. "Drogan should be here by now," I say. "He'll be in his tug, waiting for us at the end of the pier. He'll know what to do to get you away, so follow his orders and you'll be all right. And you'll start your new life with a nice little cushion, too," I say, flashing her an encouraging smile. "I've got ten grand on me. Two and a half will go to Drogan for his trouble. You can have the rest, a seventy-five-hundred dollar cushion. You can set yourself up in style."

All she says is, "So this is it," then goes quiet. Not the nervous quiet of someone about to take a trip all alone to God knows where; she's just quiet. From all I've been through with Celeste tonight, I figured she'd angle for the whole ten grand, or maybe even try to convince me to be her plaything on some tropical isle, but I didn't expect this empty silence or what she finally says at the end of it. "Your Rosie's in that warehouse back there, right? You should be going after her instead of wasting time with me."

I start to tell her she could never be a waste of my time, that if we'd met over drinks instead of over Opal's death, we might even be heading for that fantasy cruise for two, but a light suddenly glances off my side-view mirror, catches my eye, and shows me something that yanks my attention away from Celeste. Through the mirror, I see a loading-bay door of the warehouse is now open and a guy is climbing up behind the wheel of a truck, one of those square-backed short-haul jobs, the kind that delivers produce to mom-and-pop grocery stores and luncheonettes. But it's what's sticking out from behind the truck that grabs me: the front of Rosie's cab, parked inside the warehouse. I bet the cab's radio is still on. Judson's probably getting an earful. Well, after I get Celeste on her way, Judson's gonna hear one helluva drama, good as anything on the Lux Radio Theater.

Before I can figure if the trucker's just making a tomato run or if he's one of Rosie's jailers, a guy in a black coat and a gray fedora walks toward the truck.

Now I know what I'm dealing with. This second guy is pulling Rosie by the arm, her hands tied behind her back. I'm pretty sure he's the guy who was in the backseat of Rosie's cab and put a gun to her head, forced her to drive away from Sig's building.

Rosie's looking straight at him. Her head is up, her cabbie's cap at a cocky angle. She's not giving the guy an inch even when he forces her into the back of the truck. She's a gutsy dame all the way. "That's my girl," I say under my breath. The guy follows Rosie into the back of the truck. Any strategy I'd had for nabbing Rosie has just gone down the drain.

My arms take control of the situation with a will of their own. They spin the Buick's steering wheel, make a screeching U-turn on the pier. I head back to the warehouse, to Rosie, my loyal, beautiful soldier.

I tell Celeste, "Get down. Stay outta sight." She gives a yelp of terror, folds up, and hunkers down, her arms over her head like in wartime.

The truck pulls out onto the pier.

These guys are making a break, which means they were expecting me, and the only way they'd be expecting me is if Mom Sheinbaum called Sig and told him I'd figured where he's stashed Rosie. Sig must've made arrangements to move her.

The trucker's in my headlights. He sees me head straight for him and tries to swerve around me, but my arms are like motorized machines now, turning my steering wheel in unison with every move the trucker makes. His truck and my Buick lurch from side to side, swerving all over the pier as the guy tries to drive past me and I keep blocking him. I can't let him get to the pier's access road and drive away with Rosie.

I'd ram his engine if Celeste wasn't crouched so deep in the seat she's halfway to the floor. She'll be smashed flat if I ram the truck, so it's parry and thrust with the trucker, back and forth across the pier, both of us trying not to careen into the channel. My lungs have had enough of harbor water tonight.

I'm back and forth with the truck for I don't know how long. My arms ache, my muscles feel like they're tearing apart, and I'm losing all sense of time, but I don't let up, can't let the truck get by me. I grunt 'til my throat's dry, every grunt a sound as raw as the screeching tires of the Buick and the truck. Celeste's shrieks add to the racket.

"Stop!" she screams. "Cantor, stop! *Stop this!*"

She's right. This has to stop. I have to stop that truck.

My hands are clamped so tight around the steering wheel, I have to force the fingers of my left hand to unfold. Every muscle from my fingertips to my neck is on fire as I pull Pep's .45 from my waistband. With the gun in my left hand, I steer the Buick one-handed with my right. My right arm feels like white-hot gears are grinding through my joints.

Celeste must be sick and tired of all the banging around because she's trying to climb up into the seat. She tries to steady herself and pull herself up while the car lurches across the pier.

The choice I dreaded is suddenly right next to me. "Get down, dammit!" explodes out of me.

But she doesn't get down. She just keeps struggling to get back onto the seat, screaming with every lurch of the car, her body slamming against the dashboard and the door. "I can't stand all this bouncing around anymore!" Her words get tangled up with the screech of the Buick's tires as I spin the steering wheel back and forth, blocking the truck.

I yell, "I told you to get down!" but in all the tumult I don't think Celeste hears me. I stow the gun in my lap, switch to my left hand to steer the car, and use my right hand to push Celeste down hard, press her face against the seat and out of sight of the trucker. "Don't you get it? I have to keep both of you alive. You and Rosie both have to stay alive! Now get *down*."

My insides are spinning, every part spinning on its own, fast, too fast for me to think about it as I put my right hand back on the steering wheel. I use my left hand to roll down the window, then pop the door latch and grab the gun again. My door swings open. The truck and my car are still dancing all over the pier. Celeste is screaming again.

I lean out of the car, let the open door cover me in case the trucker or the guy in the back with Rosie decides it's time for a shootout, though I bet the guy in back is getting thrown around so much he'd never make it to the door. I'm barely able to hold on to the steering wheel or keep from falling out of the car, but I manage to prop the gun on the Buick's door, raise my head up just enough to see over the top, and take my best shot at the truck's front tire.

The gun's blast and the exploding tire are almost as loud as Celeste's screams and the grind of the truck's wheel rim as it makes sparks on the wooden pier. The trucker's slowing the rig down, but I blast away at the other front tire to force him to stop. With the explosion of the second tire the guy can't hold the truck, and I'm scared to death that I screwed up with that second bullet and the guy's gonna go over the side and take Rosie with him. The truck's heading for the edge of the pier, my heart's beating like fists against my chest, until the truck rams into a stanchion, stops cold. The force of the collision bursts the truck's radiator. Steam and water shoot up in the air. The driver's head must've slammed against the steering wheel at the impact. The guy's slumped against the wheel.

I run out of the car, run to the back of the truck, shouting, "Rosie!" The door swings open, her jailer is standing in the doorway, though not too steady on his feet. His fedora falls off his head. He must've taken a pounding while the truck was lurching all over the pier. Must have rattled his brains, too, because he goes for his gun before he realizes mine's already out and pointing at him. I blast his gun out of his hand. His hand's a bloody mess as he crumples to the pier, whimpering. I kick his gun into the channel.

"Rosie!" I scramble into the truck.

"Cantor…" She sounds woozy, beat-up.

I kneel down next her, cut the rope from her wrists with my penknife, then brush her hair from her eyes. "Are you hurt? Did that guy hurt you?"

"Nah, nothing like that. We were rattling around back here like dishes falling off a shelf. What the hell was going on out there?" Stray light from the warehouse touches Rosie's face and the silvery blond mist of her hair, wild now and without her cabbie's cap. It's next to her on the floor.

"My Buick got into a bullfight with the truck," I say.

"Still taking crazy chances. I worry about you, Cantor."

"I don't deserve it."

"Yeah, you do," she says, leaning into me and laying her head on my shoulder, reassuring me as much as herself. "You came to get me, didn't you? Figured where I was from hearing the trains through my radio? I managed to switch it on before those two galoots dragged me out of the cab and into the warehouse office."

"The radio trick was a good play. You're a smart soldier, my girl. C'mon, let's go home." I take Rosie's cap from the floor, help her up, and give her back her cap. Standing, getting her balance back, Rosie gets her attitude back, too, that inner snap that's tough and tender at the same time, and all of it real. I feel easy in my skin for the first time all night. I always feel easy in my skin when I'm around Rosie.

Just one more errand down the pier to meet Drogan and

get Celeste on her way, then Rosie and I can get back home to New York where we can finally relax with a bottle of scotch. Then maybe later, after we've gotten some rest, she can help me forget all about Celeste Copley and her mystery. Rosie Bliss is very good at helping me forget things I want to forget.

She puts her cap on. "Let's get the hell out of here," she says. "I'll follow you in the cab."

"You okay to drive?"

"I'm alive, I can drive." She tilts her cap at an angle, and with that million-dollar smile of hers, the one that challenges and promises in the same breath, she reaches up and tilts my cap at an angle, too.

We climb down out of the truck. The guy with the bleeding hand isn't on the ground. He's gone. I pull the .45 in case he's planning a surprise. "Stay behind me," I tell Rosie as we walk carefully along the side of the truck. When I get to the front, I see the guy pulling the driver from the rig and helping him stand up. The driver's pretty shaky. The other guy's hand is bleeding all over him.

Behind me, Rosie says, "Who the hell is that?" Her arm comes up next to me. She's pointing toward my Buick.

Celeste is out of the car and coming toward us, my overcoat blowing around her, but Rosie's still pointing, and what she's pointing at is behind the Buick: a big dark-blue Lincoln arriving on the pier from the access road. The car stops and a tall guy in a dark coat and hat gets out of the driver's seat, steps into a shaft of light from the warehouse that gives his face the hard pallor of fresh cement. He must be one of Sig's boys, maybe come to check on Rosie's transfer to another holding tank.

I don't like what I'm seeing and like even less what I'm thinking: there could be more shooting, maybe even another death, *his* death if he tries to take Rosie. I keep a good grip on the .45.

Celeste is still coming at me, running. She's close now, close enough for me to see the fear and exhaustion in those big brown eyes. Her eyes suddenly open wide, grow wild and white when a loud crack splits the air. Blood sprays from the back of Celeste's head.

She falls right in front of me. The back of her head is spurting blood. I can't take my eyes off her.

I can hear my heart beat, but I don't feel it. I can't feel it through the ice that's suddenly clogging my veins, working its way down to my stomach and up to my throat. If I don't break up the ice, I'll suffocate.

My gun arm, like the rest of me, is stiff and nearly numb. I force it to move, raise it and aim the .45 at the thug who killed Celeste. But he's not standing there now. He's back in the driver's seat of the Lincoln, closing the door, as another guy in a dark coat and homburg gets out of the opposite side of the car from the back seat. He looks straight at me, the thick features of his face catching light from the warehouse. Sig.

He says nothing. He doesn't have to. His being here explains it all. Mom Sheinbaum didn't just tell Sig that I'd figured where he'd stashed Rosie, she also told him about Celeste, that Opal is dead because of Celeste. The old lady didn't buy Celeste's story of an accident. Or maybe she did, but it didn't matter. Celeste killed Opal and Mom was going to do something about it. All it took was one phone call to Loreale, who doesn't care if Opal's death was an accident, either.

A life for a life. A life that mattered to Sig Loreale and Mom Sheinbaum and all those gossip columnists avenged with a life that mattered to no one. Except me.

I aim the .45 at Sig. My hand is suddenly warm and supple as my finger wraps around the trigger. Vengeance has melted the ice in my veins. I'm warm all over.

Even my name comes at me on warm breath. "Cantor." It's Rosie. Her hand is on my gun arm. "That's a suicide play."

Sig doesn't move. Neither does my aim. But Rosie's pressing down on my arm. Her touch is insistent, stubborn with concern for me. Slowly, I lower my gun.

Sig motions to the trucker and the guy with the bloody hand to get into the Lincoln. They make it snappy across the pier, get into the car. Sig, still looking at me, calls out, "Thank you, Cantor! You did well! You found Opal's killer. I am in your debt and I will pay you. I always pay my debts." He starts to get back into the car but stops and calls to me, "I understand you have been looking for a woman named Sophie." Then he gets into the Lincoln. Celeste's killer drives the car away.

I stare at the Lincoln until the red glow of its taillights is gone, until there's nothing to see except the darkening glow of New York's skyline in the thin gray dawn over the river.

"C'mon," Rosie says. Her arm is around my waist and she's tugging me gently. Her arm is warm and strong. But I slip through her grasp as I fall to my knees beside the woman who's cold and pale and dead. I cry my eyes out for Celeste Copley.

About the Author

Native New Yorker Ann Aptaker has earned a reputation as a respected if cheeky exhibition designer and curator of art during her career in museums and galleries. Taking the approach that what art authorities find uncomfortable the public would likely enjoy, exhibitions Ann has curated have garnered favorable reviews in the *New York Times*, *Art in America*, *American Art Review*, and other publications.

She brings the same attitude and philosophy to her first love: writing, especially a tangy variety of historical crime fiction. Ann's short stories have appeared in two editions (2003 and 2004) of the noir crime anthology *Fedora*. Her flash fiction story, "A Night In Town," appeared in the online zine *Punk Soul Poet*. In addition to curating and designing art exhibitions and writing crime stories, Ann is also an art writer and an adjunct professor of art history at the New York Institute of Technology.

Books Available From Bold Strokes Books

Courtship by Carsen Taite. Love and Justice—a lethal mix or a perfect match? (978-1-62639-210-6)

Against Doctor's Orders by Radclyffe. Corporate financier Presley Worth wants to shut down Argyle Community Hospital, but Dr. Harper Rivers will fight her every step of the way, if she can also fight their growing attraction. (978-1-62639-211-3)

A Spark of Heavenly Fire by Kathleen Knowles. Kerry and Beth are building their life together, but unexpected circumstances could destroy their happiness. (978-1-62639-212-0)

Never Too Late by Julie Blair. When Dr. Jamie Hammond is forced to hire a new office manager, she's shocked to come face-to-face with Carla Grant and memories from her past. (978-1-62639-213-7)

Widow by Martha Miller. Judge Bertha Brannon must solve the murder of her lover, a policewoman she thought she'd grow old with. As more bodies pile up, the murdered start coming for her. (978-1-62639-214-4)

Twisted Echoes by Sheri Lewis Wohl. What's a woman to do when she realizes the voices in her head are real? (978-1-62639-215-1)

Criminal Gold by Ann Aptaker. Through a dangerous night in New York in 1949, Cantor Gold, dapper dyke-about-town, smuggler of fine art, is forced by a crime lord to be his instrument of vengeance. (978-1-62639-216-8)

Because of You by Julie Cannon. What would you do for the woman you were forced to leave behind? (978-1-62639-199-4)

The Job by Jove Belle. Sera always dreamed that she would one day reunite with Tor. She just didn't think it would involve terrorists, firearms, and hostages. (978-1-62639-200-7)

Making Time by C.J. Harte. Two women going in different directions meet after fifteen years and struggle to reconnect in spite of the past that separated them. (978-1-62639-201-4)

Once The Clouds Have Gone by KE Payne. Overwhelmed by the dark clouds of her past, Tag Grainger is lost until the intriguing and spirited Freddie Metcalfe unexpectedly forces her to reevaluate her life. (978-1-62639-202-1)

The Acquittal by Anne Laughlin. Chicago private investigator Josie Harper searches for the real killer of a woman whose lover has been acquitted of the crime. (978-1-62639-203-8)

An American Queer: The Amazon Trail by Lee Lynch. Lee Lynch's heartening and heart-rending history of gay life from the turbulence of the late 1900s to the triumphs of the early 2000s are recorded in this selection of her columns. (978-1-62639-204-5)

Stick McLaughlin by CF Frizzell. Corruption in 1918 cost Stick her lover, her freedom, and her identity, but a very special flapper and the family bond of her own gang could help win them back—even if it means outwitting the Boston Mob. (978-1-62639-205-2)

Rest Home Runaways by Clifford Henderson. Baby boomer Morgan Ronzio's troubled marriage is the least of her worries when she gets the call that her addled, eighty-six-year-old, half-blind dad has escaped the rest home. (978-1-62639-169-7)

Charm City by Mason Dixon. Raq Overstreet's loyalty to her drug kingpin boss is put to the test when she begins to fall for Bathsheba Morris, the undercover cop assigned to bring him down. (978-1-62639-198-7)

Edge of Awareness by C.A. Popovich. When Maria, a woman in the middle of her third divorce, meets Dana, an out lesbian, awareness of her feelings brings up reservations about the teachings of her church. (978-1-62639-188-8)

Taken by Storm by Kim Baldwin. Lives depend on two women when a train derails high in the remote Alps, but an unforgiving mountain, avalanches, crevasses, and other perils stand between them and safety. (978-1-62639-189-5)

The Common Thread by Jaime Maddox. Dr. Nicole Coussart's life is falling apart, but fortunately, DEA Attorney Rae Rhodes is there to pick up the pieces and help Nic put them back together. (978-1-62639-190-1)

Jolt by Kris Bryant. Mystery writer Bethany Lange wasn't prepared for the twisting emotions that left her breathless the moment she laid eyes on folk singer sensation Ali Hart. (978-1-62639-191-8)

Searching For Forever by Emily Smith. Dr. Natalie Jenner's life has always been about saving others, until young paramedic Charlie Thompson comes along and shows her maybe she's the one who needs saving. (978-1-62639-186-4)

Blindsided by Karis Walsh. Blindsided by love, guide dog trainer Lenae McIntyre and media personality Cara Bradley learn to trust what they see with their hearts. (978-1-62639-078-2)

Blue Water Dreams by Dena Hankins. Lania Marchiol keeps her wary sailor's gaze trained on the horizon until Oly Rassmussen, a wickedly handsome trans man, sends her trusty compass spinning off course. (978-1-62639-192-5)

Let the Lover Be by Sheree Greer. Kiana Lewis, a functional alcoholic on the verge of destruction, finally faces the demons of her past while finding love and earning redemption in New Orleans. (978-1-62639-077-5)

About Face by VK Powell. Forensic artist Macy Sheridan and Detective Leigh Monroe work on a case that has troubled them both for years, but they're hampered by the past and their unlikely yet undeniable attraction. (978-1-62639-079-9)

Blackstone by Shea Godfrey. For Darry and Jessa, the chance at a life of freedom is stolen by the arrival of war and an ancient prophecy that just might destroy their love. (978-1-62639-080-5)

Out of This World by Maggie Morton. Iris decided to cross an ocean to get over her ex. But instead, she ends up traveling much farther, all the way to another world. Once she's there, only a mysterious, sexy, and magical woman can help her return home. (978-1-62639-083-6)

Kiss The Girl by Melissa Brayden. Sleeping with the enemy has never been so complicated. Brooklyn Campbell and Jessica Lennox face off in love and advertising in fast-paced New York City. (978-1-62639-071-3)

Taking Fire: A First Responders Novel by Radclyffe. Hunted by extremists and under siege by nature's most virulent weapons, Navy medic Max de Milles and Red Cross worker Rachel Winslow join forces to survive and discover something far more lasting. (978-1-62639-072-0)

First Tango in Paris by Shelley Thrasher. When French law student Eva Laroche meets American call girl Brigitte Green in 1970s Paris, they have no idea how their pasts and futures will intersect. (978-1-62639-073-7)